Sing Me a Song

Sing Me a Song

Virginia C. Taylor

Rutledge Books, Inc.   Danbury, CT

Interior design by Sharon Gelfand

Cover design and artwork by Erin Walrath

Rutledge Books, Inc.
107 Mill Plain Road, Danbury, CT 06811
1-800-278-8533
www.rutledgebooks.com

Manufactured in the United States of America
Sing Me a Song
    Taylor, Virginia

    ISBN: 1-58244-132-4

    1. Fiction

Library of Congress Control Number: 2001088142

Dedication

I dedicate this book to the memory of my husband, Ruel Edward Taylor Jr. Had he not saved all that pertained to Barilla, her story would never have been told.

The derelict building in West Gray, Maine, where the Taylor letters and Barilla's memorabilia were found in an old wooden box stamped with the name HORLICKS MALTED MILK, Racine, Wisconsin.

Acknowledgements

Without the help and encouragement of several persons connected with the National Historical Park Service in Lowell, Massachusetts. I could not have completed Barilla's story.

To Michael Wurm, Andrew Chamberlain, and specifically Liza Stearns, Supervisory Ranger on Education, and Martha Mayo, Historical Librarian. I thank them all for their assistance in searching out facts. Liza has developed several curriculum studies and workshops based on the life of Barilla Taylor.

To Catherine Goodwin for her research and publication of The Lowell Cemetery.

To Thomas Dublin, author of several books about Lowell Mills, for providing me with Barilla's payroll records, copied from the Baker Library at Harvard.

To Dr. June Berry, a distant cousin in Salt Lake City, Utah, who searched diligently for genealogical records pertaining Pliny Tidd.

I am truly blessed to have six children who have taught me more than I ever taught them, Especially my son Alan, a professor of history at the University of California at Davis, who taught me how to do research, and is the 1996 recipient of a Pulitzer Prize for history.

And last but not least, to my colleagues in the State of Maine Writer's Conference who have been my friends and critics for more than twenty years.

-Virginia C. Taylor

Introduction

On July 15, 1957, my husband's father, Ruel Taylor, died in Gray, Maine, at the age of 87. Six months later my husband's mother passed away at the age of 78. Thus, in the spring of 1958, three of their surviving sons tackled the job of clearing out a storage area. A truck was on hand to receive most of the contents. One brother came across a box of old letters and prepared to toss it onto the truck.

"Wait a minute, John," said my husband, Ruel Junior. "What's in that box?"

"Just some old letters. No one would want them."

Ruel perused a few. "I do," he said. "I want them."

Some time passed while the box of letters lay undisturbed in a closet in our home. In December 1970, we were literally snowed in by a four-day snowstorm. Out came the box of letters to present us with an unusual challenge Fortunately all were dated so could be arranged in chronological order. Altogether, the typed copies form a book two inches thick. About eight copies were made and presented to some of the Taylor descendants. After my husband's death in 1989, I donated the original letters to the Maine Historical Society in Portland.

The earliest document is a seaman's paper dated December 1818, Bath, Maine. The final letter is dated 1908. The patriarch and seaman was Stephen Burleigh Taylor, born in Byron, Maine, on April 4, 1797. Beginning in 1820, when he was 23 years of age, the papers recount the life and times of his friends, his children, and grandchildren.

There were twelve children born to him and his wife Melinda. All but one lived to adulthood.

They scattered to such places as Massachusetts, Minnesota, Wisconsin, Colorado, and California. Some went by covered wagon, and one by train across the Isthmus of Panama. One was a banjo player who traveled with a circus. Two worked on the railroads. One remained in Maine, and one went to Lowell. They all wrote letters home to Byron.

What is it like to come upon family letters written more than a century ago? We did have genealogical material and some photographs regarding these people. But suddenly, they were no longer one-dimensional; they had come alive.

Byron, Maine, is not easily located on a map. It is 13 miles north of Rumford. Today, travelers drive through Mexico, Frye, Roxbury, and Byron on Route 17 going to the Rangeley lakes.

Why did the Taylors go to that Swift River Valley, and why did they leave? These letters shed light on the answers with truly personal details.

Stephen Burleigh's father John, who fought in the Revolutionary War, had resided in Gilmanton, New Hampshire. He was repaid for his military service with a land grant to settle in Maine. Along with many other veterans, the exodus began. Basically they farmed, eking out a living from those virgin lands They subsisted by bartering their goods and services. Many of them, having little or no money, lost their holdings by the inability to pay taxes to the infiltrating proprietors from Massachusetts. By 1840, having a dozen children to feed and nurture became a burden. No longer could they survive by farming, fishing, hunting, and lumbering.

Thus the exodus reversed itself. There were railroads to build, factories to run, western lands to settle, and the greatest magnet of all, gold.

One area difficult to grasp was the haphazard subject of education. If there was a teacher available-that is, one who perhaps knew a little about the three R's, he or she received room and board with a family and lived in a house that served as a school. Classes were held at the convenience of the weather, never when it was too cold, nor during harvest time or spring planting. Age did not matter. One excerpt by Melinda to daughter Barilla in Lowell dated August, 1844 stated, "Florena wants you should come home and help her for she has got a great deal to do to go to school and keep her house and care for her baby." Florena was 21.

The following story is based on Barilla, the fourth child born to Stephen and Melinda, who at the age of fifteen went to Lowell to work in a cotton mill. At the time of those letters that were written by her, to her, and about her, her older sister, Florena, had married. Two older brothers, aged 17 and 19, had left home to find employment. There were six more, all boys, ranging in age from eight months to thirteen. One sister, Oliva, had died at the age of five. Another girl, Araminta, was as yet unborn.

Attempting to assimilate the essence of Barilla through her letters, and her emotions through her poetry, was not itself enough to write her story. But I had fallen in love with her and felt I had to write about her and her place in history.

1

In September 1843, frost had already killed many crops. Like busy squirrels, the harvesting and mountainous woodpile made the folks feel prepared for the coming of winter. It was hardly the time for Barilla to make an unprecedented announcement.

It was after five o'clock when Barilla drove the wagon into the barn at her Byron home. She was long overdue with supplies she had been sent to Roxbury to buy-sugar, flour, salt, and baking soda. Her brothers could unload it later. Hurriedly, she unharnessed the horse and led him to his stall.

The other family members were already at the table for the evening meal. All of them looked up at her with astonishment because her face was flushed and her eyes bright with excitement. All, that is, except her father. Being late for supper was unacceptable, and in her case, being the eldest child still at home, outright negligent.

Stephen Burleigh Taylor's attention never wavered from buttering and eating his biscuit. He spoke in a noncommittal tone.

"Did you have trouble, girl, that made you tardy?"

"No, Father," she answered calmly, as she assumed her seat. She looked directly at his silver hair and weather-beaten face as he ate his applesauce. She continued talking as she filled a small bowl with applesauce.

"There was a man outside the store. Talking loud, he was, talking about girls going to work in a mill in Lowell, in Massachusetts. He told us a lot. He..."

"Just who is the us you're talking about?" Stephen insisted.

"Emily, Climena, Malvina, and Mary. We all want to go, Father. We can earn money."

"Go?" he questioned angrily. "Go somewhere when you are needed here?" His utterance caused him to nearly choke on a mouthful of biscuit. Melinda gasped inaudibly. The other children stared at Barilla in wonderment. The baby, Philand, began to cry. Barilla, fighting back her own tears, lashed out brazenly. "You did not refuse Byron and Convers their going away to work! I don't see why I can't!"

A stunned Stephen turned his attention directly at his rebellious daughter, and spoke sternly. "Hold your tongue, girl. Your brothers are men, doing men's work and we manage the farm without them. You are but fifteen. So young you are taken in by the promises of a fly-by-night con man. 'T ain't fittin'. Now, eat your supper."

Later, their supper finished, Stephen hustled out of the room. The older boys, Morval and Marvin, followed, knowing full well they had better help with the nightly milking.

Barilla, with a firmly set jaw, cleared the table. She did the dishes while her mother put the baby to bed. The three younger boys played a game of jacks on the floor.

When Melinda returned, she moved to her rocker by the window. A forty-year-old woman, she was too active to be fat, yet the constraints of caring for her large family had taken their toll of her beauty. She appraised Barilla as she finished her tasks. Taller than she, and certainly no longer a child, the blossoming womanhood truly apparent in the girl's figure. She spoke to her sullen daughter. "Come here," she said, "and tell me more about the stranger and his story."

Resolutely, Barilla stood behind her mother's rocker and stared out at the gathering dusk. She placed both hands on Melinda's shoulders. Patiently, she answered her mother's question.

"I don't think the man was a fly-by-nighter giving out unsavory promises. He is coming back in two days time when he wants us to bring a parent to hear all he has to say. He told us to bring something to lunch on and our clothes in a satchel or trunk and he would see to our getting to Lowell. He has a first-rate wagon. I believe he is honest and that his statements are honest. Please, Mother, tell Father to let me go."

Melinda reached up to place a hand over Barilla's and said, "You are not considering how much I need you here. Since Florena is married and living with Amos, you are the only girl I have."

"But the money I can earn," Barilla argued. "You will need money for taxes and for a horse. Our horse is old. You need another."

Stephen slammed the kitchen door and stomped across the room. His anger had not lessened. "We know what we need! Do you really believe some mill is going to pay a passel of girls enough money to send any home, much less enough to buy a horse which cost forty dollars!"

"Will you just go with me down to Roxbury, Father, to hear the man two days from now? Please, Father."

"We shall see," was his noncommittal response.

Sleep eluded Barilla that night. She had a room to herself now that Florena was married to Amos Austin. Her younger brothers, Morvalden, thirteen; Marvin, eight; Jack, five; and Eugene, three; all slept in the long attic room over the kitchen. The baby, Philand, slept with the parents. She had two elder brothers. Byron, nineteen, was up in Bangor where he drove a four-horse team hauling lumber out of the forests. Joseph Convers, seventeen, was in Stoughton, Massachusetts, working for the railroad at three dollars a day. And sister Florena, twenty, with a baby boy. The only man Barilla thought about was Dana Austin, the brother of Amos. But he had gone to Boston, which was just as well. Had he stayed, she might one day marry him and so beget a life like her mother with so many children. So, too, was Florena ordained into the same kind of life.

"Oh God, Barilla prayed, "let me go adventuring like Byron and Con."

When the two days had passed, Barilla's father and brother Morvalden escorted her to Roxbury. Stephen's bearing and dour countenance contrasted sharply with Barilla's glow of anticipation. Morvalden kept a discreet silence as he held the horse's reins. Barilla had packed a small trunk, feeling confident that she was on her way to a new and exciting life.

Subsequently, the mill agent's description of the magnificent life the girls would have, along with assurances of educational opportunities, and above all, chaperones in quiet boardinghouses, finally convinced Stephen to give Barilla and her friends his blessing.

Barilla had never been beyond Roxbury before, but it was all the same-the same scattered farmhouses. Eventually they crossed the Androscoggin River on a ferry. Then the six girls, all acquaintances, reboarded the agent's brightly painted red wagon. It was beautiful on the outside with one yellow and one green strip along its length. Within the open body were only quilts. Rough, unfinished boards lined the inner walls.

After several hours of being jostled around, the gay mood with which they had started out seemed not to sustain them. They passed endless communities, each presenting a single church, a store, and a livery stable.

When the sun appeared high overhead on that beautiful day, it reminded them that it was time to eat. Climena reached into her satchel to produce a loaf of pre-sliced bread. Each of the other girls hustled out whatever meager offerings they had brought with them. Cheese and cooked sausages were passed all around. Barilla had brought a gallon of new cider from which her friends all drank in turns. Mary had brought molasses cookies.

Despite the bumping and swaying of the wagon, after lunch they became drowsy, and several lay down upon the quilts and fell asleep.

Barilla, still too excited to sleep, studied the girls lying prone, stretched out upon the dusty quilts. Climena Bradbury was the largest, a big-boned, full-chested, womanly person. Malvina, by contrast, was tall, quite thin, her pallor strikingly white against her very black hair. Louisa lay face down so that Barilla saw only her shabby, homespun dress and her splayed out hands, rough from the daily farmwork that all the girls performed.

Emily, also fifteen, was most like Barilla. The same rosy cheeks, the same deep blue eyes, which were open, looking back at Barilla. Emily smiled briefly and closed her eyes. Then Barilla fastened her gaze on Mary Bradbury, Climena's sister. She was tiny and the least spirited of them all. As Climena was their leader, Mary came at the other end of the line. Would Mary keep up with the others? Could she do the work involved? Perhaps. She was usually not a crybaby. Barilla just didn't like her.

By dusk the wagon came into a city. Here the street was lined with buildings of stone or brick; and how unusual, they seemed to be connected.

Horse's hooves clattered noisily. Why, the very road was laid with stones!

Barilla's appraisal of "a first-rate wagon" had diminished considerably as the wagon pulled up before a tavern. The agent called back to his passengers.

"This is Auburn. We stop here for supper and to spend the night."

A sumptuous dinner of roast pork was served on pottery plates at a long trestle table. Many other people were in the room, and several were girls their own age. Barilla thought it most amazing that none of them had to cook the dinner or clean up afterward.

After the meal, they were shown upstairs to a long women's room where there were several large beds. The girls paired off two to a bed. Six of the strange girls filed in to fill the remaining beds.

Climena instructed them to remove only their shoes. After all, their nightclothes were in trunks or boxes in the wagon. Neither should they undo their braids. as no one had a brush or comb. She also explained that the agent had told her they would be called at dawn for they must be in Portland in time to transfer to a larger caravan going to Lowell. A bell would awaken them.

Portland. The largest city in Maine, Barilla's visualized conception sparked her imagination to the point of eliminating the mundane events of the early-morning ritual. Raucous sounding bells had awakened them along with an admonition to hurry out to the "necessary" before a hastily eaten breakfast of fried potatoes, molasses doughnuts, and weak coffee.

The lack of water to wash and no way to tidy their straggled braids caused the fastidious Barilla some consternation. The renewal of bumps and jostling truly aggravated those aches and bruises of yesterday. Besides, they all had sunburned faces. Not one of them had salve or had brought their old broken and soiled straw bonnets.

The girls saw nothing of the city which, they were told, was up on a hill above where they met up with a large wagon. The wagon was so large in fact, that it held more than twenty people, but blessedly had a canvas top to protect them from sun or rain.

The agent and his red wagon moved away, destined for a return trip to outlying countrysides to gather more recruits.

The larger conveyance boasted benches, underneath which their trunks and satchels had been stowed. Now there were four horses instead of two, yet the tempo of progression seemed slower, for there was a greater load. All too often, rocks or ruts on the dusty roadway caused jolting and dipping so that the friends clung to one another on their precarious benches. The hours grew long.

"When, oh when?" asked Mary with abject weariness. "When will we ever get to Lowell?"

"Got another day, dearie," an older woman said.

"Let us not be discouraged," said Climena. "We shall play some games. Thus began a clapping game of "Peas porridge hot, peas porridge cold." The spontaneity became contagious and all of the passengers joined in. Eventually tiring of the game, they launched into guessing games-"What color am I thinking of?" or "What number?" or "Where have I hidden something?"

Shortly after passing a city called Rochester, there had been a noontime stop at a village farmhouse where bread and cheese, milk and cider were provided. Then, after all had made the trek out to the necessary, they were on their way once more.

Each time the terrain became more mountainous, they were told to get out and walk the uphill climb. As usual, Climena made a game of it.

"It's good for us to walk. It's a welcome stretch of our muscles."

"Besides," Barilla said, "the steep incline might have dumped us all out onto the terrible road."

She knew not where they stopped the second night, only that it was somewhere in New Hampshire. Feeling more worn out from the tedious ride than if she had done a day's work on the farm, she could scarcely recall the sorry events of that second night. Nor did she want to. Supper had been only baked beans and some watery squash. The sleeping rooms had been in no way segregated so that couples or men slept on adjacent mattresses upon the floor. Barilla and Emily cuddled together for protection.

The morning of the third day, which was October 1, the driver told them that the trip would be easier after crossing the Merrimac River in Manchester and then they would head downriver to Lowell.

"I can't wait. I can't wait," Barilla whispered joyously to Emily as they again boarded the wagon.

There were no more mountains as their course followed the river southward into Lowell.

Finally, the driver called out, "There it lies."

The girls stood up, craning their heads high to view the city of golden promise. Golden? Not at all. Barilla's joy turned into emptiness as she gazed at the fortress-like smokestacks and high buildings all crowded together. She felt betrayed.

Before long the wagon lumbered onto Merrimack Street. The driver soon turned right at Central Street. Barilla noticed the shops with signs advertising their wares. It was overwhelming. After crossing a canal, the wagon made a right turn into a lane. On the right stood a formidable red-brick building. By counting the floors of windows, Barilla deduced it to be four stories high, but the length was interminable, almost to the diminishing point of her perspective. A strange rumbling, thumping sound emanated from the monstrous building, where, close to the ground, a wagonload of cotton bales was being unloaded by two men who were bare from the waist up. Their wagon stopped.

"Here you be, ladies," said the driver. "This be the new home for those who are to work at the Hamilton."

Barilla saw then the long boardinghouse on the opposite side of the lane. The six girls who had the Hamilton designation carried their belongings and filed up stone steps into an entrance hall. A buxom woman stood there, her arms crossed beneath her breast.

"I am Mrs. Merriam," she said, giving them a pained smile of welcome. "I am the corporation's boarding matron. Now please follow me up to your rooms."

She led them up a narrow stairway to one floor, then in reverse along a hall to another stairway up to the third floor. The air had grown fetid and stale. Entering a room with three beds, Barilla saw colorful dresses hung on pegs along one wall. Two were capped by voluminous black bonnets.

A fireplace formed a part of one wall, and at the end of the room, two windows were closed. "It's very warm in here," Barilla said to the matron. "Couldn't we open the windows?"

"Just closed 'em for the season. They are not to be opened till first day of June. Rules are rules. You'll get no open windows in the mill, so you might as well get used to it." She pointed to two of the beds. "These ain't taken, so four of you pick your bedmates among you. Two to a bed. Pots are under the beds. Wash basin's over on that stand. The other girls get out in 'bout an hour, so you got time to get out of your dusty clothes and clean up before the evening victuals."

Climena then asked the question on the minds of the others. "What about baths?"

The matron's jaw tightened; her eyes fiercely penetrating, and responded decisively, "Baths provided on Saturday nights. Have to come downstairs then. Nobody's gonna carry water to fill a tub way up here." She moved toward the door and pointed to Climena. "Two of you have to go to another room. Follow me."

As Climena and Mary started for the door, Mary burst out crying, "I h-hate this place. I want to go home!"

Climena put an arm around Mary and spoke with gentle understanding. "You cannot go home. In time you will get used to it. We all will. So stop your blubbering. Tears and grime make you look like a banshee."

It was natural for Climena to admonish Mary, for they were sisters. Although Mary was older, she had not the spirit of Climena, who mothered them all, wasting no time giving orders.

Barilla felt relieved that Mary would be in a different room. She turned to her mates. "Let's get out of our grimy dresses. Just shake them out and find a peg to hang them on. Then wash hands and faces, comb and rebraid our hair, and get into a clean dress. We do not want to look like a bunch of ragamuffins when the others, the two who have that bed, return."

All of this they had accomplished when bells began to toll, and the rumbling, thumping stopped. But then another sound, scores of footsteps below and up the staircases. It was like a helter-skelter horde escaping from a storm.

Suddenly, two young women came into the room. They paused briefly to appraise the strange newcomers.

The appraisals went both ways. Barilla immediately noticed the other girls' heads. One's hair was drawn neatly back into a bun at the back and the other had bouffant side loops. She felt instinctive embarrassment because of her own long braids. Tomorrow, she decided, she would style her hair differently. But nothing could improve her sack-like homespun dress, which contrasted sharply with the others' tight-bodiced frocks and lace collars.

"Well, hello and welcome," said one. "I am Audrey, and this is Minerva."

Barilla introduced the contingent from Maine.

"We won't remember them all at once," said Audrey, as she moved to the wash basin. Because the four's grubby hands and faces had already soiled the water to a gray muck, she emptied it in a nearby slop bucket and refilled the basin from a pail beneath the stand. She splashed water on her face, then dried off on the only already-soiled towel.

As Barilla waited, she noticed something under Audrey and

Minerva's bed. It looked like a mandolin case, so she asked Audrey about it.

"Yes, it's mine. Do you play?"

"No, but my brothers do."

The Maine girls followed the others to descend the staircase. In the dining room, supper tables were already set for about twenty. Other girls rushed to fill certain places, so Barilla and her friends became separated, finding vacant chairs among strangers. The girls on either side of Barilla introduced themselves.

One was Else*; the other, Rachel.

"You new today?" asked Else, hardly pausing for breath between mouthfuls of soup.

"Yes," Barilla answered quietly. She had such a feeling of inadequacy it was difficult to swallow. She felt that the others would certainly class her as a country bumpkin. Had these other girls felt as pathetic when they first came here? She could not imagine it.

"Where you from?" Rachel asked.

"Maine."

"Maine? Where's that?"

"Up north. Three days, two nights traveling in a wagon."

"That's sure a long ways. I came up from Boston. You can come by train from there."

"I haven't seen the train, but I think I heard a whistle," said Barilla, who had begun to eat her soup.

Rachel laughed, "I don't know how you could hear anything above the racket from the mill."

"Is it always like that?" Barilla wanted to keep the conversation going even though her soup might get cold.

"Hah!" Rachel spat out the word. Then she leaned across Barilla to get Else's assurance. "She just asked if the mill is always so noisy."

Else nearly choked from laughter and placed a hand on Barilla's shoulder, saying, "Always. That is, every day but Sunday."

* pronounced Elsa

Heartened by Else's friendly touch, she asked, "What happens on Sunday?"

"Oh, that's the best day. We have to go to church, and later we are free to go walking in the town and across the bridge to walk along the riverside. You will like Sundays."

Else smiled warmly and admonished Barilla to eat her soup. Barilla ate, thinking about the promise of Sundays. She had never been to a real church. There wasn't one in Byron, or even in Roxbury. She could not even visualize what it would be like. Today was Monday, so there would be an entire week before she could have such an experience. And walking along a riverside, looking back at the city. How romantic. There was the Swift River in Byron, which only ran swiftly in the spring. It was a jumble of stones and a trickle of water the rest of the year. Perhaps living here was going to be exciting, especially if there was something she could do about her hair.

Else had neat side buns, so Barilla asked, "Would you show me how to fix my hair like yours?"

"Of course. We can do it right after supper. My room is on the second floor. You can come up there with me."

Else had brushed Barilla's long brown hair and shown her how to form it in a spiral over each ear, deftly pinning it in place. "You may keep the pins until you have money to buy your own," said Else as she proudly appraised her handiwork.

"Oh, thank you so much," Barilla beamed happily. "I shall repay you as soon as I can. I must also buy a bonnet."

"You won't be paid until the end of October. If you do not have a bonnet, you must wear a scarf on your head to attend church. But now, off to bed with you. It's lamps out at ten o'clock and the wake-up bell is a quarter to five. First work bell is at five-thirty."

"That doesn't give much time for breakfast," said Barilla.

"Breakfast bell is not until seven, then we have time to eat until a back to work bell at seven-thirty. You don't know yet where you will work, so I may not see you until breakfast."

Else ushered Barilla out of the room and quietly closed the door behind her.

Later, in their upper room, the Maine girls chattered excitedly among themselves until told to be quiet by their roommates.

Having been told by Mrs. Merriam that they would not report for work assignments until after breakfast, the six girls, entered the office of the mill agent at a few minutes past seven-thirty. Printed in large black letters on the glass window of the door to the office was the name, John Avery, Agent.

Warily, they filed into the office.

"Close the door behind you," Avery said in a loud voice.

Mary, the last to enter, carefully closed the door. That lessened the unbearable noise a bit, but not the tensing vibration. Barilla still felt the floor pulsating beneath her feet.

Avery sat in a reclining chair, tilted backward, and appraised the newcomers with a disdainful sneer. He pointed to first one and then another.

"One at a time, step forward and give your name, birthplace, and birth date," he said.

Then, for the first time, his steely, penetrating gaze wavered as he leaned forward to pick up a pen and began making entries on a pay-roll ledger.

He assigned Malvina and Louisa to the spinning room. Climena and Mary would go to the dresser, and Emily and Barilla were designated for the upper weaving room.

The girls stood immobile as Mr. Avery continued his orders.

"You are all spare hands until you learn your tasks. You will be paid fifty-three cents a week, paid on the last Saturday of the month. You will attend church service on Sundays, and obey the rules of the corporation."

He turned then and shouted, "Jamie!" to an heretofore unnoticed boy who sat huddled on the floor. The boy jumped to attention.

"Jamie," Avery ordered, "take these persons to report to their overseers. Each one has her assignment."

He dismissed the group with an outward wave of his hand.

Barilla felt a measure of relief as she followed Jamie out of Mr. Avery's disagreeable presence.

Malvina leaned down to show Jamie her paper giving their designation.

The boy shook his head. "Can't read." He looked down at the floor.

"It says, 'spinning room,' Mister Jennings," Malvina said.

Jamie acknowledged that. Then, amid the deafening noise, they all climbed the circular stairs into an enormous room. The place was filled with machines that were spinning out creamy ropes of cotton onto long bobbins.

Jamie located Jennings at some distance, then indicated that the two girls should follow him. The man appeared to be shouting at a girl tending one of the frames. Shouting, Barilla realized, was the only way anyone could hear above the clamor.

Jamie returned to the remaining four, and asked, "Where now?"

"We two," Barilla spoke loudly, "for the upper weave room, to a Mister Lord."

"And them two? Where they going?"

Climena answered him, "To the dresser," she said.

"You're next then," Jamie told Barilla. "Up to the next floor."

Here was another huge room, but different kinds of machines. They were alive with motion. Flying shuttles zipped across and back on each loom, emitting such clatter and bang that Barilla clamped her hands over both ears. Besides the noise, the air was foul, steamy hot, and gave a sense of being in a fog. And all those long belts whipping endlessly over the machines! Panic overcame her. How could she stand it, being part of such a repugnant situation? She turned to stare dully at Emily, and saw there the same abject horror and fear.

Jamie located Mister Lord, a short, bent-over man who sauntered down an aisle between the clattering monsters. Barilla and Emily followed Jamie until he caught up, then touched the peculiar little man's jacket.

"Them's yours." Jamie hollered, pointing to the bewildered girls. Moving swiftly away, Jamie, along with Climena and Mary, disappeared in the vicinity of the stairwell.

Barilla handed the slip of paper Mister Avery had given her to the little man.

"Hmm," he mused, then hollered, "new to this, I reckon?"

"Yes sir," the girls replied in unison.

"Come along then," he beckoned, and led them to the far end of the room. He stopped beside a loom without an operator.

"This is to be yours as soon as you get learnt." He looked directly at Barilla, then shifted his attention to the girl at the adjoining loom, "Else here will instruct you." He said as he moved away, beckoning Emily to follow him.

Barilla could not believe her luck at having her new friend for her instructor. She smiled broadly, but Else was all business.

"The up and down threads are the warp. The thread on the shuttle is called weft. The weft going through each way is called a pick." She stopped talking while she demonstrated threading a shuttle. "Sometimes," she continued, "the thread breaks, then you have to stop the machine with this lever and tie a knot with the broken ends."

Barilla felt her breath quicken, her heartbeat racing, and her arms and legs tighten with the tension due to inexperience. This was quite different from the handloom at home, which, being unmechanized, was tranquil by comparison.

After an hour passed during which she became mesmerized by the process, Else spoke to her. "You pay attention now while I go get a drink of water."

Barilla dared not take her eyes off the loom. And, although she was not a person with a prayerful bent, she kept repeating to herself, "Oh please God, don't let anything go wrong."

She was gratefully relieved when Else returned. What seemed

like her mouth having been filled with cotton now left only a parched dryness. She spoke abruptly, "Can I go now and get a drink?"

"All right, but we are allowed one drink each morning, and one in the afternoon. The bucket is over by the stairway."

Holding the dipper to her lips, she found the tepid water repelling. How different from the ice-cold water in the well at home. A sudden ache for all she missed at her home caused tears to form.

Immediately in her blurred vision appeared the overseer watching her with steely, gray eyes. "Only once in the morning," he warned her, "and once in the afternoon."

"I know," she said meekly. She turned away and walked briskly back to the loom. There, at least, was friendly affinity.

By observing Else closely, Barilla felt confident that she could easily learn to tend the loom herself, but the snapping, pounding noise was frightening, as if the very building shook.

Suddenly, she heard bells, which sent a shiver through her. There was immediate motion of the girls shutting down their machines, and instantaneous silence except for the pell-mell rush as they made for the stairway. Else took Barilla's hand to lead her along. "That's the ring-out dinner bell. You can't dawdle."

After dinner, bells to resume work came at 1:05. Having only a half-hour for the meal, the horde of girls hustled back to work. Barilla followed quickly in Else's footsteps.

At the loom, Else instructed Barilla to push the lever that sent the dormant monster into flying activity. The overhead belts swung the end wheel and sent the shuttle zipping through the vertical threads.

"I did it!" Barilla said, excitedly. She also realized that the floor, which had been calm and steady, was now vibrating, and the pounding racket had begun again.

"Sure you did," Else shouted, as she continued pointing out details which Barilla must learn. "Up there is a counter that measures the finished cloth." She picked up a shuttle and demonstrated how the bobbin was inserted and threaded, when suddenly a filling thread broke. Else showed her how to knot it, insisting that Barilla do it. That accomplished, Barilla felt confident to again throw the starting lever. They smiled at one another. Behind them, unseen, stood Mr. Lord. His loud, booming voice surprised Barilla.

"You're doin' good, girl. Perhaps tomorrow you can take over the loom beside you. Have Else get you started on it. It's already been shut down for a week."

Before she could respond, he had moved along the line between the black monsters vibrating rhythmically as they created sheets of cotton cloth.

The confidence she had felt at the beginning of the afternoon turned to consternation. She drew a deep breath and her hands began to shake. With pursed lips and widened eyes, she turned a worried gaze upon Else.

"Don't be concerned," Else shouted. "I'll help. I can manage both looms."

Barilla nodded helplessly. She had not breath enough to compete with the all encompassing noise.

As the hours droned on, she knew she must observe all she could. The intensity of her attention caused her eyes to smart, her arms to ache, and an uneasy tension pull taut muscles across her neck and back.

Else noticed her pallor. She smiled and said, "Water, go for a drink."

"I don't think I could swallow it." She pointed to her mouth. "It's full of cotton."

"Then keep your mouth shut."

This had been said in good humor. Barilla could not suppress a chuckle. The admonition had exacted its purpose. Both girls began to shake with laughter.

2

Barilla had never felt clock hands move so slowly as they moved toward seven o'clock. Eventually, with a clang of the blessed bells, a flurry of operatives made their way to and down the circular stairs. The pleasant hum of their chatter and clacking of hurried footsteps was such a welcome relief after the cacophonous pounding. She followed Else across the street and into the dining room. She plopped down on the hard seat and let her shoulders fall as she let out a deep sigh of exhaustion.

"You'll get used to it," said Else.

"Oh," Barilla said, "it's not the work. It's the noise, the vibration, and the long hours. But I am forgetting myself. I cannot thank you enough for your generous help and especially for your friendship."

"We have to help one another," Else responded. "After all, we are all the family we've got. My mum died while having a baby. So there's just my father and a brother somewhere. I don't even have a sister. Do you?"

Barilla told her about Florena. "Otherwise," she added, "I have brothers, eight of them."

"That's the big trouble with marriage, nothing but housework, sickness, and lots of babies. That's not for me."

"You don't ever want babies?" Barilla said. She smiled to herself, thinking of her baby brother, of his warm, cuddly body, and how he clung to her when she sometimes rocked him to sleep. So wrapped in thought, she hardly heard Else's desultory answer.

"Absolutely not"

Supper consisted of applesauce, biscuits, and honey. Both girls finished it in silence.

Then, as they stood up, Else asked if she would like to walk downtown, if she were not too tired.

"It is getting dark earlier now, but is even more exciting when the lamps are lit. I thought you might like to see the shops."

"Oh my, yes, I certainly would. But, I have no money."

"Neither do I. I put half of my September money in the bank and spent the rest within a week."

Emily joined them and was introduced to Else.

"We are going to walk downtown," said Else. "Would you like to come along?"

"Oh my, yes," said Emily,

The prospect of venturing out to see the shops so intrigued both Emily and Barilla that the mantle of exhaustion miraculously vanished. Having donned their shawls, the three girls descended the front steps. Surrounded by the pervading darkness and the chilling night air, Barilla shivered, not so much with cold as with excitement.

Lamps along Central Street were being lit by a man who carried a short ladder. Light from store windows and throngs of long-skirted women added to the festiveness.

At one open doorway, Barilla stopped short. "Look, look at all the gold jewelry. Let's go in to see it closer."

"No, Else said. "Really Barilla, haven't you ever seen gold before?"

"Of course. Gold is panned in Byron from a stream north of where I live. It is always sold. No one has it made into jewelry."

Else motioned them along Central Street until Barilla's attention was again alerted at a boot and shoe shop. "Look at the pretty shoes." Instantly aware of her own rough, country brogans, she blurted out, "I've never seen such pretty shoes!"

With every step she took, Barilla became more and more fascinated. As they turned left onto Merrimack Street, they came to a hotel where a man stood in the doorway. She had never seen a man wearing such a dazzling white starched shirt. She stopped to stare. The man smiled at her.

Else grabbed her arm and pulled her along. "You must not be friendly to men. They do bad things to young girls."

She did not question what bad things. She accepted everything Else said. She did remark on so much that was new to her-the shops, the lights, so many people.

"At home," Barilla said, "people stay pretty much to home."

"You have to understand," Else said, "it is the only time we can shop. Six days a week we are in the mills from five-thirty in the morning until seven at night." She shrugged. "How else would we shop? Or for that matter, do anything but eat, work, and sleep?"

They continued along Merrimack Street where there was another hotel and more shops, and after a time came to St. Anne's Church.

"This is where we go on Sunday. Then after dinner we have the entire afternoon free. I look forward to taking you across the river where it is very beautiful," She turned to Emily. "I hope you will come, too."

"Oh my, yes, and thank you."

Then, above the clip-clop of horses and carriages, Else directed her companions to cross the traffic on dry and dusty Merrimack Street.

Barilla looked back at the church, momentarily transfixed by the gloomy stonework whose tower thrust skyward surrounded by four shaft-like prongs. "On Sunday," she thought reflectively, "I am to go inside. Oh my."

"Come on now," said Else. "We had better go back to Mrs. Merriam's." Barilla thought that an excellent idea, for an aching weariness had begun to permeate every bone in her body.

For Barilla and Emily, the two flights of stairs up to the final comfort of their bed was an heroic effort. It was unnecessary for anyone to admonish them to be quiet and go to sleep.

Barilla faced the following day with fearful apprehension. The overseer expected her to tend a loom on her own. This she avoided by stationing herself next to Else, all the while observing everything. She did understand the principle of weaving, and to be aware of breaking threads, also of keeping the bobbin spools ready for the shuttles. She soon learned that the young girl about twelve darting around with a supply of spools was called a doffer, and a young boy oiling the machine was a grease monkey.

By late afternoon, heartened by a sense of accomplishment, she felt secure enough to ready the idle loom. When the overseer came by to glare at her, she instinctively sensed his thinking.

"Tomorrow, yes, I can do it," she hollered, pointing to the loom.

Satisfied, the overseer moved away.

Else smiled, "I know you can and I'm glad. Weaving is the best place to work."

Barilla nodded smugly with a false sense of self-assurance.

Shortly before the nightly bell, Else busied herself instructing Barilla on how to get the loom ready for pushing the lever on the following day. And when that day came, Barilla instinctively knew she could master the machine. Hers was the confident nature engendered by the necessities of farm and homework. From milking the cow to churning the butter; bringing in wood and keeping the fires; the cooking and baking; carding the sheep's wool, then spinning and weaving, and the ultimate cutting and sewing the material, were all such processes of living. The words "cannot" or "won't" were unthinkable.

Thus she accepted the iron monster as naturally as eviscerating her first chicken. She had not liked that, either, but it had to be done.

Throughout the following days she made mistakes and solved them. Threads broke and she tied them. She decided to not let the jarring, clattering noise affect her, and it didn't.

And then blessedly, the closing bell of Saturday night. Else had forgotten to tell her it rang at six on Saturday.

As she hurried across the lane, she was startled by a cry behind her.

"NO!" The scream came from the boy, Jamie. She turned in time to see an older boy trip Jamie, and he sprawled face down in the dirt. Four pennies scattered toward Barilla. She stooped to retrieve the coins before the bully could confiscate them.

Jamie jumped to his feet. "Them's mine," he said as the bully ran away.

"I could see that," she responded. "But where did you get them?"

"It's my pay. Every Saturday I gets four cents."

She handed them over, speaking kindly so that Jamie would judge her to be his friend. "And what will you do with all that money;?"

"Three for a loaf of bread and one for the priest's collection."

"I see. Well, good luck to you. You're a good boy."

She glanced once at the fast-running boy before she picked up her skirt and ran up the steps.

After supper came the long awaited Saturday night with its much-looked-forward-to bath and washing of her hair.

There was a small mirror over a washstand where she brushed and pinned up her hair. Pleased with her appearance and glorying in her cleanliness, she thought, proudly, I am going to make it in this new world.

After supper, they spent the evening listening to Audrey play the mandolin. Audrey smiled as she sang, often teaching the words to her audience.

3

Else had given Barilla a long tie to go around her dress to cinch in her waistline. So after breakfast on Sunday morning, Emily, Barilla, and Else went forth to church with all the joy of free souls bent upon a worldly excursion. Else wore a huge bonnet, which was the fashion of the times. The other girls wore scarves.

They were not alone, merely three amid the throng walking up Central Street and then along Merrimack. Church bells pealed in the distance.

Else explained that besides St. Anne's, there were other churches, a Congregational, a Baptist, and a Papist. "St. Anne's," she added, with a slight rise of her chin, "is where the corporation insists we go. It's Episcopalian."

The denominational words were new to Barilla. She had no way of differentiating them. Her prime thought was of Else's appraisal, that St. Anne's was indeed beautiful, like a castle in a fairy tale She began to fantasize about what fairylike magic would take place inside.

It began by filing through a majestically wide doorway into a magnificent hall. Mesmerized, Barilla looked upward at a raftered ceiling as high and cavernous as any barn back in Byron.

Else led her through a little door to a bench seat. She then closed and bolted the door, as one would a sheep pen. Else instructed both girls to kneel upon the floor, and said, "Now you have to pray."

Barilla looked at her blankly.

Else whispered, "Bend your head down and fold your hands together."

Both Barilla and Emily went through the motions expected of them. Soon a man appeared in the distance before a candle-lit edifice of great beauty. Because of the voluminous bonnets on most females, much like inverted coalscuttles, Barilla had to shift her position enough to see that the man was wearing a long coat, almost to the floor He went up a short stairway to a perch which was higher than the sea of bonnets and began to speak. He said many things that made no sense to Barilla until one admonition, in an ambiguous way, did make some sense to her.

"Ye have done those things which ye should not have done, and not done those things which ye should have done."

Her mind wandered, to reflect on how that concerned her. The desire to come to Lowell, for instance. Should she not have done that? Her family did need her at home And what things had she not done that she should have done? It baffled her.

But then they were off their knees and sitting on the bench. Somewhere, unseen, a violin was being played. The melody's haunting beauty stirred her deeply. She recalled how her brother, Joseph, played a violin, and a banjo, too.

Then the man-she assumed to be a teacher-began to speak. He talked endlessly in a scolding voice. It was a bit like the Sunday school back in Byron. Even though there was no church, a Sunday school was held at the school in the same building where the pupils went for daily lessons, at least whenever a teacher could be found. She herself had attended on and off for several years. She thought, rather smugly, that she could read and write and do sums, so what more did she need to know?

Suddenly, some men came down the aisle bearing collection boxes. Else, acting deviously, gave a one-cent piece to each of her companions. Barilla knew instinctively what should be done with it. That was, of course, what Jamie meant by a penny for the priest.

As they emerged from the church, Barilla pondered many questions which she assumed Else could answer.

"That man, the leader, is he a priest?"

"Not exactly. We call them ministers. Priests are those in the Papist church."

"What is a Papist?" Barilla wanted to know.

"They call themselves Catholics. The Irish, Italians, and Canadians go there. There is someone called a pope in Europe who makes rules they must follow."

"Seems to me," Barilla commented in a dour manner, "that minister makes rules we must follow."

"Oh, that," Else said in a hushed voice. "We pay no attention. Going to church is something we just have to do. So, come on now. Back for dinner, then off for walking across the river."

At dinner, Barilla had asked if her other friends from Maine could also accompany them. Thus all but Mary joined the troop heading up Bridge Street and across the river. Mary claimed that she was too sick and too tired.

Ahead of them stood a verdant forest, starkly green against a cobalt sky. The river, extremely dry, ran only in occasional rivulets. Else explained that the Pawtucket dam upriver held back the water needed to power the mills.

"It is said that they let enough water run down river to nurture the fish. I pity the poor fish in that," she scoffed.

The group of girls followed Else along the northern riverbank in the shade of surrounding trees where the air was cool. The leaves of maple and oak were beginning to color. Looking across the river, the density of trees on both sides obscured the now silent mill buildings. Alter a time of walking, the pleasant sound of the falls could be heard. One by one the girls spread their skirts and sat down. For Barilla, the serenity filled her with joy. Here one could easily forget the heat and noise of the workdays.

Else began telling a story. "A great Indian chief, Pasaconaway, ruled these lands near the falls, finding fish here in abundance. In his advanced years, his son Wannalancet became the sachem, or chief, of the region. He was more friendly to the whites than old Pasaconaway, even to accepting the white man's religion. I have a friend, James, who says that was wrong, that the Indians were happier and far better off with their own way of life. The white men meddled, robbing them of their livelihood and also their lands. For what? To build a city like this wherein hordes of people toil in hot buildings like so many ants, to fatten up the great, invested owners."

"But," Climena said, "the white, or rather, the civilized, people have to make money. We have to share in that process or we would not eat, nor live, as we would like."

"Oh," said Else, "I suppose you are right, in having the ability to buy things. Just the same, how nice if one lived in permanent freedom to hunt, fish, and canoe up and down the river."

Climena, imbued with the practical bent of her Yankee upbringing, retaliated, saying, "That is unrealistic!"

Else said no more.

As the sun lowered in the west above Pawtucket Falls, the girls grew restless, and standing up, brushed off their skirts and moved easterly retracing their steps back to Mrs. Merriam's.

Back at their temporary home, Else started up the flight of stairs, but Barilla heard voices coming from the parlor where she glimpsed Mary seated on a sofa, talking with someone. So she entered the parlor, followed by her friends. There, to her amazement, was Dana Austin seated beside Mary.

At Dana's recognition of his friends, he jumped up to greet each one affably. He hugged his sister Emily.

"I come up from Boston on the train," he said. He went on to chide each in turn with the familiarity of being brother to them all. They had all grown up together. and he was older than any of them.

"I come up to visit all of you and there wan't none of you here but Mary. She's been telling me all about the hard work you do, locked into a hot, steamy, noisy mill." Now that he was the center of attention, he continued, "Not me, though. I work on a farm in Brighton."

While he extrapolated on and on, Barilla studied him. His brilliant blue eyes glinted humorously. His hair was blond and wavy, with an occasional curl dangling on his forehead; his lips moved rapidly with his discourse.

She had a momentary flashback to the one time he had kissed her on the lips. She must have been thirteen that winter. She had fallen while skating on a flooded field. Dana helped her to her feet, skating beside her afterward, holding her hands, helping her gain rhythm and confidence. Later, beside the fire at the field's edge, they undid their skates. Then he walked beside her up through the woods toward her house. Abruptly, he had turned her to him and kissed her. Embarrassed, she had looked downward briefly before she turned away to run up through the Taylor's field. She had turned around once to see him standing where she had left him. He had waved his hand. She thought he was smiling.

And now, here they were, all grown up and out working in an unfamiliar world. And on this day, who had been here to greet him? Mary. She never liked Mary and she liked her even less now.

When sounds from the adjacent dining room indicated that supper would soon be served, Dana made excuses to leave.

"It is time to be on my way back to Boston," he said cheerily. Then turning to each girl, he kissed everyone briefly on the cheek.

At her turn, Barilla stiffened. But, suddenly aware that she was experiencing jealousy, she relaxed and forced a smile.

They said good-bye, each one no doubt feeling the poignancy of his abrupt departure.

Supper consisted of raspberry sauce, biscuits, and tea. There had never been any tea back home. Barilla did not like it. She managed a few spoonfuls of the sauce, but one bite of biscuit became unpalatable. She was in love. She wanted Dana for herself, not to share him with the others. She pushed back her chair and hurried toward the stairway, determined that no one would see the tears threatening to burst forth.

Emily was the first to enter their room where Barilla sat beside her trunk scribbling words upon paper. A nearby candle gave off its small light.

"Writing home?" Emily asked.

"No. I'm trying to write poetry."

"Oh, you mean for the Lowell Offering?"

"What's the Lowell Offering?" she asked, not looking up.

"It's a small magazine that prints what the working girls write. There were some copies down in the parlor. Everyone was reading them."

"Well, perhaps I'll do that after I see what the others have written."

Emily kneeled down and lifted Barilla's chin. "You've been crying. What's wrong?"

"I can't tell you."

"Homesick?"

"No, it's not that. It is something private. I really cannot tell you."

"All right," said Emily as she stood up. "But you know that when we get upset, we have only ourselves to turn to." Then, without pausing, she went on, "Wasn't it nice to see Dana here? To see someone else from home made the distance seem not so far."

"Yes, of course. That is so true." Those are the words she spoke. They were not exactly how she felt. To herself, she read what she had written.

> *Like the sun thy presence glowing*
> *Clothes a memory in brightest light.*
> *And when thou art not remembering,*
> *Love abjectly fades this night.*
> *All things looked so bright about thee*
> *Life is naught it seems without thee*
> *The past comes to my lucid mind*
> *And early visions are refined.*

She slid the paper inside her trunk, then stared dejectedly at the candle's flickering light.

The jarring ring of the five A.M. bell alerted Barilla to the fact that it was Monday again. A full week had passed since they had arrived. And like it or not, this was to be the routine.

She hustled with the others down the steps, across the lane, and up the spiral stairs. What had Else likened them to? A horde of ants. And she was merely one of those ants. Well, she had to work to send the loom into its banging, clattering motion. There was no room in her thoughts for anything except the monster machine which demanded full attention, responding only to her control of that lever.

At the day's end, Barilla sought Else's advice about writing a poem for the Lowell Offering. They were in the parlor where Barilla sat reading a copy.

"Sure," said Else. "Not everyone can write poetry. I think Harriet would be pleased to have something like that."

"Is she the one who puts it together?"

"One of them. A man named Abel Thomas started it a few years ago. But now some women workers get it up."

"Oh. I'll get right to it. I already have an idea."

They said goodnight and Barilla, filled with the excitement of her projected task, ran up the two flights of stairs to seat herself beside her trunk and thus begin. She struck a flint and lit her candle. It took several evenings to complete. By the third night, the candle had deteriorated into a gray mass as it flickered its own demise, drowned in smelly wax and a waft of smoke. That provided the last bit of inspiration. She ran with the finished product down to Else's room to get her opinion. Seated on Else's bed, Barilla began to read.

Epitaph on a Candle
A wicked one lies here
Who died in a decline
he never rose in rank I fear
Tho' he was born to shine.
He once was fat but not in deed
He's thin as any griever.
He died, the doctors all agreed
Of a most burning fever.
One thing of him is said with truth
With which I'm much amused
It is that when he stood forsoothe
A stick he always used
Now dripping streaks he sometimes made
But this was not enough

For finding it a poorish trade
He always dealt in snuff.
If 'ere you said, "Go out I pray,"
He much ill nature showed.
On such occasions, he would say,
"Why if I do I'm blowed."
In this his friends do all agree
Although you'd think I'm joking.
When going out 'tis said that he
Was wont to do some smoking.
Since all religion he despised
Let these few words suffice.
Before he ever was baptized
They dipped him once or twice.

Else looked up at a candle ensconced in a bracket across the room. She grinned. "It is amusing. It's different from the stories usually printed. But, tell you what; let's take it over to Harriet at the library tomorrow after supper. The library is open on Thursdays from seven to nine."

On the next evening when they reached their destination, it surprised Barilla that the library was one room of a schoolhouse.

Else found the person she was looking for, a young girl seated at a desk. They greeted one another. Then Else turned, beckoning Barilla, who stood dumbfounded at the entrance.

"Miss Harriet Farley, may I present Miss Barilla Taylor, who has written a poem for you to consider for the Lowell Offering."

"Pleased to meet you, ma'am," Barilla said, as she bowed her head slightly and offered Miss Farley her paper.

While the woman read her poem, Barilla studied the book-lined walls. She was awed by so many books. The only books in the schoolroom in Byron were on the teacher's desk. Besides Perry's Speller and Dictionary, the teacher read from storybooks as a treat when all had been diligent in their lessons. There had been fairy tales, adventure, geography, and histories, such as the lives of Puritans and how the

Forefathers once stood up to some hated British soldiers and won their freedom.

Harriet Farley looked up. She chuckled. "It's not what we usually like to publish, but I'm sure our readers will find this amusing. Thank you for sharing."

Barilla took that as a dismissal. Looking away, she saw Else across the room where a white-haired woman wearing spectacles sat at another desk. That woman handed Else a book. She was smiling.

Else joined Barilla and they walked together away from the school. Curious about the book Else carried, she asked, "Why did she give you a book to take away with you?"

"Because I am a subscriber, I can borrow a book. I paid fifty cents for one year so I can borrow a book for two weeks whenever I want one."

"Fifty cents," Barilla said. "Doesn't a single book cost more than that?"

"Of course. But when a lot of people pay fifty cents, the library can buy lots of books, so a great many people get to read the same book."

She considered this library system as quite amazing. Deep in thought, she walked along beside her companion, vaguely aware of the flickering street lamps and the rhythmic beat of horses hooves upon the street. Behind her, a train's start-up whistle blasted starkly in the cool dark night. The whistle brought a pang of memory; Dana's returning by train to Boston on Sunday night. But, how odd that she had not thought about him since then. Unwittingly, she realized that the therapy she had experienced while writing her poem, trifling though it may have been, had served a necessary purpose.

With each happening in this new life she was becoming aware that she was gaining knowledge, not only of life far away from home, but about herself. She slept well that night, dreaming of being a published poet of great renown.

The last working Saturday in October came to an end-payday! A long line of operatives wove their way through the countinghouse.

Barilla gave her name to a clerk who did not even look up. He counted out three dollars and seventy-three cents and handed it to her.

She was ecstatic. Moving along outside, she smiled broadly at Else. "I've got money.'"

"But," interjected Else, "not very much. That's because you are only a spare hand. See here. I have fourteen dollars and forty cents. That's because I have been working since last April. In a few months, you will get more."

Undeterred, Barilla went on excitedly, "Can I buy a bonnet? Tonight maybe? I want a bonnet for church tomorrow."

"Yes, of course. Bonnets cost about two dollars."

"And shoes? How much for the pretty shoes?"

"About a dollar and a half," Else said.

That was all Barilla needed to know. She decided to blow it all that evening. The purchase of material for a new dress would have to wait until next month.

Jamie caught up with them as they started up the boardinghouse steps. He held up a fifty-cent piece to show Barilla. "See," he grinned. "I get one of these on paydays, beside the pennies Mr. Avery gives me."

Barilla patted him on the head. "That's fine, Jamie. Thank you for showing it to me."

He hardly heard, for he turned abruptly and ran swiftly down the lane to Central Street.

"That kid is so dirty," said Else disdainfully. "How can you even stand the smell of him?"

"Oh, Else. He is just a little boy. I can't help but be sorry for him."

"He's Irish, so he lives in the Paddy camps, which is a stinkhole, a blot on the city. It's better not to get too friendly with the likes of him."

On Sunday, Barilla felt a new sense of pride walking to church wearing shiny, black shoes with a row of pearly buttons holding them snugly on her ankles. She had a blue bonnet atop her head, like an enormous coalscuttle, and tied demurely under her chin. It did not matter that she had no new dress.

During that day and the next, her thoughts reverted back to Jamie. He was about her brother Stephen's age. By contrast, Stephen was reasonably clean. He did have to help with the farm work and keep the wood boxes filled. Stephen went to school. He could read. She liked playing checkers with him after supper on wintry nights, and he often beat her.

Thus imbued with a sense of wrong in Jamie's life, it was after work on Monday evening that she caught his arm as he hurried past. She asked his last name.

"Dunno," he said, looking away, anxious to be on his way.

"What do they call your mother?"

"Molly."

"Not everyone, surely. She must be called 'Missus' something."

"Yeah. Missus Quinn."

"Then Quinn is your last name, Jamie."

"You think so?" he asked, looking at her directly for the first time.

"Yes, and your father's name is Mister Quinn."

"He ain't living. Got his self crushed to death working on building a canal."

"Oh, I'm sorry." She was still holding his arm. "Do you have brothers and sisters?"

"Yup, lots of them." He tried to pull away, but she moved toward the step and sat down, pulling him down beside her.

"You are ten years old and you don't go to school. You should do so. You have to learn to read."

He looked at her inquiringly, "Why?"

She launched into an explanation of what life could offer him if he had some education. All of which was lost on the little boy, who could envision nothing beyond the daily food and a particular niche in his private world.

"I gotta go," he said, jumping up and running off down the lane.

When November's payday came, Barilla, who had developed a sense of guilt for not having sent any money home, resolved to do so. That is, whatever was left after buying the cloth to make herself a new dress. By Christmas, she must have a new dress. Her pay was eight dollars.

She was elated, not only by all that money, but also the fact that she was worth it, and worth something to the company.

Sunday was cold and rainy. After the noon dinner, she went to her room, and wrote a letter to the family at home.

Lowell, Mass. December 3, 1843

Distant Parents,

It is with pleasure that I seat myself this afternoon to let you know that my health is good. It is a blustery day, but am comfortably seated where nearby a fire burns brightly in the fireplace. Yesterday was pay day. After my purchases of last evening, I have five dollars left, which I send with this letter.

I bought six yards of pretty, black and white striped, silky cloth, some pins, needles, thread, and a pattern. The whole of it coming to three dollars. I have a new friend here by the name of Else, who will help me cut out and fit the dress. She spells her name, Else, but pronounces it like 'Elsa.' I don't know why.

I like it in the mill. It is not hard work. But we must be diligent. The hours are long. The workplace is dusky with flying lint and fumes from the lamps. And the noise! You cannot imagine the noise. I cannot even describe it to you.

We are required to attend the church here. It is a large, beautiful stone building. The stones are cut square somehow, not like our round ones filling up the Swift River or what make up our stone walls.

There is a place here called a library, where they allow you to take books away, It costs fifty cents a year to join. So, next pay day, I am going to pay for that. There is a boy here named Jamie who is in the mill. He cannot read because he does not go to school. I want to get a primer from the library and teach him to read.

I hope these few lines will find you well. I would like to have you write and tell me about everyone. I miss you all so much, especially Delano, who is perhaps walking by now. Fill up your letters full. Don't leave anything out. I have wrote all I can today. I must go downstairs to use a dinner table for cutting out my dress.

From your absent daughter, Barilla Adeline Taylor

The following day began like any other. The whirring belts and wheels serviced the looms into the usual vibrating cacophony. Barilla's loom performed well. She felt good. Suddenly, above the din, a piercing scream came from behind Barilla. Instinctively she pushed her stop lever and turned around. A belt had caught the hair of another operative. Barilla was struck with chilling fear at the horrible scene as the belt and wheels tore at the girl's scalp and threatened the arm with which she reached up to free her hair.

It took but a split second for Barilla to reach the still shuttling loom and shut it off. The injured girl was a stranger. Barilla was screaming, "Help!" at the top of her lungs, as she worked to extricate the bloody mess of a crushed arm and torn scalp enmeshed in the flywheel. Mercifully, by that time the girl was unconscious, and Barilla lowered her to the floor. All the machinery had been shut down. The sudden quietness became overwhelming. Other operatives crowded around, and Mr. Lord pushed through to investigate.

With hardly time to appraise the situation, he commanded, "Get a stretcher and clear this-this mess out of here!"

"She is unconscious. She needs medical help," Barilla cried.

"More important to get these gears and belt cleared and get the machines going again," he said. He paid no attention to Barilla's horrified expression. He again commanded loudly, "Someone, get a mechanic up here, now!"

Barilla had not felt faint as she had helped the girl, nor did her blood-covered hands unnerve her, but the callous attitude of the overseer engulfed her. Now aware that Else stood beside her, she turned pitiful eyes toward her friend, and fell inertly into Else's arms, as Else dropped to her knees to support Barilla's weight against her own breast.

Someone put a dipper of water to Barilla's mouth. She opened her eyes to observe hazily that it was a strange man holding the dipper to her lips. She felt the slight pressure of a strong, male hand upon her shoulder.

"Thank you," she responded weakly, as she focused more clearly on the strange new person. He smiled, then helped her rise to her feet. The injured girl was nowhere to be seen. A boy was mopping up the floor.

Suddenly, Mr. Lord said, "Hey, you! You're not here to mollycoddle my workers. You're here to fix this belt and get things going."

Tears welled in Barilla's eyes and she turned angrily toward the overseer. "You are a hateful man! Hateful, hatefull!" She felt color rise in her cheeks. She clenched her fists to stop her hands from shaking. Then, she slowly made her way back to her loom. She would probably be let go. She did not care.

In a very short time the belts and pulleys started moving. After taking a few deep breaths, and with grim determination, she pushed the startup lever as normalcy once more returned to the room.

When work had finished that evening, as Barilla walked across the lane, Jamie grabbed her skirt. "How did the girl get dead," he asked.

Briefly, Barilla explained the accident, then said, "How do you know if she is dead?"

"I heard someone say so. Well, I gotta go, but I'm glad it warn't you."

That night before she fell asleep, Barilla resolved to block out the horror of the girl's screams, the torn flesh, and the overseer's total lack of compassion. Thus her thoughts came to dwell on Jamie. She felt a happy warmth over his parting words. The last vision that came was of the strange man, the mechanic, with deep blue penetrating eyes and genial smile. And she felt again the strong arms that had helped her to her feet.

4

At dinnertime on Sunday, the tenth of December, Mrs. Merriam announced that the day before Christmas was to fall on a Sunday. Therefore, each girl could invite a friend to join them for dinner after church. She would have to know by at least the day before how many would be accepting.

Barilla turned to Else, "Does that mean other girls, or a man?"

"A man, I guess. That is, if you know one well enough."

"I only know one. His name is Dana Austin and he works on a farm in Brighton, near Boston."

"Well then, write him a letter."

"I'll think about it," she mused, recalling the last time she had seen him…with Mary. Then, decisively, she thought it best to ask his sister Emily to write to him.

The morning of December twenty-fourth dawned bright and cold. The Maine girls, who were used to having their homes decorated with evergreen boughs, had gone across the river and brought some back. Thus they had strewn them throughout the parlor and dining room, all having been accomplished before dressing for church.

During the church service, Barilla was pensive. She recalled how Christmas at home had always been a festive occasion. And how she popped corn in a special basket popper, then threaded the kernels onto a string for the boys to loop garlands on a fir tree. They would place small red candles on its branches to be lit on Christmas Eve. Oftentimes the Austin family came by sleigh to enjoy hot mulled cider and raise their voices in carols as her mother played the old pump organ. The memories pierced her heart with an aching, empty feeling. She wondered if her older brothers would even get home.

She knew that the family would be missing her. There was one redeeming thought-Emily had received a letter from Dana stating that he would be coming today. He would be Emily's guest.

On the other hand, Else's gentleman friend, James, was to come, and he would be bringing a friend names Horace. Else had told Mrs. Merriam that Horace would be Barilla's guest. Else had so informed Barilla of the arrangement. Barilla, being stubbornly loyal to her feelings for Dana, determined to be polite, but would not give encouragement to the stranger.

Those were her thoughts as the girls left the church to return to their boardinghouse.

So now, dressed in her new striped satin dress and her pearl-buttoned shoes, she removed her cape and entered the confusion of chatter in the parlor. She found a seat at the far end of the room beside Emily. Suddenly, in the entrance, Dana appeared. And Mary was brazenly moving across the room to greet him. Barilla, stung with disappointment, watched in horror as he took Mary's hand and pressed it to his chest Oh damnation! How could he possibly be interested in mousy Mary? Ice water instead of blood coursed through her veins. Her mouth went dry. She tried to swallow, but the rapid beat of her heart made that impossible. In that moment she hated Mary and hated Dana, too.

Dana then moved around the parlor to greet his other friends, seated sedately upon sofas or chairs. Mary walked beside him, her right hand clinging possessively onto his arm.

"That hussy, that absolute hussy," thought Barilla.

He then singled out his sister Emily. Disengaging Mary's hand from his arm, he moved to greet and kiss his sister. Then he turned to Barilla. She stood up. Her hands had formed two clenched fists that hung at her sides. She could not even force a smile. She returned his warm gaze and easy smile with hardened eyes and an icy stare.

Dana, mistaking her hostile gaze as a homesick memory of Christmases past, made a wry comment.

"Not like the gay Christmastimes of our childhood, is it, Rilla?"

She tried to respond, but uttered nothing for fear of saying something laced with acid.

He reached out and she felt the pressure of his hands on her shoulders.

"It's not that, is it, being homesick?" he asked.

She lowered her eyes. He was so very close and not much taller.

"No, it's not that," she said.

"Are you ill?"

She shook her head.

"Of course you're not. Because you look so, well, so beautiful. That's one gorgeous dress."

She relaxed as she said a demure, "Thank you."

Dana's hands lifted their pressure on her shoulders and turned his attention first to Malvina, then to Louisa.

Of this, Barilla was only vaguely aware, because Else and two gentlemen were approaching, both a head taller than Else. One was blonde, the other with dark hair. She felt a flush of color rise in her cheeks.

Else bowed to her slightly. "Barilla Taylor, may I present my friend, James Gordon." Barilla nodded to the blonde one. "And Mister Horace Gailey. He had requested the pleasure of your acquaintance."

"Oh my," Barilla responded abruptly, looking up at the tall, dark-haired man. "Aren't you the loom fixer who repaired the bad situation in the weaving room?"

"I am," Horace said, his deep blue eyes and engaging grin expanding, as he reached to shake her hand. "I had to ask your name. And, fortunately, my friend James here knew Else and that you lived in this house."

Horace still held her hand as the dinner bell rang. He offered his elbow and an indication to place her hand there. She smiled up at him graciously, as two by two, everyone entered the festively decorated dining room. The aroma of roasted chicken and savory fixings drew many an inhaled breath of satisfaction. Dinner was an hour later than usual, so everyone was hungry.

There were place cards at each table setting, which eliminated confusion. Horace pulled back her chair. As she seated herself, she felt an overwhelmingly warm feeling. No one had ever treated her this way. No man or boy back home gave any deference to women as being other than chattel.

Large platters of chicken and stuffing, bowls of whipped potatoes, orange squash, and pearl onions were being passed. Except for the subdued din, the entire room seemed hushed in expectation.

With appetites partially appeased, there began the usual questioning and answers as to where each had come from, and about their respective families. Horace asked, "How do you like being in Lowell?"

Barilla, having completely dismissed Dana and Mary and succumbed to Horace's charm, spoke without guile, "Oh, I like it first rate."

"So do I. Especially now that I am seated here beside you."

Barilla accepted this without embarrassment, perhaps even with a tinge of satisfaction. If Dana did not want her company, this man did. And perhaps she was a bit smitten.

Serving girls came by to remove the dinner plates, replacing them with smaller ones, on which pie would be served. This was certainly not the custom. Usually, one merely put pie on one's empty plate. That's the way it was at home, too.

Despite the diners feelings of being stuffed, the smell of cinnamon apple pie and spicy pumpkin could hardly be turned aside.

"I am full," said Horace, "but I'm still going to have a piece."

"Me, too," Barilla said.

Any strangeness she had felt was gone, as she sat beside this new acquaintance. She had no feeling of being awkward, but rather of taking this friendly relationship as natural as breathing.

"Look out the window," he said suddenly. "It is snowing."

"Yes. I felt it was clouding up as we returned from church."

"I had hoped we could go for a walk. But now that is impossible."

"If you'd like, we can play checkers out in the parlor," she said.

"Fine, let's go." He added with a mocking smile, "I haven't played since childhood, so no doubt you will beat me."

"Perhaps not. Even my little brother sometimes beats me."

She found a spot and placed a tabletop checkerboard between them, and put the red and black checkers in position.

From the far end of the room, she could hear Audrey tuning her mandolin. As Audrey and others began to sing, "God Rest You Merry Gentlemen," Barilla spoke to her companion.

"You start."

The game progressed with the usual capture or evasive action. When he had but one checker left, she saw that she could jump it. With the captured checker in her hand, she looked up sheepishly to see amusement in eyes that were truly filled with delight.

"You are fun to be with," he said. "But I recall your furious anger that day in the mill, telling off the overseer."

"His behavior was horrid," she answered soberly. "I could not help myself."

"The overseers are not entirely to blame. It is the policy of the agents who are accountable to the blood-suckers who own the mills."

"I suppose that's true. But you don't go along with that horrid callousness, do you?." she said.

"Of course not. Mechanics don't have to put up with the degrading tactics used on you girls. In fact, I am only working until this coming Friday."

"Then what are you going to do?"

"I am going back to school. I have been before, but needed more money for tuition, so I worked here for the past six months. I leave on January first. I'll be going to a college in Boston that teaches engineering."

"Engineering?" she asked, uncertain what it meant.

"Of course. This country is fast becoming industrial. There is going to be a tremendous need for men who know about designing and construction."

"The first of January, you said? Why, that's only a week away."

"Yes. I leave a week from Monday."

"Oh!" She did not quite understand her feeling of disappointment.

"So," he said, "I would like to be with you next Sunday. It is New Year's Eve. Would you accompany me to dinner at the Merrimack House after church?" he asked, watching closely for her reaction.

Barilla's eyes opened wide in surprise. It was not her nature to be coy, so she answered abruptly, "Of course. It would pleasure me a great deal."

"Fine. Now let's see if I can beat you at a game."

Barilla grinned happily as they busied themselves placing checkers in order on the board.

As the game progressed, Barilla sensed she was winning, when into her mind came the story of Atalanta, one of the myths her teacher had read about the girl who lost her race to a desirable suitor. So she made a few mistakes. She hoped they were not obvious.

Horace won. He looked directly at her, amused by her apparent frown for having lost. Behind him came the voice of James.

"It is snowing harder, Horace, so it is best we return to quarters."

Horace laughed and rose to his feet, saying, "Unfortunately, the weather dampens many a pleasant outing."

Barilla had risen to stand opposite the two men. Horace held his hand forward and she placed her hand in it, palm to palm.

"Thank you for such a nice time. On Sunday next, I shall meet you on the church steps after the service."

Barilla nodded. her eyes dancing. And then they were gone.

Else came up beside her. "We should be thanking Mrs. Merriam."

Barilla followed her back to the dining room. After giving their benefactress profuse appreciation, the two girls moved into the hall. Else put an arm across Barilla's back, and said, "You really did have a good time, didn't you?"

Barilla turned her face and smiled happily. "Oh my, yes. I do thank you because meeting him took my mind off my…" She almost said, "troubles," but that now seemed idiotic.

When they reached the top of the stairs, Else said, "Come into my room and tell me what you meant."

"It was not important."

"You were bothered by something. I watched you when that brother of Emily's talked with you."

"I was upset. You see, he and I were childhood sweethearts and now it seems he has eyes only for Mary."

"And you were jealous? What a dodo! He is not worth thinking about. James and I sat across from him, seated between Mary and Emily. And let me tell you, he said some of the dumbest things."

"I suppose so. Dana is a great kidder."

They were seated on Else's bed with shawls over their shoulders against the cold. Else snickered. "Hmph, I think he is a buffoon. When he finished his dinner he said, 'So help me sheepshead, that was one fine plate of victuals.'"

Barilla chuckled. "Yes that is one of his expressions."

"And when dessert plates replaced the dinner plates, he said, So help me beef and onions, I never seen the like!'"

Barilla laughed aloud. "Those are words many of our Maine people use. Truly, Else, I never gave it much thought."

"I never heard you talk like that."

"No, that is because I am different now." She drew herself proudly erect. "I am no longer a country girl. I am a working girl. a city girl, and I wish to better myself. Next payday I am going to buy a library membership. I am going to learn things, lots of things."

"I'm sure you will. You've got gumption. That is one reason Horace wanted to meet you. The day of the accident I recognized him as a friend of James. When I told James about the accident, he told Horace I was your friend, and that's how it happened."

"He was nice and so good-looking. He is also smart. He is going to college."

"I know. That is where he and James met. James and his father came here from Scotland to work in the Lowell Company because they were experienced carpetmen. Mr. Gordon, the father, insisted James attend college last year. When Horace needed money, James suggested he come here to work. The three live together in the Scotch Block."

Barilla grinned shyly. "He asked me to go for dinner with him next Sunday."

"There you go. He really likes you."

"Do I have to ask permission?"

"Yes you do. Also tell Mrs. Merriam with whom, where, and when you will return."

"Oh my."

"Barilla," Else said, "you use that expression too much."

Later, in bed with Emily, both girls snuggled together to keep warm. Emily asked, "What were you so angry about when Dana tried to talk to you?"

"Oh Em, let's forget it. It is behind me now. It is not important, so let's go to sleep."

"Come on. You must have had some reason for being so unpleasant. Dana was offended."

"It was about Mary. I was upset because he liked Mary better than me."

"You are right about that. He sees Mary as a perfect lady, whereas you are spirited, independent, and set on having your own way. Girls like Mary need a man to look up to, and look after them. One who is…"

"A milk-sop, a useless drone!" Barilla insisted. "If that suits his fancy, I feel naught but pity for him. Besides, I don't care anymore, and I don't want to talk about it, so please, let's go to sleep."

In the early morning hours on Monday, after working from five A.M. until six, the operatives trooped in for breakfast, Barilla, seated between Else and Emily, noticed that Climena and Mary were not dressed for work.

"How come," she said to Climena, "you two did not work before breakfast?"

"Mary and I are all through. We finished on Saturday," Climena said.

Barilla kept eating, but between mouthfuls she asked, "So, what are you going to do?"

"We are going home."

"How will you get there?"

"By train to Boston, then in the newly opened Boston and Maine, which now goes to Portland. We'll get the stage up to Mexico."

At that, with the sudden scraping of chairs, the exodus of hurrying girls headed back to the mill.

"Well, good-bye and good luck," Barilla called back as she ran, adding, "and remember us to all the folks."

Although Emily also worked in the weave room, she was not even in Barilla's range of vision, the room stretching endlessly away. Even so, she could not have talked with her about it because the noise was too great.

It was at the noon dinner in the dining room before she could ask, "Why are Climena and Mary going home?"

Clim said it was because their mother needs them. There is to be another baby in the spring. That will be the eleventh. The poor woman has reason to be all tired out.

"My mother has had eleven and she does all right," Barilla said.

"Well, that is what they told me," said Emily. Barilla did not answer, but she did wonder.

The week passed, Barilla counting the days in anticipation of the week's end. More snow fell and she realized that with the Saturday payday she must buy overshoes and a warmer shawl. Thus, with her pay of $10.50 she purchased the items for five dollars, with fifty cents for a library card, and five dollars to send home.

On Sunday morning as she emerged into bright sunlight, after the dimness of the church, Barilla blinked to adjust her eyes. She looked around for Horace. From the sidewalk fifty feet away, she saw him moving toward her as people streamed out in the opposite direction.

He touched his hat brim in greeting, his disarming smile making crinkles around his eyes. "Good morning to you, m'lady. And is this not a beautiful day?"

"It is that, but not so good underfoot," she answered gaily.

"Take my arm and we will mush on through."

Thus they walked away through the slush of Merrimack Street.

At their destination, he steered her into the lobby of the Merrimack House and urged her to sit as he removed the new brown boots. She stood and untied her shawl of dark blue wool, and undid her blue bonnet.

As Horace took them from her, he said, "Blue complements your lovely blue eyes. Eyes which are not light like the bonnet, but as dark with intensity as the shawl."

And she, being so intrigued by it all, was oblivious to her surroundings. Not until they entered the dining room was she aware of an elegant room where tables were covered with white cloths, crystal glassware, and gleaming silver. A handsomely dressed man bowed in greeting, and Horace indicated she should follow the man.

Once they were seated, she noticed long white cards on the table. She picked one up, which said, Bill of Fare. She read down the list.

Horace, reading his card, asked what she would like.

Never in her life had she had a choice of the food she ate.

"I would like the roast beef," she said, hoping she sounded like a mature lady.

Horace ordered for them both.

While they waited for the food, Barilla looked around the room. There were a few couples engaged in subdued conversation, but mostly men occupied the room. She felt Horace's eyes watching her. She turned to face him, her head cast down a little, yet looking up. She bit shyly into her lower lip.

"I have never been in a place like this," she said.

Amused, he said, "I thought not. I trust you are not uncomfortable?"

"Oh, no. It is just that I was a country girl, and now I must be a city girl."

"Which you are doing admirably."

A waiter brought their food. She began to eat meat that was slightly pink and was pleasantly surprised that it was good and tender.

Horace, who had lived most of his life in Boston, asked her to tell him about the country life. "For instance," he added, "what about schooling?"

"Oh, I have many times been to school. There is not always a teacher. When one is hired, everyone who is not needed on the farms or in the woods goes to school. We live on the Roxbury/Byron line and can go to either school. I like Byron best. It is beside a beautiful canyon called Coos*."

"I imagine it is not very large?"

"Oh yes, a very large room."

"One room?"

"Of course."

"For how many grades?"

"I guess, about six. If a person wants more schooling, they have to go down to Canton where someone keeps a high school. You have to board there for each term. It is too far for going and coming every day."

"Did you go to the high school?"

"No. It's mostly for boys. The girls who go are those who expect to be teachers."

"I see. And you did not want to be a teacher?"

"I could not be spared. I only came to work here in order to send money home."

"I understand. My mother needs the support of my brother who works on a farm in Brookline."

"And your father?" she asked.

"He worked at the Western Railroad freight yard and was crushed to death between the coupling of two freight cars."

"Oh how awful!" she sympathized.

He looked away, deep in thought, then continued. "At the time we lived nearby on Columbus Avenue. That is in the heart of Boston,

---

* pronounced co-ahs

and where I went to school. Afterward, Mother moved out of the area to a small house west of the Back Bay."

"Do you have sisters?" Barilla asked.

"Not living. There were two, but they died young."

"I know about that. I lost a younger sister at the age of five. I was eleven. It was very hard."

"Does your father have steady employment?"

"I think you mean, does he get paid by someone?"

"Yes."

"No. We raise our food. We also have sheep for wool and cows for milk. Father and the boys cut our own wood. One cash crop is hops. Otherwise, Father barters our surplus for things like sugar, flour, and saleratus."

"What, pray tell, is saleratus?"

"A leavening to make bread and biscuits rise."

"And do you cook?"

"Of course. I've been cooking since I was eight, when my brother Melchior was born."

"And how old are you now?"

"Going on sixteen, when June comes."

She studied his face. She could not fathom his thoughts.

Then he said, "When I was sixteen, I was still in school. Now, I am twenty-two."

They had been so involved in conversation they had lost track of time, and suddenly realized that the dining room was almost empty.

She looked around wistfully and said quietly, "Do you think we should leave?"

"Perhaps," he said, rising. "It seems that whenever I am having a pleasant time with you, there appears some reason for its coming to an end."

Outside, darkness deepened. As they crossed Merrimack Street onto Central, the last rays of sun cast a brilliant orange sweeping behind the trees and the four spires of St. Anne's Church. They walked up Central Street across the canal to Hamilton Lane. After passing a lamplighter who had not yet lit the one at the corner, Horace stopped and suddenly put his arm around her, drawing her to him. She had to look up at his face so very close to hers. He untied and pushed back her bonnet and spoke with deep sincerity. "Before that fellow lights any more lamps, there is something I must do."

She knew instinctively what that was. Their lips came together, for, it seemed to her, a very long time.

He drew away slightly to whisper in her ear. "I noticed you did not mind."

She could not answer, for her heartbeat had strangely quickened. He held her head against his chest with one hand.

"I must leave in the morning so this is good-bye for a while."

"Yes, sir, I realize that."

"Hardly, sir, Barilla. My name is Horace."

"Yes, Horace."

"That's better. Now I want you to know I am not good at writing, and I will be very busy. But you must believe that I will not be forgetting you."

"Nor I you, Horace."

"I'll see you to the door and part there with a handshake. That will be best."

"Yes, of course."

After they parted, she stood on the topmost step of the boardinghouse and watched until he was gone from sight.

5

Inside the door, she stood for a moment reflecting on both joy and sadness.

A bustling noise from the dining room indicated that her coworkers were at supper. At the entrance, she caught the eye of one of the serving girls to advise Mrs. Merriam that she had returned. She then made a hurried exit up the stairway. This was not a time for irrelevant chatter with anyone.

1844 was a new year in the city of spindles. The sleep, eat, and work pattern continued despite the cold and short days. One evening after the second week, Barilla received a letter, She opened it carefully because there was no- envelope, merely a sheet of paper folded to form an envelope. It was from her brother, Con.

Roxbury, December 29, 1843

Absent Sister,

It is with pleasure that I seat myself to write you these few lines. I am well and I hope this will find you enjoying the same blessing. We received your letter in two weeks from the time that you wrote it. We was glad to hear from you and thank you for the five dollar note. The folks are well. We heard from brother Byron and he is well. I hardly know what to write as it is evening and the candle don't give a very good light. But I will tell you about Thanksgiving. They had a donation party at Mr. Knapp's and all had a merry time. I wish you had been there. Most all of the young folks in town was there, about 18. School begins next Monday. Climena and Mary have got home and they do expect to go to school. Dana came with them. He is going to work for his Uncle Asa Austin down to Canton.

The next time you write, tell us what wages you get and how much you have to pay for board. Write as soon as you receive this.

Lucky for me that my chance in Stoughton was up once it got cold. I come home two days before Thanksgiving and won't go back till spring. We had a bad storm Christmas Eve, and nobody came up or down the road. It was different without you and Byron here. The other boys missed their Rilla. Marvin, Melchior, Jack, and Gene was all as lively as so many crickets. And Bub is just as you remember him. He is almost one year old and walks with help. Come home when you see fit. Goodbye for the present, from your distant brother, Joseph Convers Taylor

She refolded the letter, musing to herself. So, Climena and Mary were escorted by Dana back home by train. Someone had to know they were coming in order to take a wagon down to meet them in Mexico. Humph, what do I care?

Coming from behind Barilla, Else's voice broke her reverie.

"Letters are more important than eating, I know. But, come on. Let's go in for supper. By the way, who is it from, Horace?"

"No. From my brother Con."

As they seated themselves to eat, pungent bowls of pea soup were placed before them. Most of the girls had finished, so the dining room was half empty.

"The folks at home are well and they have missed me," Barilla said. "I was just thinking about my being here for three months and how my life has changed. Oh, I miss my family, but now feel more grown up."

"It must be nice to have a family," said Else wistfully. "Although I do have a father and brother, I don't know where they are. The people here are my family."

"And you have your friend, James. Isn't he your beau?"

"Not a beau. He's just a friend. I don't want a beau."

Barilla continued eating her soup, then countered pensively, "That is where we are different. I do want a beau, and perhaps Horace will be that."

"Perhaps," said Else, giving her friend a mischievous grin. "But, he hasn't written to you yet, has he?"

"I didn't expect he would. He told me he'd be too busy to write," Barilla said defensively.

"Well, I know he liked you. He told James so."

Inwardly, Barilla swelled with satisfaction, visualizing the confident, smiling Horace. How often she had done that over the past two weeks. She compared his rugged type of beauty against her brothers whom she felt were about the handsomest boys she had ever known. Even Dana had a pretty face. But Horace was different. From his square-jawed chin to his almost black hair that formed in deep waves back from his forehead, she could see him smiling at her. She could even feel his lips again...

Suddenly, she smelled the strong odor of molasses and ginger.

"Come back to life, Barilla," Else said. "You have been staring but not seeing me passing the cookies."

"Oh," Barilla grinned sheepishly. "I was...just thinking."

"I can imagine. From the silly look on your face, I can tell lovesickness when I see it."

Barilla pursed her lips, gave Else a petulant look, and reached for a cookie.

There was not another missive until Friday, February 16. The unfamiliar writing so intrigued Barilla, she waited to open it until she could be alone. So, quietly, secretively, she hastened up the stairs to the sanctity of her room on the third floor. Not yet dark enough for lighting a candle, she stood where the window cast its light on the page in her hand. Supper could wait.

February 13, 1844

For Barilla,
You'll wonder who has sent you this.
But that's the puzzle for you Miss.
And yet, I have but little doubt,

That if you guess, you'll find me out.
No other motive has been mine
For sending you this Valentine
Except my friendship to express
And wish you health and happiness.

The above is my feeble attempt at poetry. I want to get away from my studies and visit you some Sunday. However, the workload is most exacting and I cannot get away until next month. And, as you know, the weather has been frightful. I hope you will be glad to see me on some nice Sunday the latter part of March. I think about you a lot.

Horace Gailey

She folded the letter back in its envelope and hugged it to her breast. She realized she should go down for supper. But how could she eat anything with such excitement stirring within her?

The next letter of significance came for Else one evening in mid-March. It was a strange letter that Amanda, one of Else's roommates, held before her as she perused the addressed envelope. Barilla never felt any rapport with the overbearingly haughty Amanda. Now the girl's eyes flashed in delighted mischief as her voice rose to give emphasis to what she read aloud to all within earshot.

"Will you just look at this. Such queer writing. Fraulein Else Weiss. The Weiss is crossed out and White written above it. It's from Germany!"

Else reached for the envelope, but Amanda waved it up high above her head at the same time as she chided Else. "So, we have all been deceived. We have a foreigner in our midst."

Else grabbed Amanda's arm, retrieved the letter, and dashed for the stairway. Several other girls stood by in stunned silence. But Barilla hurried up the stairs to follow Else to her room.

She found her seated on her bed. Tears coursed down her flaming red cheeks. Barilla sat down beside her, placing an arm around Else's shoulder.

"It is from my father," Else said.

"Well, go ahead and read it," said Barilla.

"It is in German and will take some time. It has been many years since I have used German. It is easy to forget. So, let's go down and eat supper. I'll read it later."

"Better splash water on your face," Barilla suggested.

In the dining room, Amanda seemed to be holding court, alongside her bedmate, Abigail. The entire contingent alerted their attention to stare boldly as Else and Barilla entered,

"Well," said the arrogant Amanda, "I'm not sitting next to a Kraut."

"Nor me," added Abigail.

Barilla steered Else to a distant table where Emily and Audrey sat. It was Emily who felt the undercurrent of tension and asked, "What's the fuss with Amanda and Abigail?"

Barilla, immediately defensive, answered, "They are a couple of petty-minded persons who are picking on Else."

"Why, Else, what did you do to them?" Emily asked.

"I made a gross mistake of having a German father. Thus I'm branded a foreigner."

"Is that some sort of crime?" Emily asked.

"Apparently it is with those two," Barilla said.

When they had finished eating, the four girls, led by Barilla, were accosted by Amanda as they were leaving.

"Kraut!" spat out Amanda.

That was too much for Barilla, who despite her thudding heart, countered angrily, "Such talk is uncalled for. I don't see why you persist in such meanness."

"Because Krauts are as much foreigners as the Irish. And we certainly don't want to have anything to do with them"

"Just where did your parents and grandparents come from that they were not foreigners?" Barilla demanded.

"From England," Amanda replied.

"So did mine. And is not England a foreign country?"

To this Amanda had no answer. She turned abruptly away and marched defiantly up the stairs.

Barilla insisted that Else bring the letter up to her room. There Else was left alone to read by the light of a candle. Once, she turned to Barilla and asked if she would write something down, then provided the following information: Seaman's Friend Society, 47 Purchase Street, Boston, Massachusetts. Near Fort Hill.

When Else eventually finished reading, she folded the letter back into its envelope. She studied the address a moment, then looked up at Barilla.

"Someone at the post office knew enough German to know that 'Weiss' means 'White' in English."

Barilla sat down next to her on the bed, and said, "So you felt you had to change it to get work here."

"Of course. You see, what very few people would understand is that even though my mother was English, my name comes from my father. When my mother died in Liverpool, my father wanted to live back in Germany. He was a seaman and felt out of place in England. My brother Karl and I chose to come to America. Neither of us had the German accent, so we took a packet ship going first to Philadelphia, then to Boston. Karl hired on to a freighter, and I got a maid's position. When I found out about better wages in Lowell, I came here."

"And you never heard from Karl?"

"That's why I asked you to write the address. Papa says that is where I can contact him."

"And what about your father?"

"He has married again, so has a new life."

Emily spoke up saying, "Let Else sleep here with you tonight and I'll go down to her room."

Barilla jumped up and hugged her bedmate.

"Oh, thank you, Em. That's a great idea."

When Emily returned to dress the next morning, Barilla asked, "Any remarks from the two witches?"

"If there had been, I would have threatened by reminding them they would have your wrath to contend with," Emily said, chuckling.

6

The third week of March had become instantly springlike. The girls had no need for shawls or bonnets. Barilla had been waiting for this warmth so she could snare Jamie to begin teaching him to read. She had acquired an alphabet book at the library. On Friday, after work, she accosted Jamie by grabbing his arm.

"Tomorrow is Saturday, Jamie. We get out earlier and I want you to come by and sit on the steps with me while I teach you to read."

Sullenly, he said, "Don't want to read."

"But I want you to."

"Oh, you want me to?"

"Yes, I want you to," she said.

"Well, all right, if you want me to," he said.

Saturday evening she delayed her supper for a few minutes to spend time with Jamie. He sat beside her, as close as he could get. She was dimly aware of the stares from her peers as they hustled up the steps, but determined in her task. She pointed to the first picture in the book, and asked, "Jamie, what is that?"

"An apple," he said.

"That is correct. There is a big letter beside it. That is an 'A' Say it."

"A," the boy responded.

"Now, the next page. What is that?"

"A ball."

"Right, and the letter beside it is a 'B.' Say that."

Jamie obliged and they continued on to cat, dog, and then elephant. This one stymied the boy, for he had never seen nor even heard of an elephant.

After Barilla explained about elephants, she returned to the beginning. "We will now repeat them, so far. Tell me what this letter is."

"Apple," he said.

"No, Jamie. What letter is it?"

"A," he answered, looking up for her approval. He then turned the pages rapidly, naming all five letters correctly.

"That is fine. Now, I cannot let you take the book, but here is a paper where I have printed A through E for you to keep with you, and I expect you to remember them. So, off with you now until the next time when we will go on with more."

"More? How many more?"

"Twenty-one more. Can you count that far?"

"Yes, ma'am. I can count," he said forcefully, and was off and running.

The following Saturday she sat again with Jamie on the steps, reviewed the lesson, and went on with five more letters.

"I can do more," said Jamie eagerly.

Elated that the boy caught on so readily, Barilla continued to the end.

He stopped to look up at her directly, and said, "There is a night school I can go to if...if you want me to."

"Oh yes, Jamie. I do want you to."

He stood up, but before he darted off, he asked, "I already know a lot, don't I?"

"Not a lot, Jamie, but it is a beginning."

The following day was Sunday, March 31. After breakfast when Barilla had opened the door of the house to determine the day's weather, she found it warm, even warmer than inside the hallway. Thus she realized she should wear one of the two calico dresses she had made for working in the mill. The one clean one was light blue imprinted with lacy, white flowers.

As she buttoned up the formfitting front to her neck, she thought of Horace. Would he come today? He had written that he would come the last of March. She felt a giddy elation as she hooked a new lace collar in place. She must look nice for Horace. She had at least an hour before going to church. She decided to write a few lines.

Said a beau to a lady, pray name if you can
Of all your acqaintance the handsomest man.
The lady replied, If you'd have me speak true,
The handsomest man, my dear Horace, is you.
I'll tell you some day if given the chance
Into my life you have brought me romance.

Suddenly, Emily bent over her shoulder. "It's time to leave. Else just called out from downstairs, but you didn't hear her."

"Oh, I'm ready," Barilla answered as she slid off the bed and slipped her lapboard into her trunk.

During the church service, she thought again of Horace. Would he come? He had not sent a message. Another line of her thinking, and actually more pressing, revolved around Else and her unhappiness caused by two of Else's roommates. The problem was about to be solved in that Else had obtained permission to go to another place and Barilla agreed to go with her.

It also included Judith Fox, Else's bedmate. They would move the coming week.

Finally the service concluded. Barilla and her companions emerged from the gloomy edifice into brilliant sunshine. Then, through the throng, she saw Horace coming toward her. She instinctively brightened, and eagerly hastened to greet him. She extended her hand.

"How nice to see you, Horace," she said.

He smiled graciously, beaming warmth and confidence, and said, "There is a place to eat dinner at the City Hall."

She hesitated, "But I have to report back…"

"Why can't Else make your excuses?"

Barilla turned slightly to see her friend standing beside her.

"Sure thing," said Else. "You go right ahead."

"And," added Horace as he untied the cumbersome bonnet, and passed it to Else. "She won't need this."

He offered his arm to Barilla, then steered her across Merrimack Street. As they approached the building, he said, "Not a very imposing City Hall. Its main floor is just a group of shops. The restaurant is in the basement."

"I've been here, Horace, in the stationery shop to buy paper."

"To write letters home?" he asked.

"Well, yes, but I also try my hand at verse," she answered.

He went ahead of her down the stairs and located a vacant table.

"The fish is always good here. I'll ask the waiter what is special today," he said as he held a chair for her.

"Salmon." said the waiter, promptly. "Salmon and carrots and mashed potato."

Horace turned a questioning look at Barilla.

"Salmon is fine," she answered.

He looked at her with a broad smile. "So you write poetry, do you?"

She nodded. "Nothing very great, I assure you."

"Well, how is everything else going?

"Everything covers quite a lot. But there is one disturbing bit that concerns Else."

"She looked to be all right to me."

"Oh, she is not hurt physically, but she has suffered some mental torment."

"Can't be over unrequited love. She is one icicle when it comes to romance. She won't even let James kiss her except on her cheek."

The waiter brought plates and set them down. It smelled so good, Barilla began to eat. While she ate she thought of how she would explain about Else. Finally, she said, "Life has been difficult for Else. She is afraid of love. She sees beyond a courtship to possible subservience, lots of babies, death, or even desertion."

"These things have been a part of her life?"

"Yes. She is truly alone and it has only made her very independent."

"So what is her immediate problem?"

Barilla finished eating, pushed her plate away and launched into all that had transpired since the arrival of the letter from Germany. All the while she talked, Horace watched her intently. His smile of understanding made crinkles form around his deep blue eyes.

"So you will be moving too?

She nodded.

"What about the brother?"

"Else has written to the address in Boston. Now she must wait until whatever ship he is on comes into port."

"Yes, some are gone several months."

He beckoned the waiter, paid the bill, then stood up.

"It is such a lovely day. Barilla, let's go for a long walk across the river."

He led her westerly along Merrimack Street, past the depot, onward to Pawtucket Street. They passed other churches and a hodgepodge of buildings.

Barilla was confused. "When I walk across the river with my friends, we don't go this way."

"No, I suppose you don't because the bridge near Central Street is closer. But because the river arches so far northward, that way makes for a longer walk to the falls. I like to look at the falls."

When they reached the bridge beside the Pawtucket dam, they stopped, entranced by the enormous falls whose rushing water pounded down for thirty feet, sounding like continually reverberating thunder.

"It is so loud, being this close," said Barilla.

"Loud and powerful. Therein lies the entire reason Lowell was built. That is what powers all the waterwheels, belts, and pulleys in the mills," Horace said.

"That board wall on top? I don't recall seeing those boards there last fall when we came up along the river on the other shore."

"Flash boards. Their use helps keep some of the water back. The spring thaws of March and April are the worst for high water. It causes tremendous pressure behind it and floods the fields. I doubt that the farmers think very highly of it. For the most part though, the riverbanks are high. The water behind the dam is as placid as a pond."

"Come," he urged, reaching for her hand. "Let's wander on."

After passing some farmlands, the thundering sound grew weaker until nothing more was heard except the shrill chirping of birds. They walked onward into deepening woods of starkly bare maple, elm, and oak trees, whose somber gray branches feathered stark against a cobalt sky, causing streaked shadows on the pathway and surroundings like a giant spider web.

Even though the path seemed a well-worn one, Barilla wondered if Horace knew where they were going. She looked back anxiously, seeing nothing but woods.

"You're not afraid are you, sweetheart?"

"No, Horace. I just wondered. We are so alone here except for the birds."

"No need to worry. James and I came here several times last fall to hunt pheasants. We are going northward almost parallel with the river, although a mile from it. The Indians made these trails. Now there are no Indians. At least we never encountered any."

"Oh!" she offered in a matter of fact way. "I have seen Indians! One morning two Indian men came by our farm asking for food. By hand signals they offered to help with planting corn. Mother was making hotcakes. The smell enticed them because their staple springtime diet is fish. As she offered a plateful, they grabbed them in handfuls, wolfing them down without benefit of syrup. Then held out their hands for more.

Father assured us there was nothing to fear, yet he and my brothers kept an eye on them through all the day's planting. When dinnertime came, Mother held out plates of pork and potatoes. They pushed the silverware off onto the ground and ate with their hands. Then later as the sun began to set, they were suddenly gone."

"To be sure, their ways are different from ours." Horace then asked if she was tired.

"A little, but more warm than tired."

"Up ahead there is a log. We can rest there."

"This weather is unusual for March. At home there must be several feet of snow still on the ground. What few warm days there are, sap is gathered from maple trees, and we boil it down to make syrup."

"There up ahead is our log," he said. Then, removing his waistcoat, he bent to lay it on an uprooted tree. He turned to take her in his arms. Because of his height, the first kiss came lightly upon her forehead. She looked up and their lips met, gently at first, then with greater ardor. When he released her, he looked down upon the lace collar.

"Isn't that hot around your neck?" Then, not waiting for an answer he continued, "How do you get it off?"

"By unhooking it," she responded, feeling some embarrassment. He accomplished that and laid the collar down upon his coat.

Then seating himself, he gently pulled Barilla down beside him.

She looked around enough to realize they were on a hillside that stretched downward to a small pond, where a mother duck and tiny little ones swam across its shimmering surface.

She took a deep breath and let out a great sigh. "It is so beautiful, and so peaceful."

"That it is. There, look quick, beyond the pond. There is a deer," Horace said.

"Oh yes, of course. Back home we have lots of deer. Father and my brothers kill several each fall."

He answered in a dismayed voice, "I doubt that I could kill a deer."

"Haven't you ever eaten venison?"

"No, I guess not. I'm basically a city boy."

The deer looked up apprehensively and darted away, white tail bobbing like a warning flag.

Barilla spoke pensively, "Silent the buck in yonder vale, sensing danger, flaunts a waving tail."

"Very apt, my dear," he responded, but he was again looking at her neckline and the buttons of her dress. "This still must be hot against your throat," he said as he reached to struggle clumsily to undo the small buttons.

Barilla stared, not at what he was doing, but into his eyes. She could feel that the dress was becoming undone down to the rise of her breasts.

"Horace, no! You mustn't," she said.

"Why not? All I ever see of you is your hands and your face. The female throat is also lovely. It should not be kept hidden."

She looked off toward the pond, now clear of ducks and so very calm. She was far from calm, thinking, Oh dear. I wanted to look nice for him with my new collar, and this…this undoing is not to my liking. She felt his left arm come across her shoulders as she turned a pitiable look into his eyes.

He bent to kiss her again with great passion until she realized that his right hand cupped one of her breasts.

Horrified, she abruptly drew back and, placing both hands against his chest, pushed him away.

"Please, Horace. You must not do that," she said, as she fought back tears.

"All right, sweetheart, if it upsets you that much."

She searched her mind for words to express herself, then calmly, guilelessly, with both hands folded in her lap, proceeded.

"Horace, I am not knowledgeable in what takes place between men and women who love each other, and I am not being a prude. But my mother and sister have been very definite in explaining that my body is my own to be kept private from the opposite sex, until I marry."

"I can understand that. It is a protection women need against the urgency males feel toward an object of their affection. You are very desirable, which makes it difficult for me not to explore your…uh…other charms. But, I humbly apologize for causing you anxiety."

She placed her hand on his cheek. "I do love you, Horace. And I want to be your girl. So, until I learn more about life and what is expected of me, please try to understand."

They sat quietly for a while, each with their own thoughts.

Then Horace spoke up, "This is probably the last time I can get away until summer. My studies are most demanding. and in June there will be final examinations."

"What is it that you are studying?" she asked.

"I specialize in tunnels, the planning, the engineering, and the supervision of the work. There is to be a great demand for tunnels allowing trains to go through mountains."

"Through mountains! How is that possible?"

"Oh, it's possible. In fact, one is being planned west of here, to be called the Hoosic Tunnel. I am to work there sometime this summer on surveying and planning for it."

Dejection tempered her voice to a whisper. "That means you will not be coming to Lowell to work?"

"No, sweetheart," he said, taking out his pocket watch. "It is best to start back. I have to get you to your boardinghouse, and make it to the last train, which leaves before it gets really dark." He stood up to hand her the lace collar and don his waistcoat.

It was late in the day when she finally climbed the stairs and entered Else's room, where she found her packing her small trunk.

Else looked up, "We have to move tomorrow. It is April first."

"I forgot. It came so soon. I'll go up and get my things together," Barilla said.

As she reached the top step, she heard the distant, plaintive whistle of the departing train.

7

On Sunday, May 19, Barilla wrote a letter:

Dear Parents,

It promises to be a lovely day outside, so I write this before going to church. Then after dinner some of us will go walking across the river. I have changed my boarding place. Besides Else, I have some new acquaintances.

At Mrs. Merriam's we were on the Hamilton Corporation. It was a very good place indeed. But Else had some trouble with the two girls she roomed with and she would not stay. So, the first of April, I came with her to this boarding place. Mrs. Digby, our boarding woman, done very well for about three weeks. If I may say so, she is cross, lazy, and nasty. She builds up a fire just before she goes to bed, puts her coffee on, and lets it steep all night. In the morning she gets up, builds up the fire, and goes to bed again. We get up, get our own breakfast with that awful coffee before we go into the mill. When we come out for dinner, we have what coffee is left and a little dry bread and a few crackers. We have a piece of pie once a week. She does get a decent meal for Sunday dinner. She has an iron stove which is a better way of cooking than the fireplace and bake-oven at home.

I have been sick here and I don't wonder, do you? I missed a week of work so will not get a full month's pay. They take $5 a month for the boarding woman before they pay us. But this one should feel guilty for even taking one dollar. We have complained and we expect something better soon.

When darkness comes each evening, I think of Father in the lamplight as he sits in his rocking chair, often reading the newspapers the boys have sent. And so many times I recall how I used to wander off in the lower fields, and returning, look up toward the house and beyond. Thus I send you my thought:

How oft see I from the meadow below

Where the noisy brook murmurs and the
Purple-fringed orchid does grow.
Of the lofty old pine where the Swift River flows,
And beyond where the forest climbs up "Old Turk"
That beautiful mount, his dominance shows.

I wish you could have the advantage I have of getting books from the library. When I have finished one, I get another. Every Wednesday evening we go to the Lyceum Hall for lectures. Very learned gentlemen are the speakers. So learned, that some of them have even written books.

I hope these few lines find you all well. I am sorry to sound like I am complaining, but some good home cooking would suit me first rate right now. I have wrote all I can.

From your loving daughter, Barilla Adeline Taylor

There being space left, I improve it by telling you about Ann Graham. On April 23, she got her hand tore off. It was done in the carding room of the Massachusetts Mill. I heard she has got to have it taken off above her elbow. She may even lose her life by it. The Massachusetts Mill buildings are nearer the big river where it joins the Concord River. It is a newer mill. I was told it was built only five years ago.

B.A.T

On the last payday in May, the Hamilton agent, Mr. Avery, informed Barilla that she and her friends, Else and Judith, were being allowed to move into a private house. On Monday, June 3, the three girls moved into the home of William and Abigail Elston on Central Street. Barilla had begun to feel better and naturally much happier in the homelike atmosphere where all were warmly welcomed by the young couple.

Barilla's end of May pay came to only $11.88. She spent $6.00 on material for two dresses and put the rest in the Lowell Bank.

The sewing project kept her occupied until the first week of July. When she cut the necklines, she recalled the comment Horace had made, so she cut them lower, all of two inches.

Else had received a letter from her brother Karl and had

answered telling him she would come to Boston on the Fourth of July, asking him to meet the early train.

There was to be no work on Independence Day, and the girls were excited about having a day in Boston. Emily had also had word from Dana that he was back in Brighton, and urged her to come to Boston.

The day dawned bright, muggy, and hot on that Thursday, July fourth, when Judith, Emily Else, and Barilla hurried eagerly to the station on Dutton Street. The fare was fifty cents each way. Dinner was not expected to cost more than a dollar.

Barilla, coming close to the engine, looked up at what appeared to be a formidable black giant whose driving wheels were larger in diameter than Barilla's height. Behind a car for coal were attached four other passenger cars and one for freight, the latter was covered over by canvas and tied down at the sides.

With Else in the lead, a conductor directed them to the second car, which he explained was the ladies' car. They entered to the side by going up several iron steps, an awkward feat because of long, billowing skirts. The girls seated themselves on thinly upholstered seats. Barilla observed about a dozen other mill girls, all chatting excitedly. There were several couples and one family, accompanied by two children.

The windows were small and stationary. Even before the train departed, the air was oppressive. At exactly eight o'clock, the conductor shouted, "All aboard!" and slammed the door shut. A bell clanged, a whistle blew, and the car lurched forward, jolting the passengers as it moved.

"Look," Else said, "Over there on the left. There is our mill."

"Of course," answered Barilla, now shouting. "And Mrs. Merriam's."

The latter was lost amid the encroaching din. She reflected on the unpleasant circumstances of leaving there. She hoped that Amanda and Abigail were not on the train this day.

From then on the train picked up speed. Speech was as impossible as it was inside the mill. The clickety-clack and jolting, swaying, screeching train caused everyone to hold tight to their seats and to each other. Barilla realized why the windows could not be opened, for clouds of smoke and some sparks flew past.

At some places there were double tracks, and the whooshing of a train whistling by in the opposite direction caused anxiety in some, and abject terror in the two children. Their screams of fright could barely be heard above the din.

After the passing train incident, Barilla saw mostly woods and a few farms. Then as she realized the train had slowed a little, she peered out at a village of neat white houses, a prim clapboard church with a tall steeple, and a red schoolhouse. At a main road, a horse and carriage had stopped. As the train continued without stopping, she read a sign that said, When the bell rings, watch out for a locomotive.

Hardly more than an hour passed when she noticed that they approached Boston to go more slowly across a trestle. It scared her to look out and see water on both sides. Then, by 9:15, the train had covered the 26 miles from Lowell to the station at the foot of Lowell Street near Haymarket Square.

When the door was opened, Else was the first to descend the steps onto a wooden platform. She scanned the waiting contingent of greeters until she saw her brother Karl.

As blonde as Else, but much taller, he approached her cautiously, extending his hand in greeting. But she would have none of that. She rushed at him to clasp both hands around his back and lay her head against his chest. For several minutes, both were speechless. Then Karl turned to a girl who stood meekly beside him, a very slight girl with fiery red hair and pale complexion.

"This is my girl, Patsy O'Brien," Karl said, then commanded brusquely. "Patsy, say hello to my sister Else."

"How'd ye do, miss," Patsy spoke as she performed a slight curtsey. Other greetings were happening all around them. When Dana found Emily, he gave her a friendly clap on her shoulder, saying,

"Hello, sis. I'm sure glad you could come." He then greeted Barilla casually and looked inquiringly at Judith.

Emily spoke up. "My brother, George Dana Austin, meet Judith Fox, who did live at Mrs. Merriam's, but now lives with Barilla on Central Street."

He shook hands with Judith, then turned to Emily. "Follow me ladies. We are off to the Park Street Church where there is to be a celebration commemorating our great freedom from old Mother England."

Barilla caught Else's eye, beckoning her to come along.

"No," Else said across the platform. "My brother wants me to go with him."

"All right. Be sure to be back here by six o'clock in time for the last train."

Dana offered Emily his arm. Judith and Barilla followed, walking out through a terminal building and under one of its three arches onto Merrimack Street. There were several horsedrawn coaches leaving the area. However, Dana announced that they would walk. Barilla noted the street's signs as they went. From Merrimack onto Portland Street, then Sudbury and Court.

Along Sudbury and Court had been many shops, and here and there a modest dwelling, where behind picket fences were profuse flower gardens. The gardens' heady perfume was quite refreshing after the confinement in the stuffy railroad car.

As they turned westerly onto Tremont Street, Barilla was surprised to see several mansions across the street, then a walled cemetery and the colonnaded front of King's Chapel. The sidewalk was wider now and laid of brick. It kept the pedestrians further from the dust riled up by the horses' hooves on the gravel road.

Barilla found it tiring to keep up with the long, rapid strides of a man's legs. Watching those legs thrusting forward, reminded her of Horace. Where was he now? Still in Boston? Probably not. It was summer, and he must be out working on a tunnel somewhere a long way off.

Ahead of them, Dana pointed out the spire of the Park Street

Church. Coming closer, beside another cemetery, the sound of bells pealed forth with reverberating clanging, announcing the service to begin at ten o'clock.

People alighted from carriages and others hurried toward the handrailed entrance of the church at the corner of Park and Tremont streets. Following Emily and Dana, Barilla grabbed the rail with one hand and a fold of her skirt with the other. Once inside, there seemed to be people in every pew. Dana found space at the back where nothing could be seen but the backs of men's heads and the voluminous bonnets of the women.

Immediately the throng stood up and began singing, "My Country 'tis of Thee." Everyone seemed to know the words, but it was unfamiliar to the group from Lowell. When, "Let freedom ring," had ended the song, Barilla felt the words stirring within her breast reviving the very essence of why her grandfather, John Taylor, had been one of those who fought against the hated British.

Memories of him persisted, even as she saw in the distance a preacher mount a pulpit and begin to speak. Her grandfather had died when she was eleven, having been bedridden for several years. Through all that time, both her mother and father ministered to his needs.

But in her early childhood, she recalled how he regaled the family with stories of his deeds. Born in Newmarket, New Hampshire, he enlisted under Captain John Moody in 1776 at the age of fourteen, having lied about his age. He was promised pay of eight dollars per month, which he never received. However, he was issued thirty pounds to be expended for ammunition. He vividly related a march to New York State where many others had worn through their shoes to walk barefoot, but his own boots were sturdy enough to make it. He told bitterly about the battle at Ticonderoga, where the Continental Army had been trounced by the British. But oh, how he enjoyed telling about Saratoga where the Revolutionists had regrouped.

"Our men just kept a comin', hundreds of 'em from just 'bout everywhere," he explained with delight. "We outnumbered the red-coats! Besides, we knowed full well what we was a fightin' for so we beat 'em somethin' wicked!"

After those decisive battles, he went home to eventually court Comfort Burleigh. They were married in Sanbornton in 1787. Soon thereafter the young couple moved to Wolfeboro, where other Taylor relatives lived and farmed. They had no money of their own, and the new government had none to pay the veterans.

It came about that land was offered in the wilds of Maine as payment to the former soldiers. In late winter of 1796, along with other families, the couple took off for the Rumford area of Maine to be given 200 acres of land in the Androscoggin Valley. The trip by ox cart took several months.

There was also the sad story of how those acres, along with all that had been accomplished, was confiscated by those hated Massachusetts tax people. For cash was an improbable commodity to people who lived by bartering.

After Maine separated from Massachusetts, John Taylor and his son Stephen, Barilla's father, had earned enough money to buy the farm on the Byron-Roxbury line in the Swift River Valley. It also helped that a war veteran's pension of eight dollars a month had been issued.

Barilla recalled when Grandpa John died. It was a rainy day in March when her father and his mother, Comfort, along with the two eldest boys to dig the grave, carted Grandpa's body off in the farm wagon down to the Roxbury cemetery. Florena, her older sister, stayed at home with the then-five other children. Mother had instructed them all to take apart Grandpa's bed and hang the quilts and feather mattress in the shed part of the barn.

Barilla could visualize the gravestone put up later that year, engraved with a cross, under which was his name and PVT Bell's Co. Reed's N.H. Regt. Rev. War and beneath it, March 25, 1840.

Grandmother Comfort had died one year later, unable to come to grips with the loss of her John. She was seventy-five.

All of these memories had so engrossed Barilla that none of the minister's text had come through to her except his closing words, "Let us not forget those brave men who fought. so that this new nation could be free from tyranny. Let us pray."

Barilla smiled as she bent her head, realizing she had done exactly that, had lovingly remembered, one of them.

When the assemblage moved toward the aisle it behooved the four to be out the door ahead of all others. Dana led them across Park Street and toward the Common, but Barilla had not yet stepped off the curb. She turned to observe the well-dressed congregation descending the steps. In that moment, she saw Horace and a girl whose arm held tight onto his as she held up her skirt with the other hand. The girl wore a dress of blue satin fitted close above the waist and so low cut at the bodice to expose the separating line of her breasts. Her bonnet was of unusual shape, like an upside-down basin, sprigged with flowers, which allowed bouncy curls of flaxen hair to be clearly visible. Barilla took one more swift glance at her male companion to be certain it was Horace. The man carried a shiny, black hat, which he now placed over the dark, wavy hair. There was no doubt. It was Horace.

She felt her heart drop, but it was still beating; beating rapidly and forcefully. She felt color rise in her face and her breathing labored. She turned away abruptly, and stepped off the curb to be nearly run down by a passing horse and carriage.

Dana, seeing her plight, hastened to her aid, guiding her between people and carriages to safety, where she leaned against the tall post of the Common's gate. Tears welled up, blurring her vision. She grabbed Emily's hand.

And Emily, startled, turned abruptly to the stricken Barilla to ask, "What's wrong, Rilla? Are you ill? You look as though you have seen a ghost."

"Worse than that, but I can't talk about it," Barilla's voice was hardly above a whisper.

The others were around her now, showing their deep concern, while she, feeling as though she had been whacked in the chest, responded bravely, "No, no, please, I'll be all right in a moment." Then added bravely, in a more positive tone, "Where are we going now?"

"To walk on the common," said Dana. "That is, if you are sure you are all right." His tone convinced her that the scare in the street had been what unnerved her.

She drew in her breath and swallowed hard to avoid a choking sensation, as Dana opened the gate for the girls to pass through. Emily had placed her hand on Barilla's shoulder, a gesture of true concern.

"Dana!" Emily pointed to a high-branched elm. "Could we stand in the shade of that tree for a few minutes?"

"Sure thing," he replied as he went on in an explanatory tone, "Look up there at that big copper dome. That's the state house for Massachusetts."

As all attention focused on the dominant structure, Barilla's eyes came to focus on two figures, walking arm-in-arm up the hill toward that structure. There was no mistaking that one wore a dress of bright blue and the other, of manly bearing, tall and dignified, wore a high black hat upon his head.

How could he? The very thought stabbed an instant pain within her breast. I thought he loved me, and now this, with another girl. Then, sensibly she scolded herself. "Stop thinking about it. You're here to enjoy the day."

Gradually, she heard the sound of drums approaching, heightened by a piccolo melody. The sight commanded everyone's attention to a unit representing the trio who led troops to battle back in the Revolution. Behind them came ranks of smartly uniformed soldiers marching to the rhythm. The display could hardly replicate the soldiers of almost seventy years ago, for it was common knowledge that, called rabble, they wore make-do outfits hardly more than rags.

Although the display was thrilling, Barilla found her gaze lifted up Beacon Hill, and the two-storied mansions there. The promenading twosome had turned the corner, and the fluff of blue, followed by her escort, entered one of the mansions through a white door, which seemed to have been opened by someone, perhaps a servant.

"Wasn't that something?" Dana said eagerly.

The girls all agreed, as the military contingent had passed, then smartly turned the corner to march slightly uphill, then another corner, to march along parallel to Beacon Street.

Judith spoke up, "I'm so glad we came. I have never been to Boston before, but I've heard a lot about it. For instance, I read that Paul Revere molded the plates to cover that dome with copper."

"That's interesting," said Emily, "but since this seems to be a public green, why is it fenced?"

"Oh," said Dana, "simply because this was the common cow pasture for those who lived in the surrounding mansions."

"That building across this street, with those four turrets, looks like another church," Emily commented.

"That has to be the Masonic Temple," said Judith.

"What's a temple for?" asked Emily.

"I don't know," Judith shrugged. "Perhaps it is some sort of church. There are lots of churches in Boston."

Barilla tried to keep her attention on the conversation, but that which was tearing her apart crowded out rational thinking. It nagged her like a vicious cancer. To herself, she mused, So that is what it has come down to. And why not? Why should he care anything about a mill girl, a poor common wretch who has to earn her very bread.

"Barilla, you are staring like a frightened cat!" Emily admonished her. "Something is wrong, isn't it? Now you just tell me what it is,"

"Not now, Em, I'll tell you later.

"Promise?" said Emily.

Barilla forced a smile, "All right. Yes, I promise."

"Good," said Emily, whose attention had shifted, "Will you look over there? Dana has found some friends. I do believe they are Mary's little brothers, Horatio and Hazen Bradbury."

"They don't look very little to me," said Judith. "They are both taller than your brother."

"I mean younger brothers. I guess they're about sixteen or seventeen," said Emily.

"Hazen is my age," said Barilla. "We were in the same grade in school. Horatio is a couple of years older."

"I like the looks of him," said Judith. A sly twinkle appearing in her eyes.

Dana joined the girls where there were joyous hugs and greetings all around. Judith, the bystander, watched it all, staring mostly at Horatio. Dana introduced Judith to the newcomers.

Then Dana, being the eldest, all of twenty-one, and of course an old hand at familiarity with Boston, suggested going somewhere for dinner.

8

The three couples, Dana and Emily, Judith and Horatio, Barilla and Hazen, walked the remaining length of the common where it was relatively cool in the shade of many trees whose dark green, contrasted sharply against a brilliant blue sky.

They turned left on Boylston Street, sauntering downward toward the waterfront, where a slight breeze was no longer as pleasant, for the odor had become coarse with smells from the harbor.

They soon came to Sea Street, and there ahead of them was an array of ships whose masts were as a forest, their unfurled sails securely wrapped to thwart any breeze. Docks and many windowed warehouses bulged against the sky…and the odor. That of horse-manure piled upon the cobblestones was hardly obnoxious to the farm girls, but the overwhelming dock odors were something new.

"Ugh!" snorted Emily. "Isn't that a dead fish smell?"

"Not only dead fish," said Dana, "but what's known around here as low-tide stench."

"What is a tide?" asked Barilla, concerned about being near someone or something rotten.

"Tide," Dana explained, "is when the seawater rises, called high tide. Then it goes away to become low tide. It happens once in the day and once at night."

The group kept walking. A sign painted on the side of a warehouse said, Wales Wharf.

"Look over there," Barilla said, "Men are working unloading a ship. And people and carriages and drays are all around us. How do they stand the smell?"

"Get used to it," said Dana, calmly.

Barilla thought that half of Boston milled about, paying little attention to the dock workers and nothing at all to the mixture of repulsive odors.

They passed other wharves, the Russia, the Liverpool, the Arch, and Foster's. At the latter, swarthy, half-naked men unloaded bales of cotton into a railroad car, a familiar commodity for the Lowell girls.

"So, that's how it comes to Lowell," Emily said.

"That's how," answered Dana.

As they approached Long Wharf, it appeared more like a continuous row of warehouses, which required the group to turn Northerly where they soon came to a plaza in front of the Old State House.

"Oh, my," said Judith, who stopped walking. "This must be where the Boston Massacre took place. Although..." she hesitated as she read the street sign that said, State Street. "Ah yes, it was then called King Street, referred to as the bloody butchers of King Street."

"A battle?" Emily asked. "A big battle?"

"No, there weren't many involved. But the British soldiers did kill about six defenseless men and boys. Think of it, right here where we stand."

Barilla realized that Judith possessed an intriguing amount of knowledge about Boston, so she asked, "Where did you learn all of that?"

"From books in the library. Don't you ever ask for history books?"

"Never thought about it. I read adventure or romantic stories."

"I think history is romantic."

"Bother," interjected Emily. "I'd like some dinner. And somewhere far from the docks."

"Just a ways up beyond the Old State House, to the Red Dragon Inn," said Dana as he led the group along. "There, see the red dragon above that doorway? That's where we eat."

"He certainly looks fearsome," said Emily. "See how he is crouched, ready to spring."

"That's merely a symbol," said Judith. "There are no such things as dragons. Besides, that one is so pockmarked it is left with only patches of red."

The entrance door Dana led them through stood open, no doubt to allow for passage of air. Yet there was little difference between the heat outside and the stuffiness within.

Adjusting to the room's darkness, Barilla noticed several long tables at least twelve feet in length. Dana spoke to a waiter who regarded the group speculatively. He wore a dirty towel as an apron, then used an equally dirty towel to wipe off one end of a table. He indicated they should sit.

"Sauterne, claret, or beer?" he asked. His hair was jet black, sleeked down as though with grease. He appeared to be quite young. He waited as Dana explained to the girls, "The claret is probably closest to the grape wine our parents make." He turned to the waiter. "Claret for the ladies. We men will have beer."

A man at the far end of their table, yelled, "Hey waiter," so the black-haired youth strode off.

When he returned, he set before the group a bottle of red wine and a pitcher of frothy amber. From a sideboard he brought six glasses.

"Will ya be eatin' too?" he asked.

"Yes," said Dana. "What do you have today?"

"Fried fish, hash, and stew. And there's always baked beans."

After decisions had been made, the waiter held out his hand saying, "That'll be a dollar apiece."

Each in turn handed him their money. Barilla had not thought of Horace again until that moment, for whenever she had been to dinner with him, he had paid for both of them. This was entirely different. These were only her friends, not...lovers. She looked away at a window of diamond-shaped glass, then to the far end of the room where she caught her image reflected in a large mirror. She forced a smile.

Seeing her smile, the man who had yelled at the waiter smiled back and winked. Barilla instinctively moved her head to turn toward Hazen, who was pouring wine into her glass.

"Thanks," she said, taking an immediate swallow. "Hazen? Tell me why you have come to Boston."

"Well, Dana wrote to us that we could get a chance to work where he does, at least for haying season. That's something we sure know something about. Dana told us to come by train and meet on Boston Common, and that's what we did. This sure is some big town. I never seen the like. I been a wondering what all them big buildings are for. There ain't a one seems like a barn for hay and animals."

Dana leaned over to explain. "They're for doing the business of the docks. This city has the busiest harbor in all of the United States of America."

The waiter brought their food on pewter plates and conversation stopped as they began to eat. When Barilla had her fill of stew, she spoke to Dana.

"That clock up on the wall says half after four. Shouldn't we be walking back? We came quite a ways."

"Don't worry. We have made an almost complete circle. I'll show you that it is not far back to the station."

Once outside, he pointed northeasterly, "There's Scollay Square, so we go up there, then come to Court Street, then Sudbury to Portland Street to Merrimac. We'll be there in plenty of time."

True to his word, they arrived at the Boston-Lowell station in plenty of time. On the way, he had told the girls that he and the Bradbury boys would be going back to the Common where there would later be fireworks. Thus their good-byes were brief. The three girls waved until the departing boys were out of sight, then turned and entered through an arch into the small station.

As all of the benches were already taken, each girl stood, resolutely recalling the day's events. Time passed slowly, silently, for each of them. Barilla, especially, remembering it in sequence.

"So, you beat me here," said Else loudly as she and her brother joined her friends.

Else introduced the girls to Karl, who immediately excused himself by telling her, "Now that you're safely back with your friends, I'll just go along." He kissed and hugged his sister and said, "Write to me again. I shove off in a couple of days, but should be back, perhaps by October."

He turned and the girls watched until he passed through an arch.

For the Hamilton foursome, the returning train ride bore none of the anticipation felt on the ride going to Boston. Because of the clacking sound of the wheels on the iron-clad, wooden rails, speech was impossible. So, each weary girl silently contemplated her own memory of the day's events.

Walking away from the station, down Market Street to Central, the setting sun cast its still heat-filled rays upon the backs of the girls. Upon crossing the Pawtucket Canal, a slight breeze wafted upward from the flowing falls dropping into the languid Concord River.

Emily had walked beside Barilla, so that as they came to the Hamilton Lane, she pulled Barilla aside, telling the others to go on.

"Now, you tell me what upset you when we came out of the church," Emily said.

"It was Horace. He was with another girl. A beautiful girl in a beautiful dress." Her voice caught. "I could not believe it."

"Are you sure it was him?"

"It was him, all right,"

"Well, if that's the way he is, stop thinking about him. I think he's not worth getting upset about."

"Of course, Em. You're right. I'll try."

Emily hugged her, saying, "That a girl. Now run along, it has been a busy day for all of us."

Barilla smiled graciously, "Thanks, Em. Friends like you are more important than fickle men. So, goodnight." She turned and hurried away.

Approaching the Elstons' house, she saw that William and Abigail Elston sat in rocking chairs on their front porch. Else and Judith stood, leaning their backsides against the wooden railing, both engrossed in animated conversation.

Barilla came up the porch steps, greeted the Elstons politely, and hastened through the doorway into the house.

Abigail followed, speaking to Barilla's back as the distraught girl mounted the stairs.

"I was just about to fix some cold tea and cookies. Won't you stay and join us?"

"No, thank you, Abigail. I…uh," she faltered. "I'm too tired."

Not until she entered the bedroom she shared with Else and Judith did she break apart to throw herself face down on her bed to give in to sobs. Pounding her fist upon the coverlet, in agonized whispers, she asked repeatedly, "Why, oh why, oh why?"

Else came so quietly into the room that Barilla heard nothing until she felt a hand on her shoulder.

Else asked, "What happened in Boston to cause you to behave like this? I have never seen you so upset."

Barilla turned a tear-stained face to look up at the friend who handed her a handkerchief. She bit on her lip and dabbed the cloth beneath her eyes. She tried to talk, but stared instead, with blank hopelessness at the now-dark window beyond Else's shoulder. She drew a deep breath and sighed, and went on to explain.

"At the church, I saw Horace leaving with a girl, a beautiful girl who looked up at him adoringly. And he in turn, looking at her the same way. Then I watched them walking hand in hand up to one of the mansion houses on Beacon Hill."

"So," said Else, sitting down on the bed.

"So?" Barilla replied indignantly, "I thought he loved me, as I love him. How could he be with another girl?"

Else, who herself had never allowed herself to be smitten, had little understanding of how such an entanglement got to the point of such despair. With her usual common sense, she asked, "Did Horace ever tell you he loved you?"

Defensively, Barilla said, "He kissed me and he called me sweetheart."

"Oh, sure. But did he say, 'I love you, Barilla?'"

"Not really, but I…"

"You took it for granted, didn't you?"

Barilla nodded.

Else continued in a steady voice, "It seems useless to tell you

Sing Me a Song

what a silly goose you are, but you certainly don't understand men. To them, a pretty face, an adequate figure, and flirtatious eyes are what men are attracted to. And it would appear that this other girl belongs to people of means, even possibly one of our mill's owners. Wealth and prestige draws many a man like a bear to a hive of honey."

Barilla swung her legs around to sit upright beside Else. She took a deep breath, sighed, and put her arm around Else, and said, "You are telling me things I don't like to hear. But you are probably right. I possess none of those things."

"No money perhaps," Else admonished, "but you are an attractive person. You have spirit and drive. You have compassion and caring for others, and you've got brains. Except about this Horace business," she added facetiously.

Barilla forced a smile and buried her face against Else's shoulder.

"Oh, Else, you are such a great friend. I don't know what I would do without you."

"Well, right now this 'great friend' is telling you to go wash your face, and then I want to see a big smile on it."

After Barilla washed, she turned and formed a genuine smile. The two girls embraced.

Then Barilla drew back and said, "How thoughtless I have been to burden you with my feelings and not even ask about your day with your brother."

"Oh that," said Else in a flat tone of voice. "Karl had this stupid girl, Patsy, with him. She's Irish. Of course that's nothing against her. It's just that she's such a dull wit, no mind of her own, and a puppy-dog affection for Karl."

"But she's pretty," Barilla said.

"I suppose one might say so. But besides being stupid, she's loose."

"Loose? What does that mean?"

"That upon occasion, Karl leaves his boardinghouse to sleep with her in a stinking hole of a place worse than the Paddy camp lands here."

"Wait a minute," Barilla said. "What do you mean by sleeps with her?"

"You ninny. Don't you understand how a man and woman lie together and perform the sexual act?"

"Without being married, you mean?"

"Marriage means little to a man with lust on his mind. Any snippet of a female who allows such to happen is loose. My mother used to say, 'A girl can run faster with her skirts up, than a man with his pants down.'"

"Oh, Else, there is so much I just do not understand."

"Maybe not." She smiled graciously. "But you are learning."

In that moment, Judith came into the room arid all three girls made ready for bed.

9

On Friday morning, bright sunlight awakened Barilla even before the bells rang. She sat up in a slumped position, musing on her mixed feelings. Until the moment of seeing Horace beside the girl in blue, she had felt her life had joyous meaning. Her love and what she thought was also his, was now nothing at all. The mantel of love, the complete aura of it, had been suddenly dropped, leaving her bereft and spineless.

With dispiriting lassitude, she arose quietly and dressed, thinking forlornly. 'Another day; a work day; a day of diligence and noise!'

"My life is so dull," she whispered, half aloud. "Dull, dull, dull!" Else turned over, "What are you muttering about? Or just talking in your sleep?"

Suddenly the bells rang out, bringing Barilla's bedmates to their feet.

As usual, Abigail prepared breakfast before the girls went to work. Her husband, Will, who had his shoemaker shop beside their house, always joined them for he was also an early riser. Thus breakfast was a joyous occasion. All spirits were lifted by unusually gay repartee. On that particular morning, Will joshed them by stating that he was a lucky man to live with such a harem of lovely ladies. They knew this to be in jest, because he had eyes only for his demure, pretty wife who was not much older than the three boarders.

The three girls, even Barilla, left in a happy frame of mind.

The noon bell rang and the usual shutting down of the looms, and the helter-skelter running down the stairway began.

When Barilla realized Else was not at her side, she glanced back to see her helping another operative. That's Eliza, she thought. How pale she looks.

"What's wrong with her?" Barilla asked.

"She fainted and I roused her," said Else. "Help me get her to the water bucket."

Holding each of Eliza's arms across their shoulders, they half led and half dragged her to the head of the stairs. While Else held Eliza's weight, Barilla held the dipper of fetid water to her lips, and Eliza drank. All of the other girls had gone. The entire room was empty and so very quiet.

"Come now," Else said. "You must get down the stairs and go for your dinner."

The pathetic, weakened girl took a deep breath and nodded.

Gently, Barilla behind and Else ahead, they got Eliza down the circular stairway. The three flights seemed an eternity.

Fresh air came like a blessed relief and even revived Eliza enough so that she straightened up, thanked her benefactors, and mounted the steps to Mrs. Merriam's.

Seeing her safely inside, the other two picked up their skirts and ran all the way to the Elstons.

As she ate her dinner, Barilla recalled that Eliza was new. She had only come there after she and Else had moved out. Assigned to a loom on the other side of Else's, it had been Else's duty to teach her. Barilla remembered Eliza as a quiet girl who kept to herself. A small skinny girl 'with no meat on her bones' is what her father would have said.

As the girls hustled back to work, Barilla asked Else what she knew about Eliza.

"Not much. She's quiet as a mouse. One time she did tell me she had a sick mother down in Sudbury. She said nothing about a father or other family."

"Well," Barilla said, "she shouldn't be working here because she herself looks sickly."

"She has to earn money somewhere," said Else, and shrugged.

By the time they reached the boardinghouse, they saw Eliza sitting on the steps. At the sight of her slumped shoulders and doleful expression, Else asked if she had eaten her dinner.

"A little," the stricken girl answered. "But I get a stomachache when I eat."

"Eliza," Else spoke kindly, but seriously, "you had better go up to bed. You are in no condition to work this afternoon."

But Eliza was adamant. "I have to work. You go ahead. I'll make it in a minute."

"All right," said Else. "But you know you'll be locked out if you miss the last bell. I can start your loom. I managed that one before you came. Two looms are no problem for me."

Eliza took a deep breath and nodded weakly.

Else and Barilla had reached their looms and were about to start them when, above the din of the several looms that had begun to vibrate, a shrill scream pierced the air. The sound came from the direction of the stairwell, and Else lost no time hurrying back there. Barilla followed.

The overseer, Mr. Lord, slid off his high stool and came up behind Barilla, saying, "You there, get back and start your loom. I'll see what the trouble is."

The overseer had obviously given Else the same directive because she came toward Barilla with a grim expression, and fiery anger flashed from her eyes.

"I would like to kill that man," she said. "Someone fell backward down the stairs. I got only a glimpse, but I'm afraid it was Eliza."

For all operatives, there was no recourse but to endure such subservience. Like mechanical robots, they began the afternoon's labor. The ramming of bobbins, back and forth, back and forth, a continuing reverberation of the subdued anger pulsed just as furiously through their veins. For they knew instinctively that one of their own was surely dead.

When the final bells rang that Friday evening at the bottom of the stairs Else spoke to Barilla.

"I want to have a word with Mr. Avery. You go along without me."

"No. I'll just wait across the lane," Barilla said.

As Barilla was hustled along with the departing herd of operatives, she saw Jamie sitting on the steps of their former boarding-house. When he spotted her, he jumped up to single her out. Reaching out, he grabbed her by the hand.

"Another girl got dead. I saw her taken away in a cart. I wanted to be sure it warn't you," Jamie said as he shyly lowered his head.

"Oh, Jamie, that's sweet of you. But she was sick and should not have tried to work. Even," she added in a disconsolate tone, "the stairs were too much for her."

"I ain't seen you for a long time. You moved away from this house, didn't you?" he asked, lifting his eyes to her. Too sad eyes for such a little boy.

"Yes, Jamie," she answered as she stepped aside, leading him away from the now-crowded steps and the disparaging glances of the other girls.

"Tell me about yourself. Did you go to the school? And did you learn to read?"

"Sure I did. Want me to tell you a story I could read?"

"Of course. What was it about?"

"Well, there was this fox who wanted some grapes and he could not reach up to get the grapes, so he said, 'Oh well, they were sour grapes.'" At that, Jamie laughed aloud. "Wasn't that stupid? How could the dumb fox know if the grapes were sour?"

"Jamie, that's one of Aesop's fables. It is a moral to teach us that when we cannot have something we want, it is best to just accept it. But I am pleased to know you could read about it."

In the extreme heat, she became oppressed by the stench emanating from the hapless youngster. "Jamie," she asked, "don't you ever take a bath?"

"Nope. Got no bathtub."

"Is there any soap available?"

"Guess so. Mama sometimes washes clothes with soap."

"Suppose you take a piece and go down to the river and wash

yourself all over." She had added the last with undue emphasis.

"Don't wanna," the boy said in a belligerent tone.

"I want you to. You smell bad."

Jamie sighed with resignation. "All right, if'n you want me to."

In that moment, Jamie saw Else approaching. He pulled away from Barilla, saying, "I gotta go," and was off and running away.

As Else and Barilla walked briskly out onto Central Street, Else told her about the conversation with Mr. Avery. "I at first asked if it was truly Eliza who was killed, and he assured me that it was. I then asked if her wages would be sent to the mother in Sudbury, and he assured me it would be done. Then, in came that beady-eyed Lord asking what I was doing there. Can you beat that? Such gall! 'Is this about that careless girl?' he asked, and Mr. Avery told him it was. Well, Lord went on, 'She was a sickly one. We don't need sick girls here, so what's the loss?' I turned on him and said, 'She was a human being.' I went on about it, getting more furious in my anger, and turned to tell Mr. Avery that 'Mr. Lord treats us all as if we were nothing, just the dirt under his feet.' And then old Avery spoke up saying, 'Miss!' and I said, 'White,' and he said he would take it under advisement, and I asked politely if I could leave and he said, dismissal granted. I tell you, I felt like slamming the door after me, but I didn't."

"Poor Eliza," said Barilla, as they continued on to the Elstons.

Before they entered the house, Else lowered her voice to say, "I'll tell you one thing. I'm not going to sit home tonight. I'm so mad I'm going out and buy something. Are you coming?"

"I think not. There is nothing I would buy. Perhaps Judith will go with you."

Thus it happened that after supper, Barilla continued to read her borrowed book about Greek myths. She read of Aphrodite, the goddess of love, and Artemis, goddess of the silver moon. And of Hercules and his many labors for a king who feared and hated the super-strong hero. Avidly, she wanted to learn more about how the king made life so difficult for him. She likened the king to the overseer, Lord, and Hercules and Artemis as those being mistreated. Her excitement heightened when Hercules returned from one dangerous mission with intent to fling a savage boar at the king's feet. Ah, revenge is sweet, she thought gleefully.

As she read on of more dreaded accomplishments of Hercules, the more she identified with the similarity. The old king banned Hercules from his city, never to return. So too, she thought, would the hateful overseers and agents unfairly drive some operatives out of the mills.

Judith and Else returned as Barilla undressed for bed.

"I bought a necklace," announced Else with satisfaction, as she held it up for Barilla to see.

"It's pretty," said Barilla as she admired the dull red stone dangling from a golden chain. "What is it?"

"The clerk in the store said it was a ruby, but I don't know."

Barilla turned to Judith. "What did you buy?"

"Some lemon drops." She handed Barilla a small bag. "Want one?"

"Thanks," she said, reaching into the bag.

"We met your friend Emily," Else said as she started to undress. "She told me to tell you that Ann Graham, the one whose arm got ripped off, died of blood poisoning. Kind of a gruesome day, wasn't it? Eliza dead of a broken neck, and Ann dead with a horrible infection. But, all's right with our little world, isn't it?" Her tone had become bitter with sarcasm. "We can read stories, go shopping for baubles, and flop into our beds sucking lemon drops."

She blew out the candle and the three girls stretched out beneath the sheets.

Saturday morning seemed endless. Barilla had slept fitfully the previous night, alternating between lying wide-eyed, staring into the darkness, and dreaming of heroic deeds. In dreams, the hero took on the appearance of not Hercules, but Horace. And, as she reached out to him, he just drifted away.

Her loom was jarring her mind and body. Her nerves were as taut as the warp threads through which the shuttle sped back and forth. The banging buzzed through her brain, repeating over and over, Horace, Horace, Horace. So lost in thought had she become that when the noon bell rang, she was hardly conscious of it, but rather surprised that suddenly all the others had stopped their looms to hustle for the stairs.

Else laughed at her. "Like that thing so much you hate to leave it?"

In spite of herself, Barilla laughed. Besides, this was Saturday. The afternoon would not drag on so long, for they would get out earlier.

Many of the girls planned to attend a musical at the City Hall that evening. But when Else asked her, Barilla declined.

"I need to write down my thoughts. My hand is itching to do some poetry."

"If that's what you'd rather do, all right. Judith and Emily are going, and so are the Elstons. I thought you would be going with us."

That evening when all had left, the Elston house was quiet. Barilla took her pen and ink and began to write. Although her thoughts were of Horace and the two dead girls, she knew she would not be sending her words to Horace or anyone else. It was an imperative need in her to be alone to express her thinking on paper.

> *Let us love one another, not long may we stay*
> *In this bleak world of mourning, some droop while 'tis day.*
> *Others fade in their noon; few linger 'till eve.*
> *Oh! there breaks not a heart but leaves someone to grieve*
> *And the fondest, the purest, the bravest that met*
> *Have still found the need to forgive and forget.*
> *Then ah, though the hopes that we nourished decay,*
> *Let us love one another as long as we stay*
> *There are hearts like the ivy, though all be decayed*
> *That seemed to clasp fondly in sunshine and shade.*
> *Though leaves droop in sadness, still gaily they spread,*
> *Undrained midst the blighted, the lonely and dead.*
> *How the mistletoe clings to the oak not to part,*
> *With its leaves closely round it, the roots in its heart*
> *Exists but to twine it, imbibe the same dew*

Or to fall with its loved oak and perish there too.
So, let us love one another midst sorrow the worst
Unaltered and fond as we loved at the first.
Though the bat's wing of pleasure may change, may forsake
And the bright urn of wealth into particles break
There are some sweet affections that gold cannot buy
That cling but still closer when sorrow draws nigh.
So remain with us though all else pass away
Let us love one another as long as we stay.
Barilla Adeline Taylor

She had just finished when she heard the others returning. Thus she slipped her writing into her trunk and went downstairs, knowing there would be cold tea and cookies, and a companionship which she was now better able to face.

After Sunday dinner on the seventh of July, the three girls of the Elston house, along with Emily, sought relief from the heat by strolling across the bridge beyond the Boott mill. There, along the riverbank, they found relative coolness beneath the shade of thick forestation, for there were no mill buildings on the north side of the Merrimack. A throng of others had the same idea, so the foursome soon found two of their friends, the black-haired Malvina and the plump Louisa. Since these two both worked in the spinning room, there had been little contact since Barilla had left Mrs. Merriam's. Except, of course, Emily, who still shared a room with them.

From where the duo sat, Malvina waved a beckoning arm and called out, "Come sit here. We want to hear all the news since you left us."

The foursome made themselves comfortable as Barilla answered Malvina. "Surely Emily has told you what we have been doing."

"Not her," scoffed Malvina. "We call her our closemouthed roomy. All she told us was that you all went to Boston. So, do tell us, what is a big city like?"

The subsequent chatter seemed to explode with everyone

talking at once. Before it was over, Malvina and Louisa shot amused glances one to the other regarding a confused picture of the big city.

"That's enough," interrupted Barilla as she turned to Malvina and Louisa. "Now you tell us what you have done!"

"Well," answered Malvina, speaking up so all could hear. "For one thing, we went to a meeting called by the Female Labor Reformed Association, where a group plans to demand a ten-hour workday instead of twelve to fourteen hours."

"Not so loud!" cautioned Louisa. "Remember that we were told to keep that a secret."

Worried glances passed around the group until it became obvious to Louisa to change the subject.

"Something far more exciting was a meeting in the Merrimack hotel where a Mrs. Emerson, of the Baptist persuasion, told of a chance to go West. It seems that thousands of men have gone to the Oregon and California territories and except for a few women and children, that horde of men need wives."

"Wives!" blurted Else. "Is that the reason for going?"

"That's the reason Mrs. Emerson gave. She explained that men without the stabilizing influence of women commit all kinds of immoral acts."

Malvina interrupted to say, "So that church parish in Boston will provide most of the expense, but wants each girl to pay one hundred dollars, or whatever they have saved."

"Tell us more!" urged Barilla, who had taken a sudden interest in what sounded like a fantastic adventure.

"Well," continued Malvina. "There are no roads beyond a large river called the Mississippi. After that there are miles and miles of mountains and deserts. The only way is by covered wagons. We did ask how long it took, and the lady said usually from May to October."

"Why that's six months!" said the practical Else. "What is so exciting about that?"

"It's the rich land for farming, along with a milder climate. No ice or snow or freezing weather."

"Humph!" scoffed Else. "It doesn't sound like it is a part of the United States!"

"Not yet, of course. But just imagine what a great future. Mrs. Emerson said that some nation will acquire the land, and those who settle will determine which nation," Malvina said.

Rumbles of thunder alerted everyone to suddenly look skyward. The possibility of rain pervaded everyone's thinking. Else stood up and the others followed.

"You can all dream about your land of milk and honey if you wish," said Else. "I think I'll stay here in civilization. And now we had best get for cover or get wet."

However, the impending danger of a storm proved nothing more than dark clouds passing by, causing only dirt and old leaves into cyclonic dust storms.

Back in her room, Barilla took out pen, ink, and paper. Placing them on her lapboard, she began to write.

Sunday, July 7, 1844

Dear Parents,

It is now with pleasure that I write to you to let you know that I am in good health. Not all persons can say that. There were two deaths to girls that I know about. Ann Graham was one. The other was a poor, sick girl who had not a soul of her own except a sick mother. So you can know that this daughter is thankful for my health and for good parents and loving brothers. Of course that includes sister Florena. We have been told that come the middle of August the mills will close until rains come again. That means I will come home for that time. I want so much to see all of you. If I do come, it may be for the last time. By next spring, if my health is as good as it is now, I think of joining an association and going West.

I will bring you something, Mother. When I find out when I can come, I will write again. Letters are going faster now because of the railroad. I received your last letter seven days after you sent it. I want you to write again soon. Fill up your letters full.

From your absent daughter,

Barilla A. Taylor

She folded the letter in thirds, then turned in the corners to form an envelope. She sealed it with sealing wax heated over a candle.

A few weeks later, she received a letter from her mother.

Roxbury, August 1, 1844

Dear Daughter,

I now sit to answer your letter. The folks are all well, but Florena. She was here yesterday and spent the day. She is miserable and looks miserable. Her baby, Erasmus, is very cross and wears her out. He is now two months and should stop crying so much. She does not complain, just considers herself fortunate because her first baby died. Your Aunt Louisa Hinkson was here one day with her new baby, and that one is a sweet, good baby.

We have heard from Byron who was at Bangor. He leaves Bangor for the chance to get better pay for his team, so he is mostly upriver. He sent word he was coming home soon, and we are looking for him every day. We heard you was in Boston the Fourth of July and told the Bradbury boys you was coming home soon.

Mary Ann Austin is teaching the Roxbury school now. Florena wants you should come home and help her for she has got a great deal to do at her house and go to school. I wish next time you write you would tell me what you mean by joining an association.

From your affectionate Mother,

Melinda

The hot, dry summer days continued. Then on Monday, August 16, the mill agent posted a billet on the entrance gate, announcing a universal shutdown on Saturday, August 24. Final pay would be meted out that day. It was also noted that if rain were to occur, there would be a return to operations the middle of September.

10

That evening, Barilla wrote home.

August 16, 1844

Dear Folks,

I now have the exquisite pleasure of writing to tell you I am coming home. The mill will close on Saturday, August 24. Judith Fox, Emily, and I will take the early train on Monday, August 26, which leaves at seven o'clock. We make a connection to the Boston and Maine Railroad which goes to Portland. A coach is to be had in Portland, which goes to Rumford. This can come about in one day. Imagine that. We can get off where the ferry crosses the river over to Dixfield. We want someone to come for us there. Judith found out that this should be well before dark.

I have written all I can. Do not let everyone see this, for conscience sake, for I am on the floor and my paper lies on my trunk. I have written in great haste. I now hurry to the post office.

With much affection, I remain your loving daughter,

Barilla

On that final Saturday, Barilla's pay came to $23.86 which as she pocketed it, gave her the happy, excited feeling of being able to pay her fare home with some left over.

The following Sunday afternoon, Judith and Barilla busied themselves with preparations for their trip. They had purchased canvas satchels, because they were returning to Lowell. Emily, however, said she would be taking her trunk because she was not coming back. Emily's older sister, Bernice had written glowingly of the Biddeford-Saco mills as being a better place to work.

Abigail Elston entered their bedroom carrying something in two small cotton sacks and handed each girl a sack. "These are some lily bulbs to take to your families in Maine. They are called candidum lilies and they grow quite large. You may have seen them growing in our backyard."

"Yes, of course," Judith said. "What a nice gift to take with us. We do thank you."

Barilla merely smiled gratefully. Judith had said it all. Besides, she thought smugly, she had purchased several yards of fine material to take to her mother.

Abigail then asked, with some concern, "I thought you girls would have invited Else to go with you."

"Oh, we did." Both girls spoke in unison.

"But," said Barilla, "her friend James Gordon extended an invitation to go to Revere where some friends of his, a married couple, live. They have a large boardinghouse there and James told her about how pleasantly cool it is beside the sea. That's why she left with him this morning."

"Well," Judith said, "it will also be cooler at home where we are going."

Abigail smiled then and turned away, leaving them alone.

"I think we should wear our homespun dresses. The trains can be so dusty," Judith said.

"Of course. I'll just take one of my new dresses. Perhaps we should also take our band boxes to keep our bonnet clean."

"Right. No one at home has bonnets like ours."

"Judith?" Barilla said, pensively, "how does it happen that your home is in Roxbury, but I never knew you until you came to Lowell?"

"That is because you lived further north on the Roxbury-Byron line and I lived south, actually in Frye. It was too far for me to walk to the Roxbury school, so I was sent to live with my father's sister down in Mexico. She had married a Mister Richards and there I could go with my cousins to the nearby Austin school. Besides, I was an only child, and there was no one at home to play with,"

"I see. Well, I usually went to the Coos Canyon school in Byron. But one year I went to the Roxbury school."

Alighting from the coach beside the ferry landing in West Peru, Barilla breathed deeply of the fresh Maine air, The oppression caused by the heat on the trains, and the subsequent dusty, jolting carriage ride, dropped as though she had flung off an unwanted burden. Feeling a sudden newfound freedom, she squared her shoulders, then nymph-like descended on light footsteps down the rutted roadway to the waiting ferry.

"Two cents each," said the heavy-muscled ferryman, as he held out a gnarled hand for payment.

When each of the three girls paid him, he glanced plaintively up the riverbank. "Ain't any more of ye comin'?" he asked.

They all looked back, westerly along the banking, seeing only the distant coach spewing clouds of dust as it accelerated uphill toward Rumford Falls.

"Guess not," he spoke laconically. A slow smile appeared beneath his hawk-like nose.

There were no seats on the flat-bottomed barge because few persons came on foot. It was large enough for a wagon and team of horses. A wagon driver often alighted to assist the ferryman in poling across the fast moving Androscoggin River, which flowed southeasterly toward the sea.

Barilla relished the fresh, pine-scented air that bathed her face. The crossing was not a long one. She looked ahead with anticipation of who might be there to meet her. A man was fishing on the Dixfield side of the river. He was a tall, familiar-looking man.

"Byron!" she called out. The man looked up, grinning widely.

"Byron, oh my dear brother. I'm so happy to see you," Barilla said, excitedly.

---

96   Sing Me a Song

Byron dropped his makeshift pole, jumped aboard the barge, and helped the ferryman secure the ropes to the trees on shore. Then he turned, holding out his arms to his sister.

Hugging him, her head pressed against his chest, she presented a picture of absolute joy and contentment. Her companions glanced knowingly at one another, being completely absorbed in Barilla's happiness.

Barilla drew her head back, looked briefly up into her brother's eyes, then turned to present her friends. Emily, he already knew, but Judith was a stranger. They all shook hands.

Barilla noticed in Judith's eyes the same sly twinkle that she had for Horatio Bradbury the Fourth of July day when they met on Boston Common.

Byron hoisted Emily's trunk onto his shoulder. Then the three-some followed him up the embankment to where his team stood sheltered in the cool shade of dense trees.

Barilla climbed up to the one seat, as Byron helped the other two into the back of the wagon, which he had thoughtfully strewn with hay.

"Where are you going?" he asked Judith.

"To my father's in Frye. That's on the hillside just before you get to the Swift River rapids. I'll let you know at my roadway."

He went around the wagon and moved up beside Barilla, at once pulling the reins in sudden decisiveness known instinctively by his horses.

As they trotted northerly, passing the farms of Dixfield toward Mexico, Barilla exulted in the fresh air, the quiet, the pastoral beauty, and even in seeing a few cows being directed into a barn for the evening milking. Her eyes sparkled so much, her brother smiled with amusement.

"Glad to be home, aren't you?" he said.

"Oh, yes. It's all so beautiful, so wonderful."

"Maybe you'll be staying then?"

The sun was setting directly ahead of them. Barilla shaded her eyes against the intense light and answered thoughtfully, "No, I think not. It's my way of earning money. Even though it is far from pleasant, the work is not any harder than it is at home, where I get no pay at all."

"Yes, I understand. That's why I went up Bangor way. I earn more money hauling logs with my team than I could around here."

"So, you, too, are going back again""

"Sure thing. But right now, it being so dry and the Penobscot River so low, there ain't no call for me and my team."

After several miles, the road turned right at Mexico Corner as it skirted Mann Hill. Now the setting sun profiled Byron's face. She studied him. He had been gone from home for two years. He was changed. No longer a playful tease, he was now a serious, grown-up man.

"You do realize we are going to be late for supper?" he asked.

"Of course, but Mother will see that we get something, even if it is cold biscuits and applesauce."

He laughed, saying, "The same old fare, eh? But that's what makes it distinctly our home. But now it's raspberries instead of applesauce."

After about three miles, Judith reached a hand up to tap Barilla's back. "Tell him it's the next road on the left."

When Byron finally reined in the team, he went around to help Judith down.

"Will you be all right if I don't try to take the team up there?"

"Oh yes. It's not far, really." She smiled with coyness, her eyes sparkling. "I am strong and healthy, and it's good to stretch my legs."

In parting, Barilla called down to her, "Do come up to visit if you can."

"Oh, I will," she answered as she hurried up the drive.

Soon thereafter, the golden light had gone. The sky was pale yet streaked with orange-reds and yellow. The road was alternately crooked or straight as it followed the ins and outs of Swift River, which at that time of year was devoid of water.

Several miles later, in complete darkness except for an occasional light in windows of neighbors, Byron brought the team to a halt in the road by their home. He turned to Barilla.

"You go on up to the house. I'll take Emily to the Austin place. She's got that trunk, and she will be anxious to see her folks. I'll bring your stuff when I come back."

There were no lights in her house because on hot summer evenings, the family moved outside. Her parents, Stephen and Melinda sat on a bench on the side stoop. The house faced east, and the side entrance was the preferred entryway.

It was a large white house, whose roof eaves came down to just above the front entrance door centered between two windows on each side. Two large dormers jutted out from the roof which served two spacious bedrooms. No trees blocked the morning sunshine, but on the western side, mighty elms towered high above a central chimney. On the south an ell led to a barn. The ell housed the summer kitchen, with an unfinished wooden floor a more airy room for cooking than in the main part of the house. A corner of that kitchen housed a milk room, floored with smooth, flat stones for necessary coolness. Dried corncobs filled the walls for insulation. Adjacent to these rooms was a woodshed, filled to the rafters, with only a three-foot-wide walkway to the inevitable two-holer, a necessity before the advent of indoor plumbing.

The walkway led to a cavernous barn where the cows and horses spent the coldest winter months. Otherwise the animals were pastured behind and beside the barn, down to the brook and back as far as the river.

Barilla knew that her younger brothers would be playing on the front lawn, either leap-frog, tag, or just rolling downhill toward the road. At the sound of the horses and the sight of Barilla alighting from the wagon, her brothers came whooping down to meet her, all five of them- 14 year old Morval, 10 year old Marvin, eight-year-old Melchoir, six-year-old Jack, and Gene, age four.

"Rilla, Rilla, Rilla," they all cried out in unison. Long-legged

Morval reached her first, and along with the others engulfed her with hugs and kisses.

"Me too," begged Gene, whose chubby legs were not as fast moving as the other boys.

When she freed herself from her eager brothers, she bent to pick up Gene, cuddling him in her arms. He planted a wet kiss on her cheek.

"Yes, you too," she answered him. Then, carrying Gene, she strode up to the house. Like leading a vanguard, her brothers whooped and hollered alongside in their excitement.

Her mother had gone inside the house, where through the doorway Barilla could see her lighting a lamp.

Her father arose from his bench to place a hand on her shoulder. His words to her were as noncommittal as they had always been.

"It's good to see you, girl. Now come in and have some supper."

Inside, Barilla went directly to Melinda, who had busied herself with food preparation so that her back was turned. Barilla swung her mother around, at once embracing her, realizing suddenly that she herself had become taller.

"Mother, you have shrunk," Barilla said.

"No, child, you have grown. Oh my dear girl, I'm so glad to have you home."

By this time, Byron had returned. He came in carrying Barilla's belongings. He set them to one side on the floor, and said, "Of course she's grown. She is now sixteen, a full-grown woman, even though she's still just my little sister."

"Oh, go on with you," said Barilla with a knowing smile, for like all the Taylor males, he was a natural tease.

Melinda placed food on the dining table, a plate of biscuits, a bowl of raspberries, and a redware pitcher filled with cider.

Barilla moved to the wall cupboard bent on getting porringers, spoons, knives, and cups as naturally as though she had not been gone almost a year.

"You set," her mother said as she pointed to Barilla. "The boys can do that."

Barilla did as she was told, smiling good-naturedly.

Byron sat down in the chair beside her. Morval and Marvin set the utensils on the table as the others scrambled around grabbing chairs, then, elbows on the table, gazed at her with eager eyes.

As she buttered a cold biscuit, she looked up over the table to a new lamp suspended from the ceiling. Its glass bowl was filled with ruby-red fuel.

"That's beautiful," she said. "Where did you get it, Mother?"

"Byron brought it from up Bangor way," Melinda said with pride in her voice. "Ain't it a beauty? Burns oil so there's no need of candles in here."

As the mesmerized boys continued watching her, Barilla felt an embarrassing warmth flooding her face.

"Surely you cannot all have missed me so much?" she asked.

Five smiling faces all seemed to nod at once.

She continued, "And I suppose Bub is asleep?"

Melinda, who was standing by, said, "Yes, of course. He is in our bedroom." Then she asked, "Do you two have all you want to eat?"

"Sure have," said Byron. To his sister he commented, "I've been here more than a week, and I never got all the attention you're getting, Sis."

"Aw," Morval said, "you're just one more brother."

"But I'm the eldest, so I expect to get some respect."

"Sure, sure," several voices chimed in, in a good-natured way.

"All right now boys," said Melinda, "you just clear away the table."

As they obeyed her, Barilla looked around for her father. She saw that he sat in his rocker by the window. He smiled briefly, and with pursed lips, he gave her a terse nod.

His taciturn manner had often baffled her. His manner of speaking was either an order or a comment on the weather. Now he spoke up in a voice which demanded everyone's attention.

"The hops be ready for picking, so we will get to it first thing tomorrow. So, now all of you, off to bed. We arise at first light."

He stood up and started for the bedroom, which was on the same level, but Barilla was ahead of him.

"I just want a quick peek at Bub," she said.

"Not now. You can see him in the morning," her father said curtly.

"Of course, Father, so good-night." She turned to Melinda and bid her good-night with a kiss on her cheek.

Barilla bent to pick up her belongings, but Byron beat her to it. She pointed to the small sack that Abigail had given her.

"You can leave that one. It's some lily bulbs which I will plant outside tomorrow. She then picked up a candle and struck a flint to light it. Thus Byron followed her into the hallway and up the front staircase.

11

Daylight came in its usual sneaky fashion. First rays shone on her face, then upon the pillow, until in a few minutes, the golden light swept its magic over the entire room. There had never been any shades over the double windows, for when the eastern sun rose, it was time to get up. She recalled that even when she had been sick with a cold or measles or chicken pox, she was expected to get up, wash hands and face, dress, and go down for breakfast.

She heard the others below and Byron across the hallway.

"Up and at it, Sis," he called out to her.

"Oh, I'm up. In Lowell we are often up before dawn. There, we have bells to wake us." Oh God, she thought, it's good to be away from those demanding bells.

She dressed in one of the dresses she had made in Lowell, a light blue sprigged with white, cloverlike blossoms. She folded the six-yard piece of material over her arm, a gift for her mother.

Just outside her door she met Byron and Morval in the hallway.

"So, Morval," she said, "you've been upped to the older boy's room?"

"Yep, and when Byron goes back to Bangor, Marvin is coming in to sleep with me."

"And what if Con comes home from Stoughton?"

"Then Marvin can't."

"We better use the back stairs," suggested Byron. So together all three appeared in the kitchen. The remainder of the family, except for Melinda, was seated at table. Barilla laid the gift of cloth in her mother's rocker by the window, then stepped across the room to stand beside her mother who had just placed a large jar of doughnuts on the table.

"What shall I do to help?" she asked Melinda.

"You can go to the buttery and fetch another jug of milk."

At that moment, Bub, the youngest Taylor, was bawling, so Melinda changed her directive to Barilla.

"Perhaps best that you go get him. I left him on the potty chair. I guess he's finished by now."

Gleefully, Barilla went into the bedroom to rescue the unhappy boy, who when he saw her, stopped crying. She stooped to his level.

"Well, Bub," she said. "I'll just wipe you off and..."

He stared at her with a blank, frightened expression in his bright blue eyes. Then he averted his head to one side and whimpered.

As she undid the strap that held him, she asked softly, "Oh Bub, don't you remember Barilla?"

Curious because she called him Bub, he turned to look at her again, his head held downward, but peering slightly at her face. She picked him up and held him securely, feeling his blonde curls soft against her cheek, as she carried him into the kitchen.

At the sight of his mother, he strained to get away from Barilla, reaching out both hands to Melinda.

"Put him down, Barilla; he can walk." Melinda said.

He ran to grab his mother's skirt and bury his face in the folds.

Melinda chuckled, and said, "Best to leave him alone and go fetch the milk."

While Barilla was out there, she used the necessary, which took a little time before she returned to the kitchen. Her father finished his breakfast and stood up. He stared at Barilla as she returned with the milk. His words to her were indeed dour, "That's a pretty fancy dress to go out picking hops."

"But, Father, I am not going to pick hops. I'm going to stay and help Mother, and then I'm going to visit Florena."

"Ain't no need a that," he said contemptuously, "The need is for all hands to pick hops. That's our big money crop and you know it."

"I'm sorry, Father. Perhaps tomorrow I will help with the hops.

Today I want to be with Mother, and this afternoon I am going to walk up to see Florena."

For a moment, Stephen Burleigh could not hide his astonishment that this wisp of a girl, his daughter, had become so bold. His cold recourse was not loud, but she felt its venom.

"So now it's what you want instead of what I want?"

"But, Father," she asked plaintively, "I don't understand why it always has to be that way."

"Because I say so, dammit," he answered with great contempt.

"You may do what you want away from here, but in this house I expect you to do as I say!"

Rage sharpened her resolve, for she had no inclination toward compliance. She wondered what her brothers were thinking, and how her mother was reacting. Her rage gave her strength, and she raised her chin defiantly.

"There are other persons who live in this house. And although I have always respected your wishes, I do believe that the others and myself deserve some consideration. So, I'll repeat what I said before. I will stay with Mother this morning and then go to see my sister."

The fire in her eyes, the defiance of her stance, unnerved Stephen Burleigh. He turned and stormed out the door. Barilla's brothers, even four-year-old Gene, followed meekly. Byron pursed his lips and nodded to her. She saw there a twinkle of amusement in his eyes.

Barilla stared at those of her own blood following her father's lead until the last of them rounded the corner of the barn. It seemed as though a part of her had dissolved, leaving nothing but jelly. She turned to watch her mother, who had started a bread mixture, kneading the mass and separating it into loaves in three pans.

Melinda wiped her hands on her apron and went over to her rocker by the front window. She picked up the child who had followed her and began nursing him.

Now alone, Barilla sat down at the table, poured a glass of milk, and reached for a doughnut. The strange silence of a room, so recently filled with the banter of voices, further enhanced an abject misery into her very bones. She finished eating, then stood up and began clearing the table.

Melinda had not spoken, and the only sounds wafting up from the road were those of the clip-clop of the work horses pulling a creaking wagon loaded with empty boxes to be filled with hop bracts.

Barilla moved over to sit in her father's rocker and lifted her eyes briefly to her mother's. She did not know her mother's exact age, but judging from the gray in her hair, assumed her to be about forty. She gazed fondly at the child thinking that he probably did not even know his full name was Philand Delano. She commented on that, then said, "He is such a big boy now, about a year and a half, isn't he?"

"Yes, five months short of his second birthday."

"Shouldn't he be weaned?"

"Enough time for that. You see, as long as I nurse him, my monthlies do not come. Thus, I cannot become pregnant with another."

"Another! Oh, Mother, surely you have had enough."

Melinda shrugged, then spoke patiently, "It is the way of life, Barilla. It is a woman's lot in this world."

"As," said Barilla laconically, "is the subservient manner in which Father treats you, and all of us."

"Now, now, Daughter. That is not for you nor I to question."

"Mother," she asked abruptly, "do you and Father love each other?"

Melinda's gaze dropped as she responded thoughtfully, "Love! I suppose you could call it that."

The child's mouth slipped from the breast, his curiosity aroused by the strange person his mother was talking to.

Melinda held the child up over her shoulder and rubbed his back.

"What I would really like to know is," Barilla asked, "what was it like when you first knew him, before you were married?"

"Oh that. 'Twas back in Belfast on the coast of Maine. My family lived there. My father, Joseph Hinkson, worked in the shipyard. Your father was a seaman in the new Colonial navy, come up from Bath with a captain and other seamen to fit out and launch a vessel." Melinda went on dreamily as the child cuddled in her lap. His eyes were fastened on Barilla. Melinda continued her reverie,

"My father brought him home for noon victuals. We girls were excited by those visits. He came often, until a fateful time a few days before the vessel was to slide down the ways. On that day he asked to speak with my father alone. And after a while, Father called Louisa into the front room. Soon, Stephen Burleigh Taylor left the house and Louisa came out of the parlor looking grim. 'What's wrong with you?' I asked, and she told me that Stephen Burleigh had asked for her hand, and she told Father that she did not want to marry him. She was scared about defying our father and ran crying from the kitchen. I followed her to our bedroom, where she sat on the edge of the bed. 'Well,' said I, 'if it were me he asked for, I would not be refusing him.'

Two days passed, but Stephen Burleigh, the sailor, came not for dinner, nor even a visit. I felt sad. In my mind I could picture him, tall and straight, eyes that were the color of a deep blue sky and a shock of blonde hair with a beard to match. So, being one who would not let grass grow beneath my feet, I was off next morning, after the chores were done, a walking down to the shipyard for the purpose of seeing him. A working he was, polishing the bow sprit. And me, being embarrassed by my boldness, ventured a comment about what a beautiful spring day it was for a walk, to look out upon the sea. At the time, I did not know whether my feeble ruse was being laughed at or whether he was flattered over the attention, but he did suggest that after another hour's work, he could be off and walking with me downriver further toward the sea. On the walking I was bold enough to ask a question. 'Was you angry that Louisa would not have you for a husband?' 'Not angry,' says he to me. 'Just disappointed.'

"By then we was by a large rock, having a hollowed-out natural sitting place and there we sat. He put his arm around my shoulder and drew me close against his chest. Into my hair he whispered a question 'Would thou have answered me nay or aye?'

"I did draw my head around to look up into his eyes and give answer that "Twould by aye,' before I dropped my gaze downward for the shameful hussy that I felt myself to be. He did not allow that, for next I knew, his free hand lifted my chin, and I felt his lips on mine. Oh, daughter, I tell you it was a fine moment, that kissing. When we could again look one another in the eyes, he was a saying to me, 'I will come this evening to ask Joseph Hinkson for your hand.'"

"That's a lovely story," commented Barilla. "And have you always, ever since, felt as you did that day of the first kissing?"

"Yes, daughter, always," she answered serenely, adding, "I would hope for you the same someday."

Barilla found her mother's attitude to be a conflict with what seemed to be her lifestyle as little more than a slave.

Melinda set Philand Delano down to stand on the floor where his hand held tight to his mother's skirt. She spoke to him softly.

"That is your sister, Bub, Now you walk over to her and greet her nicely."

"No," protested the child. "Falena my sister, not her."

Barilla moved toward him, and dropped to her knees.

"Florena is also my sister. You see, Bub, I did live here when you were only a crawling baby, and you did let me rock you to sleep. So, come closer now and let me hug you as I did then."

The child stepped forward and after a long hug, she picked him up onto her lap. She glanced at Melinda with a satisfied smile.

Melinda now held in her hands the bulk of material that had been laid over the back of the rocker.

"What is this for?" she asked, as she smoothed her hand across the richness of the percale, admiring the blue-green of its shimmering beneath her rough hand.

"It is my present for you. We will make a dress for you before I go back to the mill."

"Oh, no, it is too pretty for me. There is nowhere I would have use to wear such a dress. But we can make it up for you or for Florena."

Stubbornly Barilla persisted, "If it's only for you to put on whenever you would like to feel grand, that alone would warm my heart
thinking on it. But enough of that. I also brought some lily bulbs to
plant them wherever you want them to grow."

"Perhaps on the west side, beneath the back eves. Wouldn't that
be best?" She had stood as she talked, then added, "Now to the baking for me. You go along with your planting."

Barilla set the child down on his feet, then holding his hand,
stooped to pick up the bag of bulbs Abigail had given her. On her
way out through the summer kitchen, she noticed the three loaves of
dough set to rise. Both the hot fire and the making of the dough, she
knew, were done by her mother before anyone else had risen from
bed. Proceeding through the sheds, she picked up a shovel, and leading the child, walked to the back of the house.

The very fact that his new sister was using a shovel, much the
way of the other family members, somehow meant more to the little
boy than could any explanation.

"Rilla," he said, and gave her a broad and happy smile. "Rilla, sister like Falena."

"Yes, that's right," she answered happily. "And now, Bub, hand
me a bulb. See how I place it with the green shaft upward. Now you
do the same, about so far apart."

Elated by the process of doing something for his newfound sister
filled the boy with glee. After the four bulbs were placed, he hopped
gaily around her as she moved the dusty soil back into the trench.

As they returned through the summer kitchen, Melinda's fire
was apparently ready for baking. Placing her hand before the open
bake-oven, she was satisfied it would take the risen loaves of bread.

"I need some water, Barilla. Would you take a pail and go down
to the well by the brook? You see, even though I primed the pump,
naught came up but air. I fear the dryness is to blame."

"Of course, Mother. I'll take two pails, one for the bulbs which are
planted in very dry soil. They need water in order to grow."

"Bub come, too?" It was more of a statement than a question.

"Oh, I don't think you had better," Barilla said, for she knew the uneven ground would be too difficult for him.

"No," Melinda said. "He doesn't yet know how to step around the cow flops."

When Barilla returned after watering the lily bulbs, she found her mother rolling pie crust. Beside her on the table were three bowls, one of raspberries, one of blackberries, and one of green apples. The latter needed to be peeled and cut into slices. She picked up a knife and began peeling. Bub, by now in complete adoration, stood by and watched her. Occasionally she popped a slice into his mouth.

By the time the three pie fillings had been placed in the bottom crusts, Barilla added the necessary scant cup of sugar with a table-spoon of flour to each of the berry pies, and a teaspoon of cinnamon to the scant cupful of sugar for the apple.

Melinda covered each one with the necessary top crust, which she slathered with butter, Both women smiled at each other often during the process of working together.

"By now," said Melinda, "the bread should be done. Barilla, hand me the peel."

Barilla picked up the long-handled iron peel, necessary for removing the hot loaves. When her mother opened the iron door, she deftly pulled each in turn out to waiting racks to cool. Then, just as deftly, placed each pie in turn upon the peel, shoving it into the bake-oven. Melinda quickly closed the door so the heat would not escape.

Brushing the flour from her hands on her apron, Melinda stated that chickens had to be stuffed and ready to pop in the oven when the pies were done.

"And the vegetables?" asked Barilla. "Which ones shall I get from the larder?"

"Potatoes, onions, and there are some fresh green beans I picked yesterday." Thus the two, mother and daughter, made all ready in time for the noon meal, which was always set upon the table at pre-cisely twelve o'clock. On this day, the male members had arrived and washed up with not one idle moment allowed to transpire. For this, her mother had to prepare every day of her life. Barilla likened her family to animals at a trough. Not, she mused, much different from the mill girls. It was up and eat, work and eat, then work and eat again. Such was the nature of a worker's daily life.

When the last piece of pie was finished, the crew hustled outside to clamber down the incline and onto the wagon again, although the older boys walked.

When Melinda and Barilla had eaten, Melinda started to put the child, Philand Delano into his bed for a nap.

"No," he said, "Rilla do it," He grabbed her hand and lead her toward the crib in their parents' bedroom.

After she helped her mother with the washing, she stated that she would be off up the road to visit Florena. She donned her fancy Lowell bonnet, and using broad, fast-paced steps, marched northerly up to the Austin farm. On the east side, as she passed the Bradbury place, she mused over whether Climena and Mary were there. Even though their mother was her Aunt Cora, Stephen Burleigh's sister, Barilla felt it was of little consequence to stop for a visit.

She soon passed the hop fields on the westerly side of the road. She could see that a lot of the vines had been torn down, although in the distance, toward Swift River, there were still a lot adhering to their 20-foot trellises. She was pleased that none of the working crew even noticed her. The hop fields continued up to, behind, and after the Thomas place, which was a distinctive house because of its tall, white-pillared front.

As she approached the Richards' farm on the east side of the road, a man came out the front door and immediately hailed her. He called out to her, "Hello there. You a stranger in these parts?"

Without stopping, she answered, "No, not really. I'm going to visit the Austins."

"Come far?" he questioned her again. His appearance was careless and dirty.

"No, not far. Just from the Taylor place."

He hustled across the road and was soon before her.

"Wall, I swan, if'n it ain't Barilla Taylor, a come home again," he said, chuckling.

"That's right, but you must excuse me. I'm anxious to see my sister Florena."

He took the rebuff with some puzzlement, as he tilted back his straw hat and scratched his head. But he did call out to her,

"Mighty nice seeing ya."

She did not turn, just waved her hand in passing. She soon came to the Abiather Austin house and walked right in, as was the custom with both neighbors and kin. Florena was in the kitchen drying dishes while her mother-in-law Susannah washed them. Dropping the towel on the table beside the sink, she hurried over to Barilla.

"Oh, my dear, I've been so anxious to see you since Emily came last evening," Florena said.

They embraced warmly, then Florena said, "What a great bonnet. May I try it on?"

"Of course," Barilla answered, untying the ribbon and passing it to her sister.

In that moment, Emily came into the kitchen, trailed by the youngest daughter, ten-year-old Susan. They greeted Barilla, then moved over to help their mother with the washing.

Florena put on the bonnet and looked to Barilla for appraisal.

"First rate, but on you anything would look great," Barilla said.

Florena removed the bonnet and hung it over a chair. To express her joy at seeing her sister, she put both hands on either side of Barilla's waist, and said, "Oh my dear girl, I have missed you so. I am so happy you came."

"Well, Father wasn't pleased that I did not turn to and pick hops today. But nothing could keep me from an afternoon with you. And, by the way, which one of the Richards was outside ogling me when he must have had better things to do?"

"That must have been Hap Richards. His wife died in childbirth a month ago, and although his aunt takes care of the baby, he just cannot get adjusted."

"He looked pretty dirty. I did not want to have anything to do with him."

"That one is no account. He's not like the other Richards. They are all up-and-coming people. But come now into the parlor, and let's have a good talk."

Florena opened the two front windows in the little-used, stuffy parlor, then directed Barilla to sit in an overstuffed chair, while she sat opposite on a horsehair sofa. All of the furniture, upholstered in black cambric, presented a gloomy picture. But nothing could diminish the joy between the two sisters,

"How long can you stay at home?" Florena said.

"Until mid-September or until rains come again."

"Then you really are going back?"

"Yes, although it's good to come home. I no longer feel that…that I want to stay here…that is, forever."

"I read your letter to the folks saying you might go West. Is that what you intend doing?"

"It sounds exciting, and it means becoming a wife to someone who already lives there. But I have all winter to think about it."

"Have you also considered what it means to be wife to just any man who asks for you? Like you are in a lineup, and he picks you out. Really, Barilla, that is not for you."

"Well," she answered dryly, "I did have a friend named Horace with whom I thought I might someday enter the marriage state. But, I had to accept that it was not meant to be. So now, I just don't care."

"If that Horace broke your heart, he's no account. There will be others. You will meet one who will appreciate who you are and what you are."

Barilla smiled weakly, "Not around here, anywhere, and not likely in Lowell, either. So what does it matter if I go West?"

"It's odd that you should be interested in going West. Just recently, Amos has talked of going West. Southwest, that is. He's heard tell of warm climate, soil that's rich and not full of rocks, and better chances to make lots of money."

Barilla studied her with renewed interest. "You mean he would take you and your baby on the long overland trek that takes as long as six months?"

"Not us, just him, until he would get established and could send for us. But there is another way to get there. You can take a ship down to a place called Calendonia Bay where it's very hot and junglelike. Then there is a strip of narrow land called the Isthmus of Darien which goes forty miles overland from the Atlantic to the Pacific Ocean. People can go across it by mule caravan. Once across, you go by ship again up the Californy coast."

"Does he have the money for such a venture? I thought he promised you a house of your own so you would not have to go on living with the Austin family?"

"He feels that there would be a far better house and better prospects out there. But truly, Barilla, I don't believe it's going to happen right away. His father needs his help here. Right now, they are out hoeing the rows of potatoes. The only other help is twelve-year-old Peter. The older girls, Mary Ann, Bernice, and Clarinda are all married, and Dana is somewhere near Boston. So I don't fret over the 'out west fever.'"

Barilla tried to visualize riding a donkey for forty miles in excessive heat through jungle country. Better to go by wagon train. At least, she reasoned, the land could not be much different than what she had already seen. She had become so engrossed with her vision, it came as a surprise to see fourteen-year-old Lovesta enter the room carrying Florena's four-month-old baby, Erasmus. Lovesta crossed the room to place him on his mother's lap.

"Hello, Barilla," she said. "It sure is nice to have you and my sister Emily home again." She turned her attention to Florena. "He woke up, so I changed his diaper and put on a clean dress."

"Thank you, Lovesta. You are a big help," Florena said.

When she had gone out of the room, Florena went on to praise the girl. "But," she added more seriously, "Emily plans to go to the Biddeford-Saco Mills and take Lovesta with her. Their older sister

Bernice and her husband John Stockbridge worked there and said it is a better place than Lowell."

"I knew Em was not going back to Lowell. Only Judith Fox, who came home with us, is going back with me," Barilla said.

The baby's eyes had fastened on the newcomer. Barilla moved across the room to sit beside Florena. She held out her hand to the baby. He grabbed the finger she extended to him as he smiled a tooth-less grin. His mother kissed the fuzz on the top of his head, She said, "He is much more good-natured than he used to be. Lovesta amuses him and rocks him a lot so I can get some work done. I will miss her."

She had hardly finished speaking when Mother Austin, followed by Lovesta, entered the room and they sat in the chairs on either side of the sofa.

Barilla smiled as graciously as she could, feeling disheartened that her and Florena's tête-à-tête was over.

"And how have you been Mrs. Austin?" she asked politely.

"Sprite, thank ye, sprite enough for an old lady."

"Come now, surely you are not so very old?"

"Fifty-three my last birthday." She smiled so broadly, Barilla saw that she had lost several teeth. Her hair, knotted on top of her head, was more grey than brown, and her hands, crossed in her lap, were heavily veined and quite wrinkled. Although Barilla felt her presence as an intrusion, she knew that a visitor, any visitor, was a pleasant diversion from the day's routine. Susannah Austin kept talking.

"We got a letter from George Dana saying he'd seen you and Emily on the Fourth of July." Then she added with a sigh, "That Boston-town must be quite a place. Emily has told us something about it."

"Well, it is…different. But for country people like us, it is just too busy and too big."

"And Lowell? Emily has told us about that, too. I don't see how you girls stand it, such hard work and ear-shattering noise," Mrs. Austin said.

"Actually we don't work any harder than those who are still on the farms. And the noise is something we get used to." As she said it, she knew that last part was a lie. For never, never would she become used to the noise.

The afternoon wore on with questions, answers, and whatever gossip knit together such a small community.

When Emily and her youngest sister Susan came into the parlor carrying lard pails filled with blueberries, Barilla realized that several hours had passed. Erasmus had become restless and held out his hands to Lovesta, straining to reach her. She went to him, and lifted him from his mother's lap.

Barilla stood up, smiling heartily at the females of this family.

"It has been a most pleasant afternoon, and I think it best I return home." To Emily she said, "Seeing that you have picked blueberries reminds me that I should go back and pick some for my mother."

Returning along the dusty road, she found her thoughts mixed between her new life and the familiarity of the old. Although there had been joy in seeing the friends and relatives she had grown up with, it seemed as strange as looking at a drawing of something that happened many years ago.

When she came to where the crew labored in the hop field, she made her way through the tangle of vines until she located her father. Young Gene sat on the ground in the shade of the wagon, leaning back against a wheel.

Stephen Burleigh looked up as Barilla spoke to him and said, "Oh, good you came along. Gene is tuckered out, so J want you should take him home."

"Of course, Father. I'll be glad to."

The four-year old jumped up with suddenly amazing agility and reached for Barilla's hand.

She accepted the hand, knowing how sticky it would be from the yellowish-green hop bracts.

As they continued down the road, Gene practically skipping with delight, she admonished him. "You are not so tuckered out after all, are you?"

He looked up at her, speaking seriously. "I don't like picking hops. Besides, they taste bad."

"Would you rather pick blueberries?" Barilla asked him.

"Um, they taste good."

"Tell you what. As soon as we get to the house, you go wash up and tell Mother you're going with me for berries."

12

She knew that in the pinewood cuttings some distance from the house there would be good picking.

She smiled often at Gene, even though his pail contained twigs and half-green berries. He also ate a goodly share.

At the five o'clock supper that evening, the berries had been picked over, and there were almost enough to go around.

"Gene doesn't need any," Barilla said jokingly. "He ate his share in the patch."

Melinda asked Barilla, "Do you think you could get enough early tomorrow so I can make pies in the forenoon?"

"Yes, of course. That is, if Father doesn't need me to pick hops."

"Won't need you 'til afternoon," he said grudgingly. "We be a needing to clear up the dead vines and tear down more, ready for picking over in the forenoon." He then added in a more serious voice, "Lucky thing happened. Hap Richards came along right after Barilla took Gene, and he asked what he could do to help us. Likely he wants to come by for a meal sometime. He didn't say anything about wages, but I'll pay him whatever he's worth."

Barilla took in this information with an indrawn breath, yet she had sense enough not to say a word.

When supper was over, Stephen Burleigh said to Byron, "Come help me with the milking. You wasn't up when I had to do it alone before breakfast."

"Of course, Father. And I will remember to help tomorrow morning," then added in a teasing manner, "It is also high time Morval helped, too."

"By tomorrow evening," their Father said, as he pushed back his chair and stood up, "we'll load up your wagon with the filled boxes, so you can take them to Rumford first thing the next day."

After the milking and the pails had been put in the buttery, Byron and his father came back into the large kitchen. On the now cleared table, Barilla and her mother had spread out the new material which was covered with pinned-on, old, discarded dress pieces for a pattern.

Stephen Burleigh went directly to a table beside his rocker, picked out a newspaper from the pile Byron had brought from Bangor, and sat down to read by what light came in from the window. Jack and Melchoir sat on the floor playing checkers in light that fell upon their board, while Morval whittled on an apple shovel, an item soon to be needed for the upcoming cider season.

Marvin, who had been directed to keep an eye on Bub, followed behind the tyke, who pulled a small chair behind him as he circled the table where his mother and Barilla worked. The two back legs of the chair had been worn almost to sharpness as this "horsey-pulling-a-wagon" game had been part of amusement for all those Taylors who had been toddlers in bygone days.

All too soon, twilight descended. Melinda looked up to her tall son who avidly watched the dressmaking procedure and asked, "Will you light the lamp, Byron? It is beginning to get dark."

"Not only dark, but chilly," said Byron. "Some different from last evening."

"It is almost September. Could have a frost anytime now," said Melinda as she sat down at the end of the table, removed pins from the material, and placed the pattern pieces back in their box. Beside her, Barilla threaded a needle and began basting the bodice sections together, then inserting the sleeves, while Melinda gathered the bulk of the voluminous skirt pieces into the size that would fit her waist.

"Such lovely cloth you have brought me, Barilla. And such a beautiful lamp Byron has brought home. I am truly blessed with thoughtful children," Melinda said.

"What about Con?" Barilla asked, "What do you hear from him?"

"Oh, Convers sent a letter just last week. Byron, will you get it for Barilla? It's on the lower shelf of the table where the newspapers are."

Byron placed the letter on the table beside Barilla.

After a while, the youngster dropped his chair and came over to bury his head in his mother's lap."

"He's tired. I'll just go put him to bed," she said as she stood up and carried him into the bedroom.

The room gradually became quiet as each of her brothers said good night and were soon gone, except for Byron.

Stephen Burleigh got up from his rocker, yawned widely, and said, "Time for me, too, since Melinda must have gone to bed with Bub." To Barilla he admonished, "Don't stay up much longer. You'll ruin your eyesight doing such close work." And to Byron he added, "You take care to put out the lamp."

When he had gone and closed the door, Barilla draped the basted material over the back of a chair and started to read her brother Con's letter.

Saturday, July 27, 1844

Stoughton, Mass
Distant Father,

I received your letter last Friday and was mighty glad to get it. My health is good. I am not so fleshy as I was, having lost flesh 20 pounds. I am working for a company on the Railroad for $3.00 a day and I pay $11.00 a month for board. I have a man who works with me. We get up at 5 o'clock, start out with a hand car about quarter past 6. We must wait for the 7 o'clock going in to Boston. After the cars pass we can work on the tracks until 6 in the evening. I shall go as brakeman on the train tomorrow as it runs three times on Sundays, other days only twice.

I can send you some money by the middle of August. I have laid out some money for clothes, so have not much on hand. I have a first rate place to board. I board with the agent for the road. Every month he calls all who work for him into his house and pays us. Provisions are high here. Flour

costs $12 a barrel. Corn is $1.20 a bushel. Oats are 80¢ a peck. By God, a
fortnight ago I had some green peas for dinner and a week ago I had some
first rate string beans. I am glad I brought my banjo with me. I met up with
a man who is part owner of a circus and he says I should go along with him
to play and sing, as they will be taking the circus off to western
Massachusetts towns. How about that? He says we may even go up through
New Hampshire and up to Maine.

Write as soon as you receive this. Tell all hands to write, even Florena
and Amos. Give my love to all the boys. How goes it with Peaser Sis?

Joseph Converse Taylor

Barilla laughed, "I almost forgot that he called me that." Then in a stunned, but lowered voice, she looked directly at Byron. "A circus? Oh my goodness. What did Father say about that?"

"He was angry and disgusted. He made me write to tell Con not to waste his time on such a pursuit. Better to do an honest day's work than around the likes of a circus. Oh, I tell you. Father almost worked himself up to a rage."

"And Con will do whatever Father says?" she asked facetiously.

Byron responded wryly, "What do you think?"

"Con must be eighteen now. I expect he'll do what he thinks best."

Byron leaned over to whisper, "Those of us old enough to go our own way must make our own decisions. But under this roof, we have to respect Father's will."

She looked at him earnestly. Then, standing up, she sighed, "Yes, I know." She picked up a candle and struck a flint to light it as Byron turned down the lamp's wick.

The following morning Stephen Burleigh told his daughter that they would not be needing Gene to clear up vines, so she should take him with her for picking berries. Thus, right after breakfast, the duo set off with several pails. She knew her mother would use all they could pick.

After the noon meal, Barilla and Gene joined the crew going back to the hop fields. She was not surprised to see Hap Richards waiting where the next vines were to be taken down. He was smiling like a Cheshire cat and his eyes lit up like two bright coals in an otherwise bed of ashes.

"Good afternoon, Miss Barilla," he said as she and Gene stepped down from the wagon.

Barilla nodded in acknowledgment, then quickly followed her father's lead, hoping to work beside him, or at least beside Byron. As the vines were cut and pulled down, she reached immediately to remove the three-inch, conelike clusters and toss them into one of the large boxes. She tried her best to ignore the hapless Richards boy, thinking to herself that he was not only dirty, but also homely. How, she wondered, had he ever found the girl who married him? And, horrors, even had a baby with him. She shivered in spite of the heat, for she felt the penetrating gaze of his eyes filled with lust, as does a cat before it pounces on an innocent bird. The tremors caused icy rivulets to surge through her limbs.

She worked diligently all afternoon, keeping too busy to notice anything until time to quit and go home for supper.

On Thursday, the following day, Byron set off in his wagon, stacked high with the boxes of hops to be delivered at Rumford Centre. He did not return until Friday night.

On Saturday, at almost noontime as the family of hop harvesters prepared to leave, Barilla heard her father speaking to Hap, inviting him to dinner. The revolting thought that this unsightly individual would be at their dinner table caused a sickening gorge in her digestive tract.

Hap had to wash his hands in the basin on the porch because all of the others had done so. She did notice that it did nothing for the residue beneath his fingernails.

She helped her mother set food on the table, a stew of beef, carrots, and onions, with dumplings freshly cooked on top of the boiling broth.

"Beef and onions!" Hap said, loudly. "Best kind of meal a man can get."

How he could talk at all with his mouth so full amazed Barilla. She set pitchers full of milk at each end of the table, then turned away from the disheartening scene.

Melinda took her place at the table and turned back to ask her daughter, "All is ready, aren't you going to sit?"

Barilla shook her head, then hurried from the large kitchen out into the summer kitchen. She had to do something, so she proceeded out through the barn to around where she had planted the lilies.

Byron, being concerned, with plate and spoon in hand followed after her. He continued eating while he stood over her, where she had stooped to see if there had been any lily growth peeping upward.

"I could not eat," she said. "I don't feel good."

"Then you better not come back to work this afternoon." She nodded, but did not turn to look at him.

"I'll tell Father, if you want," he said.

"Yes, tell him that I feel sick."

"And what has made you sick?"

"Hap," she blurted out. "He's so dirty. And the way he looks at me with desire in his eyes is offensive."

"Him," Byron said with disgust, "That no account can't possibly think you would…" He could not continue because of the repulsion he also felt. He set down his empty plate and stooped beside her. Putting an arm across her shoulder, he kissed the side of her forehead.

"Please, Sis, don't let it get you down," he said. "You have to eat. After we have gone, you go back inside and eat something, even if it is only a little broth."

She smiled weakly and nodded her head.

As soon as she heard the wagon leave, she went back into the kitchen. She sensed that her mother would ask questions. She ladled up some of the now-cool broth as Byron had instructed and explained her feelings to Melinda.

"Well, Daughter, you are a young and pretty girl, and that fellow needs a mother for the baby."

"Not this young girl!" Barilla said, adamantly.

"I did not mean you should accept him," Melinda said, "Only that you should have a little understanding of his behavior."

Barilla expressed her annoyance at such a suggestion, "Oh, sure, a month after his wife died! What kind of man could be so insensitive?"

Melinda shrugged, "I was only stating what seemed practical."

"Perhaps so, but really, Mother, I would rather not talk anymore about it. I'll help you with these dishes and then I'll set the table for supper. I suppose it's baked beans as usual for Saturday night. I could smell them cooking in the summer kitchen."

That evening at supper, Stephen Burleigh announced that because of the chilly evening and threat of frost, they would all spend Sunday forenoon harvesting those of their tender crops, corn, string beans, peppers, and cucumbers. Also, raspberries, blackberries, and blueberries. The hours of daylight were lessening. Although the days were still warm, the evenings were gradually becoming cooler.

As was the custom, soon after full darkness descended it was bedtime. As one after another of the family said good night, Byron made a sign to Barilla of beckoning with his forefinger, a signal to follow him out onto the porch.

They sat on the bench next to the summer kitchen wall. Across the road and dark outline of treetops, a soon-to-be-full moon began its ascent over the distant mountain. She savored the loveliness, the stillness, thinking of how far away were the noisy mills of Lowell. Slowly, thoughtfully, she spoke to her brother.

"It is so quiet and so beautiful here."

Byron agreed, then added, "I was relieved to see you eat a good supper."

"Just following orders. You told me I must eat. But that's not what you brought me out here to tell me, is it?"

"No. I wanted you to know that I talked to Hap alone and he admitted that he wants you for a wife."

At this bit of information, Barilla took an indrawn breath, which came out in an audible sigh.

Byron continued talking, "I told him how annoyed you were and very much appalled at how dirty he was."

"Oh, Byron, you didn't," she answered with dismay.

"He deserved it. Even his scraggly hair hanging down beneath his hat was filthy."

"About that hat," Barilla commented, "he did not even take it off while he ate dinner. He is nothing but an ill-mannered boor."

"I'll grant you that, all right."

"In Lowell, I had a friend for a while who was a real gentleman." Her voice became wistful as she continued, "I had even begun to think…" She hesitated, then shrugged her shoulders, "Well, no matter now. Another had captured his heart, so he is lost to me."

"Apparently you have not gotten over his rejection?"

"It did hurt me and I truly wonder, does anyone really get over that kind of rejection?"

"I suppose not, but I wouldn't know. You see, there is a girl for me up Bangor way. Her name is Charlotte Gregory. She works in her family's store. They sell things to decorate inside of houses, wallpaper and such. She is adept at sewing. Makes their curtains and fancy bureau scarves. She is also a great cook. Has invited me to meals a couple of times. I tell you this because when I go back up there, I'll be asking her to marry me."

"Oh, Byron, I'm so happy for you," she said.

"So," said Byron, "now I want to tell you about my friend, Pliny. I first met him at the Gregory's store. He was inquiring about getting some special hardwood pieces needed in his business. So I told him about the Virgin family who have a sawmill at Rumford Centre. It was not much out of my way, so I invited him to come along, and I took him there before I came home."

Barilla had begun to wonder just why Byron was telling her all this, so she asked, "Is he still there where you left him?"

"Oh, yes. I saw him on Thursday after I delivered the hops. We had supper together and I slept in his room at the nearby Union House.

"That's nice. I mean to have a friend whom you like."

"I do like him. And Barilla, I'm sure you would like him, too.

Ah ha, she thought dryly, he's matchmaking. Byron kept talking. "Pliny's business is in Lowell, and he is hiring me to take him there with a load of milled and mortised hubs, spokes, and felloes for wheels. Also, hardwood panels for carriages."

"Did you say, Lowell?"

"That's right. He is employed there in the carriage making business."

"So, how come he was in Bangor?"

"That's a long story. He thinks he was born there, but his parents died when he was a baby and some relative took him to Massachusetts. All his foster parents could tell him was that his father had gone up the Penobscot somewhere to work in a logging camp. He was looking for information and expected to combine it with the prospect of finding special wood. But everything near there is logged and rafted down the Penobscot River to the bay."

When he finally stopped talking, she looked at him directly, quizzically.

"I just wanted to say that he is a gentleman."

"I see," she said.

"Do you really…see what I am talking about?"

"Oh yes, quite clearly. Now, it is getting late, so let's go up to bed."

On Sunday morning all the male family members busied themselves harvesting food, while Barilla and her mother began washing the jars, pots, and crocks, ready for processing vegetables, fruit, and pickles. Byron had brought both white and raw sugar, salt, and spices back from his Rumford trip.

By the noon dinnertime, most of the work had been completed. So their father announced that because the usual Sunday forenoon Bible reading had had to be put off, it would now be done in the afternoon.

From the lower shelf of his chairside table, he brought out the old tattered Bible that had been his father's and began shuffling through the pages. Making his decision, he looked around to be sure he had everyone's attention.

"Psalm twelve, a Psalm of David. Help, Lord, for the godly man ceaseth; for the faithful fail from among the children of men."

As he continued reading, Barilla found herself staring out the window at the distant tree-covered hill. Here and there, she picked lines she felt might concern herself; thusly, the voice droned on, "For the oppression of the poor, for the sighing of the needy, now will I arise, saith the Lord. I will set him in safety from him that puffeth at him."

Now, Barilla thought, how does that pertain to me? Or to us? These were flowery words. She could not sort out their meaning.

When he had finished that Psalm, he quickly turned pages, coming to another. He looked around at his family, seeing Gene, lying on the floor, had fallen asleep. He read on, "Psalm forty-six. God is our refuge and strength, a very present help in trouble."

Barilla found herself being lulled to sleep, but that wouldn't do. For four-year-old Gene it was excusable, certainly not for the others. Keeping alert and interested, she again stared out the window. Oh, who was that just passing by? She was certain she saw someone, but knew better than draw attention away from the Bible-reading.

Suddenly, there came a knock on the side door. Melinda went over to see who it could be. When she turned around, a cleaned-up Hap Richards followed her in. The entire family stared at him, hat in hand, clean shaven, long hair shorn, and his clothes, the entire outfit from shirt to pants, were clean.

"Well, Hap, come in and sit," Stephen Burleigh said. "We are just having our Sunday Bible reading."

Obediently, Hap pulled a chair away from the dinner table and sat down facing the man holding the open Bible. Hap looked neither right nor left, but stared, mesmerized and listened to words which, Barilla was certain, had little understanding for him.

Finally, the Bible was closed and replaced on the shelf. Stephen Burleigh appraised the visitor with a critical eye.

"What brings you to our door on this Sunday afternoon?"

"Begging your pardon, sir, but I'd like a word with you in private."

"Certainly, Hap," he answered, rising from the chair, "Come into the parlor."

Barilla watched them enter the parlor. As the door closed behind them, she looked in panic toward her mother and then to Byron.

The latter stood up, took her by the arm, and led her out onto the porch, indicating that she sit on the bench.

"You are as white as a ghost," he said, "and you're trembling."

"How else do you expect me to be? You must know what that's all about, don't you?" she asked.

"I'm afraid so. But you do have a mind of your own and you are an idiot if you don't use it."

"But the man got himself cleaned up, actually presentable. That alone, makes me feel like an idiot" she said.

She looked past him toward the doorway where Melinda stood watching them and, Barilla was certain, could hear their conversation.

There was a wry smile on her mother's face, an understanding smile. She stepped out onto the porch. Byron vacated his seat in deference to their mother. Melinda put her arm around Barilla.

"Your concern is unfounded. Your father and I had a talk about you last night before we went to sleep, and I am sure he'll give that one short shrift," she said.

"Oh, Mother, I do hope so," Barilla said earnestly. "I…" she started, but was interrupted by the irate, very sour, very mad, Hap Richards coming through the doorway. He stomped down the steps, hastened down the hillside, and was soon out of sight beyond their house.

Barilla felt herself go limp. She could not help feeling compassion, yet, neither could she deny the relief she felt. And her father. This was a different side of him. Always the gruff, demanding person, and now this, quite obviously an understanding, more humane person than she had ever given him credit for.

"Go in and talk with your father now," Melinda said. "You will both feel better."

Barilla stood up, braced her shoulders, and walked through the kitchen into the parlor where her father sat in thought, pensively staring out the window.

"I can imagine," she said, "that from the expression on Hap's face, you told him I was not interested in him."

As she talked, her father turned to face her.

"It was not easy for me. The man did clean himself up, and he did the honorable thing in asking my permission to court you. Those were his words, 'I ask your permission to court Barilla.' You must understand. It's not easy for a father to tell a well-intentioned young man that he is not good enough for his daughter."

Barilla, taken aback, asked, "Is that what you told him?"

"Not my exact words, but enough so he understood my meaning."

"Oh, Father, I am so relieved."

"I understand. You see, Daughter, that youngun has that farm and he lets it run down around him, till it's good for nothing. A kitchen garden was planted last spring which has gone mostly to weeds. The one cow left alive was not bred, so the milk supply has petered out. The man's got no gumption. Any man worthy of my daughter has to prove he's a go-getter. A couple of those Richards fellows have gone off and got themselves an education. And the eldest one, down in Mexico, is a right upstanding, well-respected one. This one here isn't."

"Oh thank you, Father," she said gratefully. She wished she could put her arm around him so that he would also embrace her. But some instinct warned her that it would be more reserved to just place her hand on his arm.

He smiled graciously and said, "Your letters told us you were reading a lot of stories. Perhaps we can gather the family around and you tell us about them."

That prospect so delighted her, she answered gleefully, "I'd like that. I'd like that very much."

13

She went to bed that night in a mixed-up state of mind. It had been a delight to have the family listen to her stories of Greek mythology, but she felt anguish over the rejection heaped on the unfortunate visitor.

Instead of going right to sleep, Barilla thought long and hard about men. Specifically, what she wanted from them, or, more importantly, what they wanted from her. She thought of those who had touched her life. Dana Austin, who wanted a meek, docile girl; Horace, one of wealth and distinction; and poor Hap, just any female willing to cook, weed a garden, mother his baby, and share his bed. Also Byron, wanting to foist her off to his friend. And marriage, oh, how hard her mother worked, and Florena too. Did either of them have the right to express what they wanted? No.

Because that's the way it is. What men wanted, and whatever they decide, is what women have to expect. Well, she decided, I don't have to. She finally fell asleep, assuring herself over and over, I don't have to.

At breakfast time the next morning, she asked her father if she could stay at home and help her mother instead of picking hops.

"There are still cucumbers to pickle and if there is time, I would like to sew on the dress I am making for Mother."

Her father thought a moment, then without looking up from his eating said, "Yes, you may. Your mother already asked if you could be excused."

Then suddenly there was urgent knocking on the side door. Barilla, who was standing nearest the door, opened it to see a strange woman holding a baby in her arms.

"Come in," she said automatically, for the expression on the woman's face was one of anguish.

Melinda came up beside her daughter saying, "Yes, do come in. Will you set and have a bite of breakfast?"

"Oh, I do thank ye Mrs. Taylor, but I'm too upset to eat," the woman said.

"Well, now," Melinda said, "you let me have that little one and sit down and tell us what we can do for you."

The woman did as she was bid, while Barilla studied the small package in her mother's capable arms. It squirmed and began to cry lustily.

"The baby, she's hungry. Please ma'am, could you spare some milk? I have an empty bottle here." The woman produced the bottle, which Barilla took and filled with milk.

The other family members all stared at the newcomers in wonder as to what would happen next. The youngest, Philand Delano, stood at his mother's knee where she sat feeding the baby, in absolute wonder at this strange being.

The woman sat down and launched into a bizarre tale.

"It's because of Hap that I be needing help. And I was wondering if somebody could take me and the baby down to Mexico. It ain't fittin' for me to leave her with a gone-amuck boy."

"Why?" asked Barilla. "Did something bad happen?"

"Bad as it gets," she answered angrily. "He come home yesterday afternoon and began drinking. From that keg of hard cider in the cellar he brung up a jugful and lit into it like it was better than a plate of victuals. I knew he had been to visit you folks and knew why he had come. After a while I set a bowl of applesauce in front of him, but he pushed it away and said for me to leave him be, so I did. There wa'nt nothing for the babe to drink but some potato water, and she was howling something awful, being that hungry, she was. Well, he began yelling that I should shut her up or he would. And then, Mother of God, if he didn't start stuffing her blanket into her mouth. I grabbed her out of her basket, coughing and like to choke, and ran into my bedroom and barred the door. The poor little one crying so hard and me trying to soothe her by rocking her." The woman paused as tears ran down her cheeks. She wiped her eyes on a rag tucked in her sleeve and continued her story, "I had to wait until dawn when I snuck out and here I be, with nowhere to turn but to the Richards family down to Mexico."

She stopped for breath when Barilla placed a cup of coffee on the table, along with a bowl of sugared raspberries She placed a spoon in the woman's hand, whereupon she began to eat. The woman glanced around, seeing the baby sucking contentedly, then her gaze went from one to another of the Taylor family, eventually to the master of the house.

"I'll be thankin' ye for taking me in like this. I swear I did not know what to do," the woman said.

The master of the house spoke up reassuringly.

"Now don't you fret about anything. My son, Byron here, will take you down to Mexico as soon as both you and the baby have eaten." He then added in a tone of genuine interest, "My daughter, Florena Austin, told us you were Hap's aunt, and we do not even know your name."

"It's Mary. A blessed lady is that Florena. Many times bringing us food and milk, also claddings for the babe. But, I am not kin of the Richards' family. I was aunt to the baby's mother Hephzibath, who was maid working for the Richards family in Mexico. That Hap found her out in the barn one day, sweet talked her I guess, and when 'twas known she was a growing in the belly, she owned up that it was Hap done her in. So they married and I guess you know the rest."

Melinda finished the feeding and placed the sleeping baby girl up to her shoulder. Bub, seeing that, attempted to climb up in his mother's lap, but she pushed him aside.

Barilla asked Mary, "What's the baby's name?"

"Name?" said Mary. "Ain't got no name I know of."

"Then perhaps she should be named after you. Mary is a pretty name."

"I don't rightly know as I ought."

"I can't see that anyone has a better right," Stephen said. "So we will think of her as Mary."

That caused more tears from the woman. Barilla smiled, for she considered these to be happy tears.

Arising from the table, Stephen spoke to Byron, "Take the gig and the mare. It will be a more comfortable ride." He went over to Mary, placed a hand on her shoulder, and said, "You are a brave lady who has endured a great deal. Go now with our blessings and our best regards to the Richards folks in Mexico."

Melinda passed the baby over to Mary, and Barilla handed Mary a refilled bottle of milk.

The woman responded gratefully, "You are good people and I do thank ye." She started to follow Byron, who headed out through the summer kitchen, but paused long enough to turn, saying, "God bless thee, one and all."

Barilla followed along, ostensibly to help Byron harness the horse, but actually wanted a word with him.

"Would you stop at the Fox place and ask Judith to come for a visit? She could return with you in the gig," Barilla said.

"Of course, Sis." He smiled knowingly. To her, that smile conveyed the thought that he understood her need for the friendship of a girl her own age.

Walking back into the house, she reflected on this last unsettling occurrence. Now it was Monday. She had left Lowell just a week ago. Could so much have happened in less than a week? Now what will become of the misguided boy, being left so alone on the Richards' worn-out farm. No matter how distasteful the entire situation, she felt concerned. After all, he was a neighbor, and neighbors were supposed to help each other, but, she sighed resignedly, he is such a weakling. I don't think anyone can help him.

Byron returned with Judith in time for dinner. The two girls hugged one another. Then Barilla introduced her family. The girls had no time alone to talk until after the washing up and Melinda had taken Bub into the bedroom for a nap.

Barilla picked up her sewing and began the lengthy tale, telling of the past week's events.

"I remember Hap," said Judith, "from when I stayed at the Richards' place in Mexico. He was perhaps a year or two older than I. In school he could not seem to learn anything. So after a while he dropped out. We had given him the name 'Hapless.' I don't even recall what his Christian name was."

"Just the same, I feel sorry for him." Then in order to end a useless discussion, she abruptly asked Judith how things had gone for her.

"All right, I guess," she answered. "Nothing exciting, but it has given me a chance to know my father better. In the past, I was a small child living a separate life. Now I am a grown woman of eighteen years. As he had been uncomfortable dealing with a child, he has no difficulty conversing with what he considers an equal. Truly, Barilla, this past week has been good for both of us. Besides helping him with the crops and cooking the meals, I have cleaned the house, which has suffered years of accumulated…stuff!"

"He must be truly glad to have you home. It must be lonely living so alone."

"True, but he keeps busy with the farm and woodcutting. And there is a neighborly friend who drops by every evening. The two men have a great time playing checkers." She chuckled as she recounted the checker game. "There is a jug of hard cider and two cups on the table beside the checkerboard. As each game ends, the loser has to pour a cupful for the other. Sometimes all goes pretty evenly. But there are times when one gets a little peppier than the other. And their language! I've been learning some words and phrases I knew nothing about."

Barilla smiled, feeling quite relaxed. She heartily enjoyed Judith's story.

Melinda came out of the bedroom and Barilla asked her, "Come, let me try this bodice on you."

It was like putting on a jacket, because buttons were not yet on the front. Barilla could put it on over the meager, homespun dress.

With some dismay, Melinda called attention to the sleeves, "Those are too big."

"Not at all, Mother. That's the latest fashion. Big sleeves are supposed to make the waist smaller. It makes a lady look more feminine."

"I am what I am," Melinda said. "I don't need any fur-be-lows or other stuff to make my body look different,"

"The sleeves stay," said Barilla adamantly. "This is to be your Sunday dress. And a little of current fashion isn't going to change who you are, my beautiful, wonderful Mother."

"Oh, go on with you," Melinda said with embarrassment as Barilla removed the bodice, laid it aside, and hugged her.

"Now that I know how it fits, we can attach the skirt. Then put on buttons. Will you pick out what you want from the button box?"

Melinda went into the bedroom to sort out appropriate buttons.

Barilla glanced at Judith as she again picked up the material, seeing a plaintive expression on Judith's face.

"You are lucky to have such a mother," Judith said. "I envy you."

"Whatever happened to your mother?"

"I don't know. I cannot remember anyone called Mother. Oh, different women took care of me, but they were always Aunt this or that."

"And you have not asked your father?" Barilla said.

"No. I don't rightly know how to ask him."

"And the Richards family members?"

"Nothing there either. Besides, what difference does it make now?"

"Of course," Barilla said, "it makes no difference."

"By the way, that brother of yours is a mighty fine gentleman."

Judith's eyes had come alive, sparkling with interest.

"Don't get any hopes up about him, Judith. He's spoken for. Has a girl up Bangor way he's going to marry."

"So, have you seen Hazen and Horatio Bradbury, the two who came to Boston on the Fourth of July?"

"Not yet. I shall visit the Bradburys sometime. Their mother is sister to my father," Barilla said.

"That means those boys are your cousins," Judith said.

Melinda, returning with some buttons, answered Judith's question.

"Yes. We are all family." She turned to Barilla to ask, "Didn't you stop in there when you went to see Florena?"

"No. I suppose I should have, but…"

"Well, then, suppose you just drop what you are doing and take Judith and go along up there now."

"All right, Mother."

Laughing together in a lighthearted manner, the two girls strode along the dusty road. Then suddenly their mood changed somberly as they noticed the western sky had darkened ominously. They were halfway between the Taylor and Bradbury houses when thunder rumbled and gusts of wind forced the dust into cyclonic whirls. A bolt of lightning flashed a streak of jagged light down through the western blackness. They held up their skirts and ran, coming breathlessly into the Bradbury's open shed as raindrops pelted the driveway behind them. In the distance, Barilla saw her father's wagon, loaded with her brothers, hastening to shelter in their own barn.

From the vantage point of safety, they looked out to see Horatio Bradbury running full tilt across the road to also enter the shed.

"That sure came up sudden, didn't it?" he said breathlessly, then added, "It's good to see you Rilla I heard you was home."

"Yes," she said, laughing, "and I brought Judith for a visit."

"First rate," he said, giving Judith an openly beaming look. Close behind him, entering through the barn's side door, came his father, William, followed by Horatio's brother, Hazen.

"Hey," said Hazen when he saw Judith, "Ain't you the one that came to Boston last Fourth of July?"

"Yes, of course. And I'm glad to see you again, too," said Judith.

Barilla presented Judith to her Uncle Will, explaining that she also worked with her in a Lowell mill.

Sing Me a Song

A sudden, deafening clap of thunder and instant flash of light sobered the joviality. From inside the barn a horse whinnied and clomped his feet against a wall.

"Come in. Come inside," Will urged them. "The family will be anxious, hoping we are under cover out of this storm."

Barilla, first to enter the kitchen, immediately moved over to greet her Aunt Cora. Surrounding their mother stood young Will, fourteen; Albert, twelve; Abigail, ten, Hiram, eight; Oliva, five; and John Quincy, three. Every one of them was so excited they all seemed to be talking at once.

Barilla burst out laughing. "If you will all just quiet down, I want you to meet my friend, Judith Fox."

They all spoke up as one voice, "Glad to meet you, Judith."

Then Cora said, "Since all are safely in out of the storm, what do you say to a cup of raspberry juice? Then we'll just sit down and have a cheery talk."

Young Will went to the pantry, bringing back a pitcher of juice. Albert put a jar filled with cookies on the kitchen table, and Abigail placed an earthen cup in front of everyone seated around the table.

As Will poured the juice, he couldn't resist telling how he and Albert had been hilling up potatoes and hustled inside at the first sound of thunder.

Not to be outdone, Abigail shook her head, swinging her pigtails from side to side, and said, "Look at the rain splashing against the windows like someone throwing buckets full of water at them."

The youngest, John Quincy, sat in a high chair, which brought him up to the level of the others. "Rain, rain, rain," he said. "Puddles, puddles, puddles."

This outburst caused laughter among them all, recalling that at their own ages of less than five years, they had been permitted to splash around barefoot in puddles. Judith sat next to Barilla, and Horatio just opposite. He spoke up next.

"I was helping Uncle Stephen with the hops, when all of a sudden little Gene piped up that we should look at the black sky over

Old Turk Mountain. Well, there it was, hanging there above white sky below, the black streaks hangin' down like teats on a cow's udder. All to once, the Taylors beat it for the wagon, Byron drivin' them off for home. And me, I just bolted on home quick as a scared rabbit.

"When will the hop picking be finished?" Barilla asked.

"Soon, I expect Got to do over by the river. And then clear out the dried up vines. Funny thing," he added. "Hap Richards had been helping, I knew that, but he did not show up this morning."

Barilla shot him a strange look and said, "I hardly expect he would."

"What do you mean by that?"

"Oh, nothing. You know how careless he is."

But Horatio persisted, "There's something going on there I don't know nothin' about, isn't there? I asked your father about why Hap didn't show up and he said, 'Twarnt important.' He's as close-mouthed about it as you are."

"Now, now, Horatio," his mother said. "Show more respect for my brother. When he gives you an answer, that's all there is to it. He was always the leader in our family. What Stephen Burleigh says, goes. What he thinks, he keeps to himself."

"No lack of respect, Mother. I was just a tellin' it like it was."

After a while the thunder faded to distant rumbles, but the rain continued.

"And where is Climena now? Barilla asked.

"Down to Mexico," Aunt Cora said. "Likely, she'll be back tomorrow. She's visiting the Wilsons for a few days. And Mary, she's working for a family in Brookline, near Boston. Seems that Dana Austin was working on a farm there and the lady of the house needed a hired girl. So he wrote asking Mary. And off she went."

William, the father, shook his head sadly, and said, "And we miss her something awful. She's the eldest, but never been the strong one."

"I know," said Barilla. "The mill work was too much for her."

"But," said Cora, "it's mighty nice to have Climena here to help out. She's as strong and healthy as a horse."

Barilla, noting that the rain had slackened, stood up and said, "We'd best be off now, Judith and I."

"Oh, my dear Barilla," said Cora. "Couldn't you stay for a bite of supper? I am about to make some cornbread."

"I do thank you, Aunt Cora, but 'tis best we head for home. It has been a nice visit."

Horatio had gone to fetch two oil-skin slickers. He handed one to Barilla, then proceeded with putting the one for Judith upon her shoulders, then place the hood upon her head. He turned to face her, grinning widely. Barilla, observing this, saw that Judith smiled shamelessly into Horatio's eyes.

After saying their good-byes, Horatio followed the girls out to the shed entrance where he was speaking quietly to Judith. Barilla, being discreet, paid no attention to their conversation.

The outside air smelled sweet from the wet grass, clover, and goldenrod. The rain had lessened and the trees' leaves glistened as warm sunlight filtered through. The road beside where the girls walked was no longer dusty, but muddied, the ruts filled with water. Arriving at her home, it was necessary to cross the road Although Barilla and Judith stepped cautiously across, their feet became mired in mud. Before entering the house, they sat on the porch bench to remove their shoes, then walked into the kitchen.

Greeted with the smell of hot biscuits that her mother was taking from the bake-oven, Barilla took in all at once the scene around the room-Byron dropping a load of wood with a thud into the large box near the fireplace, Morval and Marvin setting the table, Melchior and Jack on the floor playing checkers, and Gene running behind Philand, who dragged his chair, trying out a new word Gene had taught him, "Giddy up, giddy up."

Her father arose from his rocker. Then all moved as a group to their places at the supper table. The whole of it gave Barilla the comfortable feeling that this was home, a haven of kindly providence where she belonged, for these were her people, individuals who loved her.

As she ate her supper, she glowed with a happy feeling of security.

It was not until she and Judith were in bed together that they began to talk. "I enjoyed this day with your warm and friendly family, and especially visiting the Bradburys," Judith said.

"Uh huh. No one could miss the interest you and Horatio showed for one another," Barilla said.

"Oh, wasn't he sweet? He asked how long I was staying, then told me he would take me back to my father's whenever I want to go."

Barilla said, "That's nice. Now, let's be quiet and get some sleep."

Next morning at breakfast, Stephen brought up the subject of Hap Richards by telling Byron, "I want you to go up there and find out how he's doing. We can't let him starve or drink himself to death."

So it was Byron who found no sign of life inside the Richards' house. The place smelled damp and musky. After searching the barn and all around outside, he went across to the Austins. His sister, Florena, greeted him.

"I be looking for Hap," he said.

"The last I saw of him was before the storm, ambling along, quite unsteady, going north toward Byron village."

"I'll go along up there. Likely he found some place to get in out of the rain.."

He bid her good day and strode off along the heavily wooded area, wishing he'd come on horseback.

Rounding the curve, he came to Gum Corner, a village of several houses, all close together, a cemetery across the road, and beyond the bridge over the canyon, the Coos Canyon School where all of the Byron children went to school.

After inquiring at various homes, it was at the Youngs where a boy said he'd seen him at the height of the storm heading upriver on this side of the canyon. "I tried to hail him, be he paid me no mind. And I warn't going out there in that kind of weather."

So it was Byron and the boy going close to the canyon's edge who looked down at a body lying face down in what water flowed in the bottom of the canyon.

Byron turned to the boy saying, "Run back and get a long rope, and alert everyone. I'll climb down there. We're going to need help bringing him up. Try to get some workers from Bancroft's sawmill."

14

"It's all my fault," Barilla cried out when Byron came home and told his story. She had been helping her mother get dinner ready when she heard a wagon coming down the road with neighbors following on foot, and Byron jumping off, allowing the wagon and the curious to go on their way.

"Of course it's not your fault," Byron tried to set her straight. "He slipped on the banking and fell. He was undoubtedly drunk and knew not where he was going. Hap must have somersaulted down to that protruding boulder and hit his head, which was split open, and then he must have catapulted over to fall face down in the water. The rain, you know, caused the river to swell, and the water rushing over him washed away the blood."

"It's still my fault...that he started drinking. I think he fell down on purpose."

Because it was time for the noon meal, before taking his seat, her father came close to Barilla and laid a hand on her shoulder and said, "We have to believe that he slipped. What Byron is saying makes sense. That's the story and it best be let alone."

Barilla said nothing. Tears rolled down her cheeks, which Judith, standing on the other side of her, dried on a handkerchief. Then she hugged the distraught girl as Barilla laid her head against Judith's shoulder and sobbed openly.

The younger children could not understand the goings on. They stood around, wide-eyed, staring at the strange commiseration.

Melinda, hoping to change the gruesome subject, told everyone to sit down for dinner.

But grief had so pervaded Barilla, a tight band closed around her ribs. The thought of food sickened her. She turned to face Judith and said, "Please go and eat dinner. I'll go and sit over here. Truly, I just want to be alone to think."

She sat in her mother's rocker, dreamily going over in her mind everything from the time Hap had first hailed her on her way to visit Florena, and finally to Byron's words as he had told the details of the brutal end to a young man's life. She could see it all, over and over. No matter how Byron and her father tried to gloss over it, she felt it was her fault.

That night in bed with Judith, Barilla tossed and turned, hoping to fall asleep. Inadvertently her thoughts circled back to the previous evening, to the delight she had felt in the love of her family, then back to the present day's events, until sleep finally overcame the turmoil.

She awakened to the sound of Judith's voice, "It's still dark outside. But listen, it's raining again."

"Makes you wonder," said Barilla, "if it is raining way down in Lowell. If so, we'll have to think about going back."

"Remember, they told us the middle of September."

"That's another week," Barilla mused. The thought of returning to work sustained her. Thus she slept soundly until, with the dawning, a gray sky appeared. But soon thereafter bright sunlight flooded the east window.

Judith stayed the next day and night until Horatio came by at breakfast time to take her home. He had walked down the evening before to ask if she wanted to go because he would be going by horseback down to Roxbury for the local mail. So here he was, tethering his horse to a post on the porch and coming into the kitchen while the family ate breakfast. More than one voice issued an invitation, "Pull up a chair and have something to eat."

"I'll do that," he answered, grinning widely. He was thanking his Aunt Melinda, but his smile was all for Judith.

As they prepared to leave, Judith thanked the family for her pleasant visit. Then, followed by Byron and Barilla, she went out to where Byron untethered the horse and handed the reins to Barilla. He then lifted Judith up to place her astraddle on the cushion, pillioned behind Horatio. Judith knew instinctively that she had to hold her arms tightly around Horatio's waist.

Barilla smiled with amusement, knowing that Judith would not mind the closeness to Horatio's body.

"That's the first time I've seen you smile in the last two days," said Byron as the horse trotted slowly down the driveway.

Barilla sighed. Drawing in a deep breath, she said, "I know most things that happen we have little control over. And I have to believe that everything that happens is for the best."

"Atta girl," he said, smiling broadly. Then, placing an arm across her shoulder, he led her back inside.

In the kitchen, their father was giving orders for the day. "Since it has dried off a little, we will harvest the carrots, beets, and parsnips this morning. The potatoes can wait a week or two. Then in the afternoon, we will go back to see how the hops survived the storm." To Barilla, he directed, "You cut what cabbages your mother will want to fill the crocks for sauerkraut. Then pull up a half dozen to hang in the root cellar. We'll gradually feed the rest to the pigs. Now about the pigs," he continued, addressing Byron. "We need some fresh meat, so tomorrow, we will kill a hog. We must begin salting the shoulders, hams, and bacon. We will share the fresh meat with the Austins and the Bradburys. But I'll want you to take the ground meat to make sausages down to your Uncle Abel on the Mine Notch Road when you take the next load of hops to Rumford."

The boys followed their father as he proceeded out through the summer kitchen and woodshed into the toolshed where each of the boys took up a tool most proficient for each task. Morval and Marvin took charge of two wheelbarrows. Barilla came last, choosing a short, sharp knife and a cart for hauling cabbages.

Working with her mother as they sliced, salted, and layered cabbages filled Barilla with delight. When they had finished and placed clean rocks on top, Barilla went out to pull up those cabbages which, when hung upside down by their roots, would keep in the cellar for several months.

The boys came and went, bringing loads of vegetables into the various bins. Leaves would be needed to cover them, so Barilla went out with a rake and an old sheet to gather the colorful leaves that were falling more and more each day. The air smelled fresh, crisp, and clear. Although the nights were frosty, the days were warm.

When she had raked up a pile in readiness for picking up the corners of a sheet, along came Gene to dive into the middle of the leaves.

"Come on, you scamp," Barilla said, "get out of there, or I'll dump you, leaves and all, in with the carrots and beets."

"Oh goody," said Gene, "I'll get a ride."

"Oh no, you won't," she answered, tickling him until he righted himself and scampered off to join his brothers.

She pulled up the sheet corners and, hauling it over one shoulder, went down the hatchway into the cellar and laid her bundle on the floor which was paved with smooth, slate-like rocks. She threw an armload of leaves into each bin, and some into the largest one saved for potatoes, leaving enough on the sheet to cover the next deposit of vegetables.

Satisfied with her morning's work, she crossed into the main cellar and climbed the stairs into the kitchen.

"Now I'll help with the dinner," she told her mother.

"You are such a sweet girl, Barilla. It would be so nice if you would stay home instead of going back to Lowell."

Barilla had just placed two blackberry pies on the table. She could not answer her Mother immediately. While she contemplated what she might say, she picked up a pile of heavy stoneware plates and set each one around on the table. Moving back to the cupboard drawer, she counted out the pewter utensils.

As she set the forks and knives beside each plate, she finally answered, "Please understand that it is a new kind of life for me. A different world. And besides the work and the pay, I am learning a great deal."

She was interrupted by the male family members trooping up the cellar stairs. Melinda admonished the younger ones to wash up.

To Byron, she said, "You haul those roasted potatoes off the spit before you wash. You'll get black enough doing that." She handed him a large tin bowl and a pair of tongs. To Barilla, she said, "You dish up the string beans." And to Morval, she said, "As soon as you wash, set Bub in his chair and put on his bib."

Barilla picked out two large bowls, and using a slotted spoon, she swung the crane out away from the fire and dished up the combination of long, grayish-green beans and chunks of salt pork. She placed them at each end of the table and did the same with two butter dishes and two loaves of bread.

Barilla set mugs before each person, then proceeded out to the pantry and brought back two pitchers of newly pressed cider. Only then did she and her mother sit down.

After dinner, Melinda took her youngest into the bedroom to nurse and put him down for a nap. The boys cleared off the table, then followed their father, bent on going off to the hop fields. Barilla was left to wash dishes. As she heard the wagon clatter away, she felt relieved that she had not been asked to go along.

The prime occupation of the following days was the preparation of the pork and related products. Barilla, using a hand-operated meat grinder, spent hours grinding the parts intended for sausage. Thus on Saturday morning, Byron made his trip to deliver the meat to their Uncle Abel and proceed with a load of hops to Rumford Centre. He did not return until Sunday dinner and the subsequent Bible reading.

"Father?" Barilla started to ask, as her father picked up the old, tattered Bible. "May I suggest a chapter?"

Showing his annoyance, he became blunt, "What do you, a mere girl, know about choosing proper Bible reading?"

"Because in Lowell, I attend church service every Sunday. So I hear a lot of Bible reading. So I am suggesting the First Epistle of Paul to the Corinthians, chapter thirteen."

Her father did not look up. His very countenance seemed cold and defiant. Nevertheless, he did shuffle through the pages. Coming to the requested chapter, he placed a hand with extended finger on the chosen chapter. He turned his gaze toward Barilla, his eyes burning like two sharp points of light. He then began to read.

"Though I speak with the tongues of men and of angels and have not charity…" his voice droned on with no inflection or meaning to the words.

Barilla bristled, thinking to herself that she could have read it far better.

Eventually Stephen came to the end, speaking softly, "And now, abidith faith, hope, and charity, but the greatest of these is charity."

He again looked over at Barilla and spoke with his usual authority. "In the following chapter is a lesson, my daughter, which you seem to forget." He ran his finger down the next page and began to read, "Line thirty-four. Let women keep silence, for it is not permitted unto them to speak, but they are commanded to be under obedience, as also sayeth the law."

He slammed the Bible shut and shoved it on the shelf underneath his newspapers. He leaned back in his chair, gazed not at any of his family, but out of the window, and said, "That's the end of today's lessons. You are all now free to do as you wish."

Barilla felt her face becoming flushed. She stood up and with squared shoulders, went out through the kitchen onto the porch. Byron followed her. He was laughing. His eyes sparkled with mischief. No doubt he was ready to tease her about their father's putting her in her place. He said, "So, how's the 'mere girl' handling the reprimand?"

"Not very well. Honestly, Byron, I have changed. I don't belong here anymore. I will be happy to leave and get back to Lowell."

"About going back to Lowell. I found out that the stage leaves the Union House at six every morning. So, while I was with my friend Pliny, he asked if I could bring my wagon down next Sunday morning so that we could have it loaded and he and I leave for Lowell on Monday. What do you say that I take you and Judith with me next Sunday where you can spend the night at the hotel and get the stagecoach on Monday? That will be the fifteenth of September."

"Oh, Byron, that's great. But we will have to get word to Judith."

"Sure, I know a way. Come on. We are going for a walk."

"Where?"

"Up to Bradbury's."

"Of course, Horatio!"

Her depression had dropped. Her expression brightened. She smiled knowingly up at Byron.

Eager to complete their mission, the twosome set off up the road.

On the Saturday evening before their departure, the annual harvest dance was to be held in the schoolhouse. During the day, Byron had cleaned his wagon of the sticky hop residue, and by in-stalling two benches, was ready to take any who wanted a ride up to the Coos Canyon School.

The only Taylors to go were Byron, Barilla, and Morval. Horatio had borrowed the Taylors' rig and gone after Judith. He had asked if she could stay the night with Barilla because the girls were leaving Sunday morning.

Dressed in her blue, white-sprigged dress, her hair smartly pinned up, Barilla felt great pride in herself. Seated up beside Byron, they called for Climena and young Will Bradbury, then for Amos and Florena Austin.

Arriving at dusk, Byron tethered his horses to one of several posts. Music wafted out from the open door and windows of the school.

There were greetings all around from former schoolmates, Shaws, Reeds, Thomases, Youngs, Bancrofts, and Hustons families. Two fiddlers, one mandolin, and one five-string banjo player provided the music. The jigs and reels kept everyone hopping.

At a brief rest period, many out-of-breath participants hastened out onto the porch to the cider barrel. The pungent smell of stick cinnamon added to the enticement.

Barilla, having just danced with John Shaw, walked with him to the cider barrel. As she drank from the dipper John handed her, she was acutely aware of the friendly chatter all around and the distant rush of water over the falls of Coos Canyon, almost drowning out the chirping crickets. She avoided looking toward the chasm below the falls, hoping that John would not refer to the body so recently found in the gorge.

She handed the dipper back to John and said, "So many of the young people have left the valley to work elsewhere, this place seems different to me."

"It's that, all right. My brothers have gone and my sisters married. But it don't seem fittin' for me to go and leave my folks to manage the farm alone. So, I'm stayin'."

"Not I," she answered. "My brother Byron and I are leaving tomorrow."

"Tomorrow," he said thoughtfully, "We have to move the benches and desks back in here. School starts on Monday. One of the Reed girls is to be teacher. She can live at home, so the school board don't have to look for a boarding place."

The musicians were moving back to their places, so John said, "Excuse me, I'm goin' to ask the teacher to dance." He grinned, showing a wide expanse of teeth. "It don't do no harm to cotton up to the teacher."

To herself she thought, I wonder if she can teach him the proper use of verbs. Also not to use double negatives. Then again, perhaps not. That is because his parents and friends talk that way, and he'll never leave Swift River Valley.

Will Thomas, the banjo player, began with a solo, singing, "Barb'ry Ellen." Byron, who had not yet engaged in the rapid, gyrating jigs, now took his sister's elbow and steered her inside.

"This is more my speed," he said as they waltzed around in a more sedate manner.

When Judith and Horatio waltzed nearby, Horatio smiled broadly and winked at Barilla. As the couple turned, the expression on Judith's face was just as joyful.

Feeling happy and secure in her brother's arms, Barilla relaxed, being truly content with this, her last evening with relatives and neighbors.

Later, when Barilla and Judith were undressing for bed, they spoke softly.

"I saw you," whispered Barilla, "in the darkness, on the porch. Byron and I watched you and Horatio saying good-bye, and him kissing you before he went on up home."

"Of course. He is a lot of fun and he likes me. And I like him."

"You did say like, not love?"

"Oh, Barilla, you don't have to have love. The way I figure it, just enjoy what comes along and see what happens next. By the way," she added while climbing into bed, "if Horatio gets a chance to work near Boston, he promised to come to see me in Lowell."

"That will be nice, won't it?" Barilla said as she blew out the candle and got into bed. "So now we had better go to sleep. It's up and away early in the morn."

During the past week, Melinda's new dress had been finished. Barilla insisted she put it on after breakfast, saying, "So that I can always remember your wearing it when we have to say good-bye."

After breakfast, Judith and Barilla cleared the table and washed dishes while Melinda changed. All of the family stood around expectantly until Melinda emerged from the bedroom.

Although no taller than Barilla, her mother carried herself erect, shoulders squared and head held high. She smiled shyly at Barilla, then turned around once for all to admire. The shimmering, percale skirt changed color from blue to green as she moved.

Bittersweet tears formed in Barilla's eyes. She could not resist throwing her arms around Melinda. She stepped back and said, "It's beautiful. Look, Father. Isn't Mother beautiful?"

Stephen's comment was as bland as usual, "Your mother is a mighty fine person. She doesn't need finery to make her beautiful."

For a moment, her father's prosaic statement baffled Barilla. If his comment was expected to unnerve her, she vowed not to show it in any way.

Byron said his farewells and, taking Judith with him, went out to hitch up his horses.

The moment of departure was at hand. The family had come out onto the porch. Ripples of excitement ran through Barilla. She now realized what was meant by, "Parting is such sweet sorrow." The boys in turn hugged and kissed her.

Her father laid a hand on her shoulder and said, "Come back when you can, girl." Then he kissed her lightly on the forehead.

Bub, realizing this was an actual parting, hung onto her skirt and said, "Rilla no go way."

She stooped down, picked him up, and held him tightly. She spoke gently, "I must go now. But I'll come back sometime."

She handed him to their mother, turned away, and hurried out to the wagon where Byron and Judith waited for her.

Her emotions were in such turmoil she could say nothing as Byron helped her up to the seat beside him. They turned only to wave as the horses galloped away.

Quietly, Byron spoke to her, "I hate good-byes. I see that you do too."

She looked up and said, "He kissed me, Byron. Father kissed me for the first time in my whole life."

Byron chuckled, "Deep down, Father loves all of us. It is sometimes difficult to understand his way of expressing it."

15

After crossing the Swift River near its junction with the Androscoggin, it was almost noon, so they stopped to eat. Byron helped Judith down from the back of the wagon and asked her to bring the blanket she had sat upon to spread it out on the riverbank. To Barilla he handed a basket containing three large tin cups, three spoons, some slices of buttered bread, and three molasses cookies. As he joined the girls, he carried in one hand a lard pail filled with baked beans. The other hand held a jug of fresh cider.

The respite dispelled any gloom the three of them had felt. They were quite gay, as at the river's edge each of them washed out the cup and spoon that had been used to eat the beans.

Resuming their ride along the road to Bethel, Barilla noted that they first passed the meager settlement of Rumford Falls; then East Rumford, slightly larger, even boasting a post office; to arrive in midafternoon at the largest village of all, Rumford Centre.

Byron stepped down and tied the horses. He then carried the girls' canvas bags through a doorway beneath a sign that read, Abbot's Union House.

He made arrangement for a room for them. Speaking to Barilla, he said, "I have to go along up to the mill to begin loading the wagon. I'll be back in time for supper." Then looking directly into her eyes, he said "I'll have Pliny with me. We will all eat together in the dining room."

Barilla showed no reaction, merely nodded. The two girls turned away, picked up their canvas bags and, holding up their long skirts, went up the stairs.

As soon as they were in the room allotted them, Barilla took off her dress, shook the dust out of it, and laid it across a chair along with her other belongings. She then went to the washstand to wash away the dust of travel. Drying her hands and face, she said, "Byron has the idea that I am going to like his friend, Pliny. Well, I can like him easily enough, but as for any earnest relationship, I am not interested. What I have learned of men is that they have no consideration for women. Whatever a man wants, he expresses it. Do men ever even ask what we want? No."

She had whipped the towel back and forth and now threw it to Judith as she moved to sit on the bed. Taking off her shoes, she abruptly flopped backward.

Placing her hands beneath her head on a pillow, she continued grimly, "Well, from now on I will not allow myself to pay any man more attention than ordinary politeness."

The tirade amused Judith. As she washed herself, she commented laconically, "That is until the next handsome, charming man like Horace comes along."

"Oh, no. Never that again. I have long ago dismissed him from my thoughts."

"Uh huh."

"I mean it, truly, That will not happen to me again."

Judith came around the bed to flop down onto the other side. Staring at the ceiling, she remarked quietly, "If you never marry, you will learn that loneliness can be a bitter pill. My father is an example of a lonely man."

"Did you ever ask him about your mother?"

"Yes. And it was difficult for him to tell me." Judith hesitated as she recalled his telling of it. "You see, Barilla, when I was less than two years old, my mother just left. No one knew where she went. There was a search party out looking for her. After a while Father gave it up, figuring that someone must have helped her. That is, taken her away. Father said he could think of no reason except that she cried a lot, so she must have been unhappy."

"That's a sad tale. I can tell it bothers you."

"What bothers me is not so much her leaving me, a mere babe, because at the time I did not know the difference. The worst of it was how very much it hurt my father."

Barilla rolled over to grasp Judith's hand. "I remember your telling me it was best to accept whatever comes along and see what happens next."

Her words caused Judith to respond with a chuckle, "That, my friend, is the only way to face up to life."

It was nearly six o'clock when Byron knocked on their door. Both girls had changed into their one good dress. So now following Byron, they descended the stairs and entered the dining room.

Seated alone at one of the tables was the stranger who arose from his chair and came forward to greet them. Barilla noticed at once the sleekness of his red hair before Byron began introductions.

"Pliny Tidd, may I present my sister, Barilla Taylor, and her friend, Judith Fox."

Pliny smiled delightedly and said, "I am pleased to meet you both, Miss Taylor and Miss Fox." He offered his arm to Barilla and led her to a seat, then held out a chair until she was comfortably seated.

He explained that the supper this evening was chicken pie. He hoped that was acceptable to the young ladies.

"Oh, yes," said Barilla. "It is quite a while since our noontime picnic, so that sounds first rate." On the table before her she noticed a lighted candle and a bottle of wine.

"Would you care for some elderberry wine?" Pliny asked.

To answer, she had to meet his gaze, to look into light green eyes with tiny flecks of gold as reflected by the candle.

"Thank you," she said, holding up a glass. "I will have a little."

"The same for me," said Judith, as she offered her glass.

When Byron had filled his own, Pliny held his glass to clink it against Barilla's. "A toast to Lowell, where after Byron and I get there, we shall have a pleasant reunion."

In unison, they all nodded agreement, although for Barilla, it was not without trepidation.

A woman with a tray approached the foursome. She deftly removed individual pies to place one before each diner. A dish of pickles was set in the center.

"Pickles, Miss Taylor?" Pliny offered her the dish.

"Thank you," she said, forking over several pieces onto a side dish. Then, savoring the odor of the steaming chicken through the slits in a nut-brown crust, she began to eat.

The only other sounds in the room were the steps of people leaving, all of them men. Several glanced in the direction of the newcomers. Female clientele was an oddity in such a place.

Pliny, addressing Barilla, said, "It was a lucky day for me when I met Byron in the Gregory's warehouse in Bangor. I had been trying to locate the kind of seasoned oak needed for wagon wheels, where they also had the know-how of mortising hubs, fitting the spokes and the rims to the specifications of the Day Company in Lowell."

"Where is that company in Lowell?" Barilla asked.

"On Central Street, number 137. That is on the south side of the Pawtucket Canal."

"Oh, I must have passed by there, not knowing what was being made. I like to stop on the bridge over that canal and look down on the lower' locks and gatehouse." She laughed, "I seem to be aware only of stores that show merchandise in the windows."

"We make carriages. The demand is so great, it is impossible to have even one to display out front. Anyhow, our shop location is not obvious, being down hill, nearer the gatehouse. We do have a large sign hanging between two posts, with the name, Day, Convers and Whittredge on it."

"Can you have opened windows and look out upon the spillway?"

"Yes, of course," he said.

She gave him a long. serious look. "We cannot. We must suffer both from heat and noise."

"Ah yes, the noise. I have heard the noise whenever I have walked by outside a mill."

Judith smiled wryly. A look of all-knowing understanding passed between her and Barilla, a look of knowing full well that only those who worked inside could believe the horrifying heat and noise.

It was time to leave. The waitress brought a bill which Pliny signed. The foursome went out into the entrance hall.

A brief awkward moment ensued, so Barilla said, "We have to be up so early, it is best now to say good night."

Pliny reached for her hand, which he held onto as he said, "Until morning then. We will be up for breakfast and seeing you onto the coach." He released her hand, mounted the stairs, and was soon out of sight.

"Byron," she admonished her brother, "you should not have let him pay for supper."

He laughed. "My dear sister, his company is paying all the bills including payment to me for using my wagon, a wage for the time it will take until the delivery is made and I can leave Lowell."

Barilla smiled and shrugged her shoulders. Judith had already climbed the stairs.

Byron leaned over and kissed his sister on the cheek. "Off to bed with you two. I'll knock on your door to waken you a little before five o'clock."

Later, in the darkness when the two girls lay in bed, Judith whispered, "I watched that Tidd fellow gazing at you. All starry-eyed, he was."

"You imagine things." She paused, then said, "Didn't you think his looks were rather odd?"

"What do you mean by odd?"

"Green eyes and hair the color of carrots. Across his nose and cheeks are freckles. Truly, Judith, I never saw anyone who looks like that."

"At least you did…look at him."

"I could not help that. He was talking to me."

"I thought him rather nice. Polite and well-mannered. I doubt we have seen the last of him."

"We can't avoid it. His business is in Lowell. Now, enough talking. Go to sleep."

True to his word, Byron knocked on the door to waken the girls. They donned their traveling clothes, repacked their bags, and were descending the stairs along with other travelers and local businessmen.

In the dining room, Pliny and Byron both stood up, smiling - eagerly as the girls entered.

"We ordered some flapjacks and bacon," Byron said.

A pot of coffee had been placed on the table. As soon as all were seated, Pliny filled their cups. He then passed a sugar bowl and creamer to Barilla. He said, "You will get to Lowell long before we do. There are still some crates to pack in the wagon. We should get started in a couple of hours."

"Then," said Byron, "it will take several days over through New Hampshire and down into Massachusetts."

Barilla nodded. "I can recall going by wagon just a year ago. I am thankful that the coach and train are much faster. Not any cleaner or less rough going, but faster."

They heard the sound of horses' hooves, and the scuffling of footsteps. "The coach has arrived," said Pliny. "But, you don't have to hurry. The coachman usually comes in for a cup of coffee while a boy waters the horses." He paused long enough to finish the food on his plate, then asked, "Where do you stay in Lowell? I want to call on you, if I may?"

Barilla knew she could not be evasive, "Judith and I stay with the Elstons. That is further out on Central Street, beyond Warren Street. There is a sign hanging on the front porch that reads, William Elston, Shoemaker."

Everyone stood up to follow the coachman out of the dining room. Byron carried the girls' canvas bags. The farewells were brief. The girls entered the wagon followed by two strangers who sat down on the opposite seat. An elderly man and woman were already aboard. A man came alongside and hurriedly threw a mail sack atop the coach. Barilla, seated next to a window, waved. The coach lurched, turned around in the road, and headed down to the ferry across the Androscoggin River.

The road on the south side followed the valley going easterly. After the calmness of the ferry ride, the rough road was often a quagmire of potholes stuffed with log pieces and pine boughs. Because it had so recently rained, the passengers did not experience the usual choking dust.

Swaying and jostling prevented conversation. It was not until stops at Canton, Livermore, Turner, and Auburn that the six travelers could communicate.

The coach finally reached Portland to circle around the high ground on the left and onto Commercial Street along the waterfront. Coming to a stop by the railroad station at the foot of High Street, the coachman stepped down, opened the carriage door, and held out his hand to accept his passengers' fares. Two men from inside the small station pulled down the mail sacks, which had been picked up from the various towns, and took them inside. The coach disappeared around the corner of the building.

The travelers now found themselves on a busy street, surrounded by hordes of people, vending pushcarts, and wagonloads of various produce and wares. An acrid smell came from fish and rotting vegetables in the cobblestone street.

Beyond crowded buildings on a long wharf, Barilla could see tall masts, but now she noticed the coachman, who had evidently tethered his horses, enter a nearby saloon. Then her attention focused on a group of rowdy paraders, some of whom carried placards. Then to the movement of a man who made his way to the stoop of the saloon, turned around, faced the crowd, and in a strident voice berated strong drink as the evil scourge of mankind.

Someone behind Barilla muttered, "That's the Quaker do-gooder Neal Dow."

"A lot of good his rantings ever going to come to," interjected another.

Barilla turned to Judith, "There is all this to-do going on around here, but where are the houses?"

The voice behind answered her, "Up on the hill, m'lady. That's where the high mucky-mucks live. Us common folk live on the streets below. You can't see any of 'em because of the trees. Yep, Forest City, they calls it, cause of all them trees."

The voice of the man called Dow had risen to a harsh, metallic tone. "Men! Listen to me.' For shame it is that men in this state of Maine consume more liquor in proportion to its people than in any other state. More women are left widowed due to drink than any other state!

Wham! A yellow squash hit the speaker on the side of his head. An accomplice of Dow's helped the unfortunate orator down from his temporary pulpit and wiped away the insulting debris.

A sudden shrill of a train whistle's numerous toots caused an immediate lack of interest in the disagreeable scene. An official of some sort hustled out of the station to shoo people away from the tracks. All attention centered on the approaching train that backed up to a blockade and stopped.

Judith turned to Barilla, "I almost forgot," she said, "that it had to make a 'Y' turn to back in here."

"Of course," Barilla laughed, "how else can you turn a train around?"

As the incoming passengers alighted, the coach, which had come down from Rumford, along with several others, now came alongside. The passengers waiting to board had been lined up awaiting directions. Mailbags were being tossed both off and onto the train. An agent passed among those waiting to sell them tickets. On the opposite side, roustabouts loaded produce aboard a boxcar.

That accomplished, the travelers soon heard the call, "All aboard."

Barilla and Judith, pushing through an unmannerly throng, managed to find a seat together. Then, the Boston and Maine train was on its way along Fore River and across the Eastern Division Bridge before picking up speed.

Barilla gazed out at the light-brown, drought-damaged fields where beneath trees and near creeks patches of green held bravely forth. Her concentration narrowed. Men, she decided as she relaxed against the seatback, are a sorry lot. I certainly don't need one in my life.

When the two girls stepped off the train in Lowell, dusk surrounded them. As they walked down Market Street, the lamplighter ahead of them performed his nightly task. Darkness descended rapidly as they turned onto Central Street, crossed the Pawtucket Canal, and on to the Elstons.

Abigail greeted them with delight, throwing her arms around each girl in turn. Else came bounding down the stairs. Barilla and Judith received more greetings and hugs.

"Have you had any supper?" Abigail asked.

"No, nothing since dinner, beside a railroad stop," Barilla said.

"Hours and hours ago," Judith added.

Abigail asked, "How about bread and cheese and blackberries?"

"Great," both girls agreed.

Seated at the table, the three girls buzzed excitedly about the time spent away from one another, then Else said somberly, "James asked me to marry him."

"You don't sound very enthusiastic about it," Judith said.

"I had decided I would not marry. But during the two weeks with him at his friends' house, I had time to think. That couple who own the place, Walt and Alice Burns, seemed to be in a happy, loving union. That is probably what motivated James to ask."

"How did you answer him?" asked Barilla.

"I told him I would think about it."

"So, you're still thinking?" Judith said.

Else nodded her head.

After their supper, Barilla said, "I am heading for bed. Such a long day we have had. I am exhausted."

"Will you two go into the mill tomorrow?" Else asked.

Barilla turned questioning eyes to Judith, who said, "Sure, we can do that."

On Thursday evening, Barilla and Judith had been back to work for three days. As the reunited group had just finished their supper, there came a knock on the front door. William went to investigate.

"How do you do, sir. I am Barilla's brother, Byron Taylor. And this is my friend, Pliny Tidd."

"Come in, come in," said William eagerly as he offered his hand to each of the newcomers.

Barilla, alerted, sprang to her feet and came forward to be gripped by Byron in a bear hug. She nodded politely to Pliny. She saw that his left hand held a banjo whose circular diaphragm rested on the carpet. "When did you get to Lowell?'" she said to Byron.

"About noon," he answered.

The others had followed Barilla. She introduced Else and Abigail. Judith said, "Hello again."

"Would you two gentlemen like a bit of supper?" Abigail asked.

"No, thank you, ma'am," Byron said. "We ate before we came."

"Well, then, won't you please sit down." She motioned her hand toward the furniture.

"Yes, yes," William said with a broad smile. "Do make yourselves at home."

The parlor contained a pair of two-seaters covered in maroon velvet. There were matching side chairs. Abigail went to the dining room and brought back another chair.

Byron moved quickly to take it from her, saying, "Pliny can use this. That is, if you don't mind his playing a few tunes?"

Enthusiastic affirmative answers came from everyone.

Pliny sat down. William and Abigail sat on one sofa, Else and Barilla on the other. Byron and Judith each took one of the chairs.

As Pliny tuned the instrument, he said, "I have not played this for months, so I hope you will bear with me and my mistakes." He began playing a lively Irish jig. Barilla watched his hands, how deftly they moved. The left, fingering across the frets, the right, strumming across the lower; strings. Even as the music ended, Pliny began another tune, and this time he sang, "Yankee Doodle." His voice was strong and quite precise.

Barilla could not avoid studying him. His face was thin, nose, aquiline, the slim line of his lips moving with the music of the words as he sang. Despite this, he was smiling, and his green eyes blazed as lively as the tune.

The applause, amid laughter and genuine delight, was spontaneous and lengthy.

"Thank you," Pliny said. "I love to play and I am glad you enjoyed it."

"Oh, yes!" William exclaimed. "How about another?"

"Certainly. There's an Irish one I learned a long time ago."

He sang the whole of "The Wearing of the Green" unto the last lines,

"Where the cruel cross of England's thraldon never shall be seen.

And where, thank God, we'll live and die, still wearing of the green!"

With that final strum, Pliny said, "You see, the Irish were as defiant against the British as the American heroes were."

Pliny thought for a moment, then spoke up again. "I learned a new song while I was up in Bangor. It was being sung in a tavern there. It is quite lively and repetitious, so if you can catch on to the chorus, please sing along with me."

Barilla bit on her lower lip. The man's charm was getting to her. Had she really thought he was odd-looking, as she had expressed to Judith? On the contrary, he was downright enchanting. She could not suppress the delight she felt as, inadvertently, a broad smile and twinkling eyes relayed just such a message.

Pliny began to play and sing,

"Let Bachus to Venus libations pour forth, Viva la compagnie!

And let us make use of our time while it lasts. Viva la compagnie!

Oh! Vive la vi-ve la vi-ve l'amour,

Vi-ve la vi-ve la vi-ve l'amour,

Vi-ve l'amour, vi-ve l'amour, vi-ve la com-pag-nie."

There were five more verses. By the second verse, three of the girls had caught on to the chorus. By the third, Byron, William, and Barilla joined in. Thus the final chorus became so joyous it was even rowdy.

"That's enough for now," Pliny said as he finished, stood up, and bent over in a sweeping bow. "I would not want to wear out my welcome."

"Not at all," said Abigail. "You are most welcome to come again anytime." She turned to William and asked him to light a lamp.

Byron stood up and said, "That's mighty nice of you, ma'am, but I cannot come again. I have to leave at first light in the morning."

After the shuffle of laughter, shaking of hands, and good-byes. Barilla led her brother and his friend out onto the porch. It had become dark.

To Byron she said, "Why must you leave so soon?"

"There was a letter from my girl Charlotte waiting for me at the carriage shop. Her older brother Edward is being a bit difficult. I left two of my horses with them and money enough for the feed and care. I also had paid money down on a piece of land in Levant. So Edward jaws away at Charlotte about when I am going to get back and take the damn horses up to Levant."

"Oh, my dear brother, that is upsetting."

"He's right in a way." Byron chuckled. "There is more grass up in Levant than on Union Street in downtown Bangor. So. because it will take more than a week to get there, I have to start tomorrow."

He bent to kiss her as she wrapped her arms around his back.

"Safe journey, dear brother," she said as he stood back away from her. To Pliny, she offered her hand. "This has been a very enjoyable evening. Thank you for the music. You are quite talented."

Pliny held onto her hand and asked, "Would it be possible on Sunday for you to have dinner with me?"

Taken aback momentarily, she paused to answer slowly, "I have to go to church at Saint Anne's."

"May I meet you there after the service?"

She did not smile, but answered soberly. "All right, if you so desire it."

"I do desire it." He withdrew his hand and said, "Good night."

Before retiring, she had a brief discussion with the Elstons regarding the pleasure and excitement provided by Byron and his friend. As she went toward the stairs, she said, "My brother's friend has invited me to dinner on Sunday."

Was there a knowing glance between husband and wife? She continued up the stairs being certain of it.

From outside the girls' bedroom door, Barilla heard a merry voice singing, "Vi-ve l'amour." She opened the door quietly and slipped inside. It was Judith, dancing around in her nightgown singing the lively song Pliny sang. Barilla shook her head from side to side, yet there was the hint of a smile on her face.

"Hey," said Judith, "you enjoyed the singing too. I watched you. Actually, I never saw you so happy. That Pliny is quite a gent." At that she flopped down backward on the bed. Else stood there laughing at the excited girl.

Barilla undressed and took the pins out of her hair to let it fall onto her back and shoulders. Then she blew out the candle and climbed into the bed she shared with Else. A long time elapsed before she fell asleep. Not only the tune persisted in going round and round in her brain, but also the vision of the man who had taught it to them.

16

On Saturday, when the girls returned from work, Else found a letter addressed to her. She studied the unfamiliar writing, then ran hurriedly up the stairs. Barilla and Judith went to the kitchen to help Abigail with supper.

Abigail had just finished sprinkling salt, pepper, and a dash of vinegar into a bowl filled with sliced cucumbers. She handed it to Judith.

To Barilla she said, "You can take this platter of sliced tomatoes in to the table while I take biscuits out of the oven."

Barilla stopped to watch her. "That stove is a great invention. I wish my mother could have one like it."

"Not all older people want stoves like this," said Abigail. "Why my own mother calls it a newfangled contraption."

Barilla laughed, "You may be right. My mother seems content with what she has. Oh my, don't those biscuits smell good."

William had come in to wash up. "Mmm," he said, "what did you put in them to smell so good?"

"Cheese and a few drops of juice from a clove of garlic."

Barilla went into the dining room with the tomatoes. Abigail brought the biscuits and William followed. The four sat down.

"Where is Else,'" Abigail asked. "Didn't she come home with you?"

"She took her letter upstairs," Barilla said, rising from her seat. "I'll go call her to come down."

Barilla found her seated on the bottom stair, her head bent over. She held the letter in her hand.

"What is the matter?" Barilla asked with great concern.

Else looked up. Tears streamed down her cheeks. She attempted to wipe them away on her sleeve.

Barilla fished a handkerchief out of her pocket, saying, "I have never seen you cry before. It is usually my tears that need wiping away." She sat down beside Else and placed an arm across her shoulder.

The disconsolate girl held out the letter to Barilla, who began to read the crudely printed missive. The letter was from Patsy. It said that Karl had been killed by pirates who came aboard, robbed, and burned the ship.

Barilla hugged her friend. "Oh, my dear. I am so sorry."

"Karl and I had just found each other and now," Else sobbed, "now I have no one."

"You have me," Barilla said boldly. "And you have Judith and the Elstons. Also lots of other friends. Now, you come out and eat some supper." She helped Else to stand up, adding, "Just wait until you smell the biscuits."

"All right," Else said, wiping her eyes and blowing her nose.

As Barilla made certain Else was seated, she told the others what had happened. Barilla continued, "Now she is going to eat something because there is nothing that can be done about it."

Else managed to eat a little. Otherwise, it was a very solemn meal.

On Sunday morning, Else told Barilla that she did not feel like going to church.

"Nonsense!" Barilla said. "It is better to go, to get out and walk with the rest of us, instead of moping alone here. Besides, look out the window. It is a beautiful day."

Else sighed. "I suppose you are right."

"Of course I am right," Barilla said, then added, "You seemed to sleep well last night."

"After a while, yes. Although I visioned the tussle with pirates and the burning ship."

"Well, Patsy may be uneducated, but she did the right thing in letting you know."

"Yes, she did. I will write her a note."

"You better keep it simple," Barilla chuckled, "or she won't understand."

"One thing I can well understand is how lonely and miserable poor Patsy is feeling."

As the three girls entered Saint Anne's amidst the throng, Barilla spotted James. Thus she held back in order to speak quietly with him.

"Else just received word that her brother is dead. So she needs…" Her words were lost in air as James hustled to single out Else and take hold of her arm.

He whispered in her ear, "Come sit with me, please."

Judith entered a pew halfway down the sanctuary. Barilla slid in beside her, and Pliny Tidd moved in beside Barilla.

Despite her cumbersome bonnet, she turned to say, "Good morning. Isn't it a lovely day?"

"It is that," he said, with a wide grin.

A tap from behind came on Barilla's right shoulder. A female voice, speaking softly, admonished her, "No talking in church."

Barilla nodded her head.

Because she could not speak further, she harbored her thoughts. Here she was, seated beside a man, a single man. Else sat elsewhere, also beside a single man. Now what would the gossips make of that? Or the minister? Usually the mill girls sat together in a body on the right side halfway down the cavernous edifice. The young, single men were at the rear, on the left.

Gleams of light came through the side windows and an arched window above a large wooden cross in the altar area, thus creating semidarkness. Each pew had a door that latched shut. One felt shut in, trapped, until the service was over.

So, how, she thought, had Pliny found her, enough to now be seated beside her, unless he had waited on Central Street for her to pass, then followed close behind? All these thoughts so clogged her mind she paid little attention to the service. That is until near the end. A flute player was introduced and began to play a majestic yet sweet

melody. She sensed, more than heard, that Pliny hummed the plaintive tune. She smiled inwardly, actually amused. This was the first
time she had heard music inside the church.

The service over, Pliny stepped into the aisle, allowing Barilla,
Judith, and two other girls to pass. In front of them, a crone, by her
appearance, now cast a look of obvious dissatisfaction directed at
Pliny.

The throng progressed slowly down the aisle toward the narthex.

Once outside the entrance, the crone's voice spoke out loud and
angrily. "Music in the church. What's this world coming to? Next
thing you know they'll be dancing, And young men a sittin' beside
mill girls. Oh, my soul, what next?"

Barilla glanced at Pliny, who had offered her his arm with such a
twinkle in his eye and suppressed amusement on his face. In fact, he
seemed to be withholding a pent-up explosion.

They turned left. Not until then did Pliny burst out laughing.

"I could hardly be disrespectful, but that old woman certainly
holds a distorted sense of religion," he said.

She answered, "You seemed to know the melody. I thought I
heard you humming."

"Sure. It is a lovely hymn." He began to sing the words to "O God
Our Help in Ages Past."

"That is lovely," she said when he finished. She then turned to
Judith, who walked on her left. "I neglected to tell you that I had been
invited out for dinner. I already told Abigail last Thursday. Would
you be kind enough to take my bonnet home?"

"Of course," Judith smiled knowingly. "Go, both of you, with my
best wishes." She ducked behind and crossed Merrimack Street.

"We could have asked her to join us," Pliny said.

"Well," she shrugged, "I didn't know."

"But I am satisfied that I'll have your company all to myself."

By now they had reached Merrimack House. They paused on the
curved portico surrounding the entrance.

"Have you ever eaten dinner here?" he asked.

"Once," she answered, briefly recalling the dinner with Horace. "Last January. New Year's Day it was."

Pliny said nothing as they passed through the entrance and into the dining room. Since nice girls did not frequent such places unaccompanied by a gentleman, Barilla realized exactly what he was thinking.

After he had ordered their dinner, two glasses and a decanter of wine were placed on the cloth-covered table. Pliny held up his glass to clink next to hers.

He took a sip of wine, then spoke seriously, "So, what happened to him?"

"To whom?" she said.

"The man you had dinner with last January?"

"Oh that," she scoffed offhandedly. "We are no longer friends. The fact of the matter is, he found someone he liked better than me."

The lines around Pliny's sparkling green eyes crinkled with amusement. "He was a fool. A damn fool, if you'll pardon my expression."

"Perhaps not. You see, she was a member of the rich Boston people, while I am only a farm girl, a mill girl."

"Only!" Pliny said in disgust. "Apples are apples. There are nice, wholesome ones and there are rotten ones. Do you follow me?"

"Yes, of course," she said meekly.

The waiter brought two plates filled with fried shrimp and chunks of roasted potatoes.

With her fork she picked up one of the shrimp. She studied it for a moment, then said, "I have never eaten these."

Pliny explained, "Shrimp are brought into the port of Boston, and come to Lowell by train. You have to pull off the tail pieces because they are hard. See, like this," he said as he demonstrated.

When she tried a chunk of potato, she said, "These are delicious. I wonder how they are cooked." She smiled brightly. "You see, Abigail Elston likes to experiment with food. I would like to tell her about these."

Pliny beckoned the waiter. "Would you kindly ask the cook how he prepares such delicious potatoes?"

"Certainly, monsieur," the waiter said.

When the waiter returned, he handed Pliny a slip of paper. "The cook was so pleased that you like the potatoes, he offered you this."

Pliny handed the recipe to Barilla.

"Thank you." Her smile was wide and her eyes sparkled, "That was a nice thing to do."

"You have a beautiful smile," he said.

"I can't help it when someone does something that pleases me."

"I hope that I shall always do things which please you."

Disconcerted by such an earnest statement, she sobered, casting her eyes downward.

"Hey," he said suddenly. "You stopped smiling."

Embarrassed, she smiled once more. "You are so amusing, and entertaining, Mister Tidd, that I will try to keep smiling."

"Please call me Pliny. Actually, my entire name is Caius Plinius Tidd."

"Could that be from the Greeks?"

"No. I looked it up. It's from the Romans. Caius Plinius wrote about natural history. What I find tantalizing is the fact that my mother must have had more than a common-school education to name me that.

The waiter came and removed the plates, asking if they would have some apple pie.

"Thank you, no," said Barilla. "I have already eaten far too much."

Pliny paid the bill and asked the waiter if it was all right to sit there for a while. Then he continued his story.

"I was raised in Wrentham, Massachusetts, by an aunt of my mother's named Deborah Briggs. My great-aunt Deborah told me only what she wanted to, and always in a voice of disapproval. At first I was told only that both parents were dead and that I should not ask questions."

"I think I was six or seven when I was taken to a school for orphans in Boston. And when boys became fifteen, they could no longer stay there. Various tradespersons came to the school to apprentice the boys. Thus William Day of the company I am now associated with took me to Lowell. However, several months before I was to leave, I inquired at the school's office as to who brought me there, and was given the name of Hiram Briggs, husband to my great-aunt Deborah. I wrote him a letter asking about my parents and received some information."

"My mother, Matilda Todd, along with two other girls, had gone by ship out of Boston up to Castine in Maine. It was the beginning of the booming lumber industry on the Penobscot River. Somehow the girls were swept up in the frenzy of that industry whose center was Bangor. My mother worked in one of the taverns, possibly as cook, but more likely as a barmaid. She had written one letter home in March of 1823 in which she mentioned having a friend who had been a woodsman working in the great forests north of Bangor."

"A year later the Briggs received a letter from a woman asking if there was a relative who could come up and take a three-month-old baby boy who was now an orphan. I was born in mid-December in 1823, and apparently cared for by some woman there until April of 1824. With no other information to go on, I was always anxious to get up to Bangor. In June, Mister Day allowed me leave to go. Thus I took the ship out of Boston harbor bound for Bangor."

"So," Barilla said, "that is how you happened to be there when you met my brother."

"Yes, but hunting up records was to no avail. There are no employment records for either barmaids or woodsmen. And unless one belongs to the wealthy families or similar important personages, birth and death records are unavailable."

Pliny became pensive, so Barilla said, "Probably then, it is best for your peace of mind to follow the great-aunt's advice and stop asking questions."

Pliny ran the fingers of one hand casually through his hair. "There was one consolation in the letter from Hiram Briggs. My mother had a nice singing voice, so I can imagine her entertaining the clientele of a Bangor tavern."

"That is nice for you to know. You have also inherited her musical talent."

"Yes, it does give me that connection."

"And perhaps," Barilla hesitated, noticing that the usually slicked down hair was springing into curls. "Perhaps she also had red hair."

"Red curly hair, which I cannot control without pomade."

"The curls are natural, why try to hide them?"

"Curls are all right for women, but not for men."

He reached for his pocket watch and showed her the time.

"Half past four," she said.

"Yes. Too long I have worn our your ear and your patience listening to my tale of mystery."

"Although discouraging for you, I found it quite interesting." She remembered to smile.

Before crossing Merrimack Street, they paused as a coach, drawn by four horses, passed by to turn onto Bridge Street. As they walked along Central Street, they passed the home of William Day on their left, directly across from Middle Street. Pliny pointed it out to her as being where he lived, and had lived ever since he first came to Lowell. Then across the Pawtucket Canal, he pointed out his place of business. And almost opposite, she showed him the lane that led to the Hamilton Mills on their right.

When they reached the Elstons' front steps, Pliny stopped to face her He looked intently into her eyes. He said, "Thank you for this day, and for your patience in listening."

"It needed no patience I thought it intriguing."

She hoped he would not try to kiss her. After all it was not yet dark. She extended her hand which he heartily accepted.

"Until next Sunday, dear girl. Perhaps we can do this again?"

"All right. But after church. It would hardly be advisable to be seated together."

"I know." He laughed. "The disapproving lady and other gossips. Good evening, Barilla."

"Good evening, Pliny."

Later, as dusk descended in their bedroom, the three girls chatted about their day. Judith stood at the window staring down into the garden and the river beyond. Barilla sat on the bed, talking directly to Else, "During supper, I noticed that you were smiling inwardly. A smile of secrecy, wasn't it?"

"Yes. It is about James."

Judith turned away from the window and listened more acutely to the others' conversation.

Else continued, "He was most kind about my brother Karl's death. After church we walked out Merrimack Street to the Old Stone Tavern, where we ate dinner. Then we went to sit by the embankment of the Northern Canal. It was cool beneath the trees and very quiet. James had one arm around me and with the other he put his hand under my chin and lifted it so as to kiss me. It was only the second time he did that. I found myself responding by wrapping both my arms around him. The first time he kissed me was as a rising moon spread its beauty over the water at Revere. That was the night he proposed. And," she smiled shyly, "this time I said yes."

"Oh, Else," Barilla said as she hugged her with delight. "When will you be married?"

"At Christmastime," Else said.

"I'm happy for you. If it is what you truly want," Barilla said soberly.

"I believe it is meant to be. We are to live with his father in the Scotch Block. It means I will finally be part of a family again."

Judith said, "I spent an interesting afternoon with John Abbot. "You remember him? His wife Carrie died of consumption about two months ago. He caught up with me as I started walking alone down Middle Street. It was the first time since her death he had been to church. I think he was lonely, needing someone to talk to. He came all the way here, so I asked Abigail if he could join us for dinner. After all, you two were not showing up to eat. John ate very little. Afterward we sat on the front porch talking. He is not well. He coughed a lot. Told me he had bleeding lungs. He left before supper.

He said that the night air was bad for his condition. I felt sorry for him." But then she changed her tone, "How about you, Barilla? What was your date like?"

"Well, Pliny is very nice. He told me something about his life. It was an interesting afternoon and he was a perfect gentleman."

"Uh huh," Judith chided her, "And are you going to see him again?"

"Yes. Next Sunday. But now I am tired and we have to work tomorrow, so I am going to bed.

On Saturday, the twenty-eighth of September, the girls were paid. As they walked away from the paymaster, Barilla spoke to Judith and Else in a disparaging tone, "Only five dollars and sixty-one cents."

Else said, "That is because you worked less than two weeks this month. You should have full pay next month. I got seven dollars and six cents. That is enough to buy cloth for a wedding dress, so let's go shopping tonight."

After church on Sunday, the three girls came out the door, being instantly aware of mist in the air and a cloudy, darkened sky.

John Abbot, leaning against a tree, became alert as he spied Judith and came forward to clasp her hand. Abruptly behind the girls, James commandeered Else. And there, with a beaming smile, stood Pliny. Barilla had to admit to herself that she was glad to see him. Her two roommates had gentlemen friends, so, she thought, do I. That is if we can just be friends.

"It is apt to rain," said Pliny as he offered her his arm. "So let's just cross the street to have dinner downstairs in the city hall."

"That is a good idea," she answered as they hustled across Merrimack Street.

A poster was tacked to the outside of the city hall. Attracted by the name O'Toole, Pliny halted to read of the brothers Johnny and Denny O'Toole who would perform in the hall there on Saturday, October fifth, at seven-thirty.

"I know those two," Pliny said in a joyous voice. "They were in the orphanage when I was there. Oh, Barilla, I must attend. That is next Saturday. Will you join me?"

"It states that they are Irish Vagabond Singers," she said.

"That's right. We used to play and sing all together until they had to leave there. They are older than I. Will you attend with me, please?"

She laughed, "Yes, of course."

Seated downstairs in the dining room, they were served the special of the day, roast pork baked with potatoes and onions. Barilla occasionally glanced up at Pliny's face, neat and clean-shaven, the green eyes sparkling, looking into her eyes significantly.

She looked away and inadvertently noticed Judith seated at a distant table with her friend, John Abbot.

She was forced to again look at Pliny as he was speaking wistfully, "Your brother Byron told me about your family. That is something I never had, a family of brothers and sisters and loving parents."

"My mother and my brothers do love me dearly," she said. "But because of my year away, I found my father too domineering and deeply rooted in the theory that women were lesser beings."

"A lesser being certainly does not apply to you," he said adamantly. "You had to have initiative to come and work here. And after your sojourn home, to return again to Lowell. However, I'm sure your father loves you." He smiled brightly, and said, "How could he help it?"

Pliny's directness prompted her to look downward soberly.

"Now, Barilla, I did not say that to upset you. I merely said what I thought. Sometimes I speak too quickly. That harks back to my orphanage days when any thoughts or expressions were promptly squelched. Not until William Day sort of adopted me and treated me like a son did I loosen up to feel like a person of any consequence."

"Oh, but you are. A valued person to Mister Day and to his company. Byron told me so."

"Yes, I have proved that. But there is this nagging feeling that except for the biological fact that a man had to be involved with my mother," he hesitated studying her intently, no doubt to observe if she were shocked, then continued, "I was born the first of December in 1823, and my mother's name was Janet Todd. The similarities of Todd and Tidd does cause me to wonder if…"

A sudden commotion occurred as Barilla watched in horror as John Abbot, coughing violently, fell sideways off his chair and lay semiconscious in spasms on the floor. She dashed across the room to where Judith had knelt beside him, placing her hand beneath his head.

Behind her, Pliny also rushed to aid the stricken man. Seeing Judith, he instinctively knew these were friends of Barilla's. Other diners had gathered into a semicircle.

Judith gave Pliny a helpless look as he lifted the stricken man to a sitting position and addressed Judith.

"He certainly is not well. We should get him home. Do you know where he lives?"

"Yes, in Mrs. Dean's boardinghouse. It's not far down Merrimack Street."

Pliny turned to the group. "Is there one among you who will help me get him up the stairs?"

With the help of a waiter, Pliny managed to half carry John up to the street, where the stricken man, refreshed by the cooler air, revived somewhat. Judith thanked the waiter as she pulled one of John's arms across her shoulder and Pliny did the same with his other arm.

"He lives at Mrs. Dean's on this side of Merrimack, just opposite John Street," Judith said. Thus the foursome made their way until Judith turned to Barilla and said, "His doctor, Silas Doane, lives here at 118 Merrimack. Please ask him to come to Mrs. Dean's, it is at 104 Merrimack."

Barilla's errand proved to be curt and to the point.

The busty woman who answered the door informed Barilla that the doctor would come along after he finished his dinner, then said, "If that Abbot fellow would only stay abed like he was told, he would not be in such a fix!" Then she slammed the door shut.

Barilla turned toward the street and felt sudden rain pelt her as she hastened on to arrive at Mrs. Dean's as the landlady ushered the group along a hallway into John's room on the first floor of her house.

"I told him not to go out, but no, he wouldn't listen to me," she said.

Pliny managed to lay John on his bed, then removed the man's jacket as Judith removed John's shoes.

"You, girl," Mrs. Dean said to Judith, "You're Carrie's friend, aren't you? May her soul rest in peace. And this one here, he ain't far behind her."

Judith thanked Pliny and Barilla and told them to leave. She would stay until the doctor came.

Approaching the entrance door, Barilla told Pliny it had started to rain hard.

"In that case, you should stay here while I run around the corner to my place to get an umbrella," Pliny said.

"If it is that close by, I can run with you," she said, laughing. "I can pick up my skirts and run when I have to."

That was how they arrived breathless at the door of the house where Pliny lived. The sounds of two out-of-breath persons alerted William Day. He came into the entry to greet them.

"Ah-hah, Pliny, you and your young lady got caught in the rain."

"Yes. We just stopped by to pick up an umbrella. I do want you to meet Byron's sister, Miss Barilla Taylor. Barilla, this is Mister Day."

She held out her hand to the man, who clasped it warmly between both of his.

"I am pleased, very pleased to meet you, Miss Taylor," he said. "The short time your brother stayed here were pleasant moments. I look forward to becoming better aquainted with you, also."

At a loss for words, Barilla merely nodded, but did remember to smile.

"We'll be off now, Will," Pliny said. "Barilla lives not far out Central Street."

"Good-bye then, Miss Taylor, until we meet again," Mr. Day said.

The two young people were soon outside as the door was closed behind them.

Holding up her skirts out of the muddy walkway, they hastened up Central Street. It was not until they arrived under cover of the Elstons' porch roof did they let out a simultaneous sigh of relief. Barilla's bonnet had kept her head dry, but it had taken on enough moisture to be uncomfortable. She untied it and took it off.

"Do come in, Pliny," she said, "Perhaps I can fix you a cup of tea?"

"It is rather chilly out. Tea would be most welcome," said Pliny.

She wiped her feet on the mat before the door. Pliny did the same.

Abigail was seated at the kitchen table slicing chicken off its carcass as Barilla entered. Pliny had followed and was close behind her.

"I want to put the kettle on and make tea for us. Is that all right," Barilla said.

"Of course. Just add wood, and hustle up the fire a bit so the water will boil. Hello, Mister Tidd." Abigail smiled up at him. "Or may I call you Pliny?"

"I would be honored if you would, ma'am."

Abigail looked at her messy hands and then back to Pliny. "If my hands were clean, I'd shake hands with you. I want you to know how welcome you are to come here."

"Thank you, ma'am.

"I am fixing chicken to make sandwiches for supper. Since not one of our girls showed up for dinner, there was a lot of chicken left over." She smiled graciously, and added, "I hope you will stay for supper with us."

He glanced at Barilla whose back was turned as she fed wood into the stove. So he answered Abigail.

"I would like that. I'd like very much to stay."

When Barilla knew the stove fire would catch, she turned to Pliny, "Perhaps you'd like to sit in the parlor until the water boils. I'll bring the tea when it is ready."

After a while, she entered the parlor carrying a tray which she set down on a small table. Sitting down, she poured from an ivory colored china teapot, asking if he wanted sugar and milk.

Sing Me a Song

"No sugar. Just a little milk, thank you." He sipped from his teacup as thunder rumbled in the distance, and said, "This is quite cozy, being comfortably inside."

She nodded and smiled.

"That fellow John?" he asked. "Isn't he a lot older than Judith?"

"Oh, yes. I'd guess he is twice her age."

"Yet somehow she feels responsible for him?"

Barilla cast her eyes downward as she related what she knew. "That's because of his dead wife, Carrie. She and Judith came here to work a year before I did. Carrie had a husband back in Maine who beat her. One day she struck back, bashing him on the head with a cast-iron pan. Him being unconscious, she ran away and stopped the first wagon she saw, which happened to be a wagonload of girls bound for Lowell. Judith was among them. She comforted the distraught newcomer. They both worked on the warper floor, winding bobbins ready for weaving. One night Carrie felt faint and lingered at the drinking water bucket. The overseer, thinking no one else was around, forced his attentions on her, and she hit him with the dipper. She screamed as she backed away from him and fell, breaking her wrist. John, a mechanic, heard the commotion and rushed to assist her. Judith, who had gone down the stairs, also heard the scream and hustled back up the stairs. The overseer got off free by blaming John for Carrie's broken wrist. With a broken wrist, Carrie could not work. And Judith asked to be transferred to the weave room where I work. Later on, Carrie and John got married. She never knew nor cared whether she was committing bigamy."

She lifted her eyes to study Pliny's very serious face, and said, "Life for many can be tough. Carrie died in July with a lung disease. John is lonely. That is why he seeks, and needs, Judith's friendship."

"I can understand that," he said as he put the teacups on the tray. Rising to his feet, he carried the tray out to the kitchen.

Barilla followed, then looked beyond him, out of the window. "Look," she said, "the rain has stopped. The sun is even shining."

"So it is," said both Pliny and Abigail in unison as William came in through the back door.

At that moment, Judith and Else entered from the dining room. Judith was laughing and teasing Else, "I had to walk back here, but do you know how Else got here? On the back of a horse, sitting astraddle behind James Gordon."

Else's mood was such that she also had to laugh, as did the others in the kitchen.

Abigail interrupted by suggesting they could all help by setting the supper table and carrying in the food she had prepared.

While the group ate, Else felt she should explain, "The horse belongs to James's father. After church James insisted I go to his father's place for dinner. Mr. Gordon cooked the dinner. It was indeed very pleasurable. Besides a kitchen and parlor, there are two bedrooms. One for the father," she blushed a little as she added, "and the other for James, and for both of us when we get married at Christmastime."

"Why, Else," Abigail said, "why didn't you tell us sooner?"

"I did tell Barilla and Judith," Else said.

Abigail continued, "You could be married here. Would you like that?"

"Oh, yes. Yours is the only real home I have known since coming to this country."

"At Christmas, you said?" Abigail stood up to look through the months of the wall calender. "Christmas comes on a Thursday. So you girls do not have the day off. How about doing it on the Sunday before, December twenty-first?"

"That would be fine if it is all right with James. We did talk about a preacher. James does not think much of the Reverend Edson of Saint Anne's, so would prefer Reverend Blanchard of the Congregational Church."

"Oh what fun, planning a wedding." Abigail stood up and put her arm across Else's shoulder. "Thank you, Else, for allowing me the pleasure."

Else bit her lip as tears of happiness formed in her eyes.

Pliny, seated across from her, stood up, went around the table, and offered his hand to Else. "My congratulations." Then he spoke to Abigail. "And thanks to such a gracious hostess. But now I feel I must be leaving."

Barilla accompanied him out onto the front porch. The setting sun cast an eerie light on the trees and beyond to the stark mill buildings. In the semidarkness, Pliny turned to face her, his expression so grave, she was taken aback. She reached out to touch his arm, and said, "Pliny, just before John fell ill, you started to tell me something important to you. Was it because you think your mother and father were never married?"

"Yes. That is what I believe."

"And I can tell that it bothers you. But that is no fault of yours." She smiled then, wholeheartedly, "You have made a good life for yourself, and have the respect of many people. Why not forget the past?"

Pliny pulled her to him. Allowing his umbrella to drop on the porch floor, he wrapped both arms around her. Her forehead came even with his chin.

She felt his jaw's motion as he spoke softly, "For someone of your age, you have a tremendous amount of compassion and understanding." He released her, picked up his umbrella, and said, "I will come for you Saturday about six-thirty to go to the O'Toole concert."

"Oh, no. That will not be possible. We have to work until six-thirty on Saturday. I had better meet you at the city hall as soon as I can get there."

"All right," he said as he extended his right hand to shake hers.

"So, for now, good evening, Barilla."

"Good evening, Pliny."

She stood still, watching until he was out of sight. Reflecting on their parting, she thought that maybe, after all. they could be just friends.

17

On Saturday, Barilla hurried to the city hall. There, seated on the boardwalk at the entrance, she noticed the Irish; boy, Jamie.

"Why, Jamie, what a surprise. I have not seen you for a long time," she said.

"I go to school now," he said proudly, "and I'm clean too," he added, even more proudly.

"I can see that. Well, are you here for the concert?" She asked.

Jamie lowered his head. "I got no money to go inside. So I was hoping I could hear from out here."

In that moment, Pliny came through the entrance, extending his hand to Barilla.

She accepted his hand, then turned her attention to the boy. "Pliny, I want you to meet Jamie Quinn." To Jamie she said, "Please stand up and shake hands with Mister Tidd."

Jamie did as he was bid and spoke with shyness, "Hello, sir."

Barilla turned to Pliny, and spoke quietly, "He wants to go in, but cannot afford a ticket."

"Well, I can solve that quite easily. I had bought two tickets and find that I need not use mine. I came early with my banjo to practice with Denny and Johnny. They asked me to be part of the show." He passed the tickets to the boy. "I would appreciate it if you would use these to accompany Miss Barilla."

Jamie's eyes shone. His smile was so broad it showed his gleaming white teeth. Barilla was proud of his being clean and presentable.

There were scarcely a hundred persons in the audience. Two brightly lit lamps hung from the ceiling on each side of the small stage. At precisely seven-thirty, three performers moved swiftly onto the stage. The middle one, shorter than the other two, held a guitar as he presented an introduction.

"Good evening, ladies and gentlemen. Welcome to our show. We are your devoted servants here to entertain you. I am Johnny O'Toole. On my right with the banjo is my younger brother, Denny. I used to call him my little brother, but as you can see, he is no longer little. On my left, well, what do you know? Another banjo player, an old pal from our childhood, and now a Lowellite, Pliny Tidd."

The amused audience applauded as all three bowed low.

The trio started off with, "Mine Eyes Have Seen the Glory." Throughout each chorus, a charming descant was sung by Pliny. After all three verses, the performers bowed amid tremendous applause.

Then Johnny began a repartee, "Brother Denny, and do you know why the Irish left the old sod?"

"I do not. But I'm sure now you'll be telling me."

"That I will, me lad. It was because of the impossible language."

"What language?"

"Gaelic. Now we are going to sing, 'I wish I had the Shepherd's Lamb.' But do you know what it is called in Ireland? 'Is Trua Gan Peata An Mhaoir Agam.' It's no wonder the Irish came to this land. Few knew what all they was talking about."

Amid laughter from the audience, the trio began to sing.

"I wish I had the Shepherd's lamb, and Katy coming after" complete through several verses. While all three strummed their instruments, Denny voiced some off-the-cuff words to his brother.

"Katy'll not favor the likes of you 'cause you're too short and too homely."

"Them's fighting words, little brother. I would remind you to respect your elders, and I am your elder."

"Now now, boys," said Pliny, "you don't have to prove what they say about the fighting Irish. Let's go on with singing about your old Irish potatoes, 'The praties grow small over here.'"

After that Irish ditty, Denny said, "I like sad songs. Let's do 'Barb'ry Ellen.'"

The ballad of the haughty Barbry who declined the love of the man from Dublin ended with the twined lovers' knot which had grown over their graves, symbolized in a red rose and a brier.

The trio continued with love songs, sad songs, and several ribald ditties to finish with an ode to the taxing of the tea, while encouraging the audience to clap to the rhythm.

With a final twang to his guitar, Johnny added in spoken words, "The Brits made a big mistake, man, when they put a tax on that tea."

Some in the audience were so amused, and impressed, that amid the final applause, they stood up.

There followed handshaking all around as the O'Toole brothers mixed with the audience.

But Pliny came directly to Barilla and Jamie. "Did you enjoy yourself, young man?"

"Oh, yes," Jamie responded happily. "When I grow up I want to be a banjo player."

"Maybe you will, lad. Now all three of us will go downstairs for dessert. Because you had little time for supper, Barilla, I imagine you are hungry."

When they had finished having pie and tea, Pliny handed Jamie a handful of cookies to take home with him. Then they climbed the stairs into the darkness of Merrimack Street.

"I thank you very much, sir," said Jamie, "but now I hafta go." He turned and ran off in a great hurry.

Barilla and Pliny walked in the opposite direction on Merrimack Street. At the corner of Central, Pliny said, "We should stop by my place to drop off my banjo."

"Yes, of course," she agreed, then said, "I want you to know that I did enjoy the evening. You and your friends were a great team."

"For something like this evening, fine. But the life of traveling musicians is too chancy for me. Ah, here we are."

Freed of the banjo, they continued on Central Street. As they crossed the canal, Pliny placed his arm across Barilla's shoulder to pause and gaze momentarily at the lower falls and a rising, lopsided moon coming up over the distant trees.

"This is so beautiful," he said, "I love moonrises."

"It is indeed beautiful. But I am also thinking of how nice it was for you to treat Jamie as you did. The boy reacts to kindness. He will remember it all of his life."

"Tell me how it happened, your befriending him?" he asked.

While they continued walking onward, she told of all that had transpired in her relationship with Jamie. Having by that time arrived at the Elstons, Pliny placed his hands on her shoulders, and said,"Seems to me, your kindness is something he will not only remember all his life, but also benefit from."

She smiled. Her eyes twinkled in reflected moonlight. He picked up her wrist and kissed the palm of her hand. "Good night, Barilla. I'll see you in church tomorrow." "Good night, Pliny."

After church the following day, Pliny suggested they walk to the north end of Merrimack Street to have dinner at the Stone Tavern. "It being such a lovely, warm day for walking out. The distance is about three-quarters of a mile. Are you agreeable to that?" he asked.

She smiled dutifully, "Of course."

On the way, Pliny pointed out the Congregational Church telling her it was the one, which up to recent times, he had attended. Thus he asked if she would accompany him there next Sunday, stating that she would find the service more relaxed and friendly. "Besides," he added, "that is also the house of worship which your friend Else and her intended frequent."

"I realize that," she answered. "Else told me."

Thus it happened that on subsequent Sundays up to the time of Else's wedding, the new church became Pliny and Barilla's place of attendance.

An oft-frequented tavern on nearby Worthern Street became a habitual place to dine, occasionally making a foursome with Else and James.

Barilla came to realize that her attitude and even her way of life had gained new perspective. Not only maturity, but the secure feeling of having such a friend as Pliny filled her with pleasure and assertiveness.

In mid-December, two weeks before the wedding date, the Reverend Amos Blanchard singled out Else and James as Barilla and Pliny stood nearby. He advised them that there should be a rehearsal the following Sunday at the designated place.

"You must secure a license at the city hall. Also it is required that each of you have an attendant as witnesses," the reverend said.

Else reached for Barilla's hand, and said, "Barilla Taylor, sir, will be my attendant."

"And the gentleman?" the Reverend asked James.

"A friend who will come up from Boston. His name is Horace, Horace Gailey."

Barilla's shock caused her to pale. Her indrawn breath induced chills to race through her arms and legs. Knowing that she should not be observed by the others, she averted her eyes to stare stoically through the open doorway at the departing parishioners and the waiting carriages. Inadvertently, she moved toward the opening. Pliny followed.

She turned to him and said, "I would rather go to city hall or Merrimack House for dinner. Would you please make excuses to James and Else?"

"Of course," he said, his voice tempered with concern.

Bitter cold penetrated both of them as they walked easterly on Merrimack Street. Barilla was noticeably reticent. Pliny asked no questions until they were seated at a table in the Merrimack House and had ordered dinner.

"What is wrong, Barilla?"

"Do you recall my telling you about a man who let me down by preferring a Boston socialite?"

"Yes. Go on," he said.

"He is James's friend, Horace Gailey. When I just learned he will attend James at the wedding it came as a shock."

Pliny stared at her and asked, "So, you still care for him?"

"No, of course not," she said angrily, then softened it by placing her hand over his. "The feeling is more like being uncomfortable. But surely, Pliny, it will be a help to have you, my true friend, there at the wedding."

He turned his hand over to grasp her palm, squeezing it gently. "I want to be more to you than just a friend."

Taken aback, she uttered a surprised, "Oh" as the waiter brought their dinners.

With downcast eyes and serious mien, she ate what had been placed before her.

Pliny, sensing her discomfort, spoke up playfully, "You are not smiling. I've told you before that you are less beautiful when you stop smiling."

She laughed, smiling broadly as she looked directly into his eyes. "My dear Pliny. What would I do without you?"

"That's better. I don't want you to ever do without me. Now, finish your dinner." He poured coffee from a carafe into her cup. "You will need this when we face the cold out on the street."

Arriving at the Elston home, Barilla suggested that Pliny come in to get warmed with hot tea.

He removed her cape and hung it on the hall coat tree, placing his overcoat on another hook.

During the tea drinking, she asked Pliny if he cared to play pachisi. "It's an old Hindu game played on a board using dice to move pieces."

She set up the board on the tea table, explained the rules, and thereby they spent a pleasant afternoon.

When Pliny looked out a window at descending dusk, he announced that he had best be leaving. He stood up and said, "It gets even colder at night."

Her gaze never left his face as he wrapped his scarf around his neck and donned his coat.

She found herself being pulled into the circle of his arm while he spoke words of comfort in her ear.

"You and I have spent a truly pleasant day together. Think on that instead of feeling upset over anything, much less a past friendship gone awry," he said.

He kissed her lightly on the forehead, released her to place his hand on the doorknob, and said in parting, "I'll be with you every minute that fellow is within your sight."

"Thank you, Pliny. I depend so much on your kindness," she said.

Then suddenly he was gone. She leaned her back against the door and tried to sort out her thoughts. Pliny loved her. No doubt about that. She thought of the past year, of the heartbreak Horace had given her. And of how hard her mother worked, and so many babies! Also her sister Florena, dominated by her husband Amos. Her last thought was of how, after all the flowery words of love, men eventually subjugated their women to what they wanted.

No, she told herself adamantly, I will not be such a slave!

She felt pressure from the other side of the door. Stepping aside, she allowed the door to be pushed inward by Judith, who moved inside speaking, breathlessly, "It is damn cold out there, and getting dark. However, I did pass Pliny on my way."

"Have you been at John's bedside?" Barilla asked solicitously.

"Until he died, yes." Her voice became so matter-of-fact as she went on. "Don't know how they will bury him. The ground so frozen, no one can dig into it. Is it time for supper? I need something hot."

After church the following Sunday, the Reverend Amos Blanchard arrived at the Elston home in his horse-drawn brougham. Also alighting from the coach, besides the minister, were James and Else. Pliny and Barilla, having walked the quarter-mile distance, arrived at much the same time.

Abigail had prepared a hearty beef and vegetable soup that was ready immediately so that the directions for a rehearsal could begin promptly thereafter, being that the minister declared himself to be a very busy man. Exactly what it was that made him so busy could hardly be rational, given that he himself decreed the Sabbath to be a day of rest.

Barilla was relieved that Horace had not put in an appearance. James explained that Horace was unable to be on holiday leave until the following weekend.

After all the instructions, the Reverend Blanchard prepared to leave. Pliny escorted him to the door and asked, "Would it be permissible for me to sing two selections for the service?"

"Well now," he answered in hesitation before putting on his hat, "and what two would those selections be?"

"Because Else is of German heritage, I thought it appropriate to sing 'So Many Stars in Heaven Are Seen' as she comes down the stairs. Then after the vows are completed, to sing 'Loch Lomond' for the Scottish James."

"Good choices," the Reverend said, adding, "quite appropriate, indeed."

Barilla had been watching from the archway between the hall and the parlor. After the Reverend had departed she spoke to Pliny, smiling broadly.

"That was very thoughtful of you. I'm sure James and Else will be delighted."

He came closer to her and spoke quietly, "I want to give them something. My music is all I can think of. Shall we keep it a secret until the time comes?"

"How delightful," she whispered as she glanced to where James and Else were seated on the parlor settee absorbed in conversation. "Come now," she said to Pliny, "let's find out what we can do to help Abigail."

They moved through the parlor and dining room where Barilla noticed salt cellars, pepper mills, and unused silver still on the table. Picking them up, she placed them on a sideboard. Then she proceeded to the kitchen where Abigail washed dishes while Judith dried them.

Pliny had gone to the kitchen ahead of her to seek out William. As she entered she heard Pliny ask William, "Perhaps I could help you on Saturday to gather some evergreens to decorate the parlor and dining room?"

"That is a fine idea," said William. "Could you come to the shop about two o'clock?" He then turned to his wife to ask what further he could do.

Pliny, thus dismissed, came toward Barilla, who had picked up a crumber and gone back to scrape crumbs off the tablecloth.

He sat down in one of the chairs and said, "Rilla, as soon as you finish that, please sit down here."

He had never called her Rilla before. She stared at him with a puzzled expression.

"Your brother calls you Rilla," Pliny said, "so unless you object, I find it comes quite natural to me also."

"No objection. It just came as a surprise. All of my family call me Rilla." She added dryly, "All except Father."

She sat down as he had bid her, clasped her hands together on the tablecloth and fastened her gaze on the crumber lying within reach. She spoke up pensively, "Pliny, I think it best that I do not attend church next Sunday. I will be needed here."

"Yes, of course. I was thinking the same thing. There is something else I wanted to tell you. William Day has bought a new house and is moving his family further out Central Street. He only rents where we are now. The present house, along with several others, is to be torn down because some business establishment is to be built there. The Days have to be out by New Year's Day."

"I see," she said, now looking directly into his eyes. "So, you will be moving with them?"

"Perhaps. Mr. Whittredge lives closer to our shop. That is one reason why I should live with him, because in the future I'll be opening the shop each morning. The two men will decide. I have no choice but to leave it up to them."

"Does Mr. Day have a large family?"

"Just his wife Martha, seven-year-old Sarah, and four-year-old Lucretia."

"And Mr. Whittredge?" she asked.

"That is the dilemma. Alfred Whittredge is a widower. His wife died two years ago. His daughter Nancy, who was his cook and house-keeper, died last Monday. The concern is that he is now alone and I should live with him for that reason. He has a widow lady, Mrs. Mansur, keep house for him. He is over sixty, and he is in charge of the blacksmith work at the shop.

Impulsively, she put her hand over his. "You really do mind not having family members of your own? Much like Else who has no one but us her friends."

He smiled at her. "I like to think that you and your friends, and of course the Elstons, are my friends. Believe me, Rilla, that means a lot to me."

"I'm glad," she said gently. Rising, she picked up the crumber and brush and went toward the kitchen. Abigail, standing in the door-way, stepped aside to allow Barilla to pass.

She thanked Barilla, then speaking casually said, "Now that everything is cleared up in good order, I must think about supper."

Pliny stood up and said, "I should be leaving. The dinner was delicious and the company first rate."

Abigail, smiling graciously, moved closer to Pliny. She placed her hand on his shoulder. "You have become like another member of my family. So we would like to have you stay as long as you wish."

Barilla returned to stand slightly behind Abigail. Her blue eyes twinkled and she grinned widely.

After the supper of applesauce, bread and butter, and tea, the girls cleared the table as Pliny, William, and James stood aside talk-ing. Then Pliny spoke up saying, "I really do have to leave now."

James turned to Pliny. "I'll walk with you as far as Market Street."

"Of course. Glad to have you."

After thanking their hostess, the two men walked through to the hallway. Else and Barilla followed. After the men donned their coats, James bent to kiss Else ever so lightly on her lips. Pliny did the same to Barilla. Then each put on their hats and mittens, and were soon out the door amid a blast of cold air.

Later when Barilla and Else were in bed together and Judith

seemed to be asleep, Barilla spoke quietly to Else. "I noticed that while you and James were seated together in the parlor that he appeared as happy as a lark, but you were sober and pensive?"

"I am overwhelmed by it all," Else said, then in a whisper added, "I'm also scared. Scared of what it is going to be like being in bed with a man."

"I don't know, either. When I was home I asked my mother. She said, 'When you love a man it will all come naturally. There is nothing more I can tell you.' Then I asked my sister and she said the same thing."

Else sighed deeply. "That's just it. I don't love James that way."

"Then why are you marrying him?"

"To be part of a family."

"Oh," Barilla was shocked, "I hope you will be content. Now, let us get some sleep."

She turned over, instinctively recalling the many farewells between herself and Pliny, thinking of the series as a progression of his affection.

On Monday the girls were up at first bell, dressed hastily, and ran down for breakfast as usual as though Sundays were merely an incident.

When they returned after last bell they found letters, one for Barilla from her sister, the other for Judith from Horatio. Barilla set hers aside until after supper. Judith opened hers immediately and read parts of it to the assembled group.

"Horatio has a chance to work in Brookline in the spring. He says that his sister Mary is contented in her work there and the family she works for can use me about the middle of March. Dana has gone to work in the city of Boston getting eighteen dollars a month and his keep. He is to work for a man who builds houses. So I am to stay here to help out with the farm and woodcutting for now. Then he adds, 'If you would like to have me come to Lowell sometime, I could come up with Dana.'"

She refolded the letter as they all had started to eat supper.

While Else and Judith helped Abigail, Barilla went upstairs. By candlelight, she read.

Dec. 10, 1844

Absent Sister,

I seat myself this morning to write a few lines while my washwater is heating, to let you know that my health is good. The reason why I have not written to you is because I have not had time. Father had bad luck and so did Amos. The first of November Father was drafted to Paris (Maine) as jury-man. He had been there a fortnite and calculated to return home the follow-ing week. But on Sunday returning from meeting had got to his boarding place, turning up under the shed, his horse took fright, tacked short, turning the gig over, throwed him out and broke both bones in his left leg. It was some time before he got over his ride home. His leg gains very slow. He can bear no- weight on it. He is very pale, feels poorly and has not been out anywhere since he got home. He wishes you were home. He needs someone to rub his leg oftener than Mother can get time to. Please come home on Father's account. He has been childish about this because he has been sick so long. He says he wants his Barilla and his Byron to come home where they belong.

Amos bought the Richards place. After much cleaning it up, we now have our own house. By the time we got fairly settled Amos twisted his knee out of joint and separated the bones from his knee. His colt had jumped out of the yard. Amos caught hold of the halter and the colt sprang partly be-hind him to get away. Amos sprang to brace himself which brought a sud-den yank upon him to cause the accident. After two weeks now he can hob-ble a little without crutches. You can see why I have found no time to write.

You and your friends remember to be good girls, mind your manners and beware of worthless, miserable chaps. I would not give one good steer or plow-jogger for all the Mass-fops that might stand between here and Lowell. Write as soon as you receive this to let Father know when you calculate to come home.

Your loving sister,
Florena

Barilla folded the letter, slipped it into her trunk, blew out the candle, and sat on a chair before the window. Looking out, she could see nothing but stark limbs of trees vaguely distinct in the dark sky. Any feelings or emotions she had so recently experienced had faded as she felt overwhelming guilt regarding the family back home who need her there.

Memories of past years so flooded her mind that the passage of time had no meaning for her until she heard her roommates coming up the stairs. She sprang up, lit her candle, and began to undress for bed.

As both girls entered they carried candles that they placed in wall sconces.

Judith spoke to Barilla, "That was a nice letter from Horatio. Who was your letter from?"

Barilla sighed audibly, "From home. But I don't want to talk about it now. There is something I want to do. To give both of you."

She knelt to open her trunk and drew out a flat box. Because of the dim light, barely discernible printing read "George F. Tibbets." She sat on the bed and opened the box to reveal a string of gold beads, a pair of pendant earrings, and a ring containing a small, rose-colored stone.

Standing over her, Else and Judith stared in wonder at the shimmering array.

"What in the world have you done?" said Else, while Judith merely stared.

"I bought them out of last October's pay," she said, with some degree of indignation in her voice. She picked up the earrings and handed them to Else.

"When I learned you were going to marry James I wanted to give you something. So these are for you to wear at your wedding."

"My, oh, my," said Else as she bent to kiss Barilla's cheek.

Barilla then picked up the ring and handed to Judith, and said, "I wanted you to have something, too."

Judith slipped it on her finger, stared at it for a few seconds, then sat down on the bed beside Barilla.

Placing an arm across Barilla's shoulder, she said, "This is so sweet of you. Are you sure you want to do this?"

"Very sure."

"The beads?" Judith asked.

"Those I will wear for the wedding. And when I go home, I'll give them to my mother."

She saw that Judith stared at something on the floor near the head of the bed and explained, "That is something else I bought, a Bible for my father."

"But," said Judith, "it has your name imprinted on it."

"That," Barilla said with a smug smile, "is to remind him of who provided it. And now, I am getting into bed." Before she could snuggle under the covers, both girls hugged her as they thanked her profusely.

18

As long as she lived Barilla was going to remember Else's wedding day. To remember the gently falling snow as the three of them hurried home on Saturday. How the descending snowflakes dissipated as they dropped into the warmth of the gas street lamps. At the entrance to the house, to be greeted by a large wreath, tied with a huge red bow, then inside the house, to see the rooms lavishly festooned with evergreen boughs, the deliciously fresh scent as redolent as the forest back in Maine. The odor from the wood fire in the Franklin stove also caused reminiscence, but could not compare to her family's wide, yawning fireplaces with huge logs ablaze.

In the morning the snow had stopped. Outside the frost-etched windows, brilliant sunlight shone on branches covered with velvety ermine which here and there dropped to fall silently below. While still in their bedroom, Else asked Barilla to twist her hair with rag strips which she wore as she came down for breakfast. Shyly, she apologized for the rag-wrapped curls.

William had laughed, "It is well that James cannot see you now."

"Happy is the bride the sun shines on," said Judith as tempered with great excitement, they all ate breakfast.

After clearing away the breakfast things, they shooed Else away upstairs. The table was lengthened by William inserting several leaves. Abigail told them to set it for ten persons, which they proceeded to do using a new, white linen cloth, fine china plates, and newly polished silverware. In the center, William placed a bowl filled with greens, augmented with bright red holly berries.

"Pliny fixed that," said William as he also opened a box of four greens-and-holly-decorated corsages. "Pliny also brought these for you girls and Abigail to wear."

After that, Judith stayed downstairs to help Abigail as Barilla, overwhelmed by Pliny's thoughtfulness, took three of the corsages upstairs. There she helped Else with her copper-colored dress, puffing up the bouffant sleeves, then standing back to admire how the copper color shimmered to tones of honey as Else moved. The full skirt was enhanced by several petticoats beneath it. Then together they worked on her hair, lightly brushing it into strands by curling around the fingers.

"Could we put the corsage on top of my head?" Else asked.

"I'll try," Barilla said as she worked it into the shining blonde hair using a lot of hairpins.

"Because I don't have a mirror, Barilla, you have to tell me how it looks."

"It's beautiful, truly it is. The red and green set in your golden hair makes you look like a fairy princess."

Barilla changed into her blue dress, the one imprinted with tiny white flowers. It had a lower neckline, which showed off the gold beads to better advantage. She adjusted the beads, and asked Else to clasp them.

"I am getting nervous," said Else, "I'll go down and get a drink of water."

"Oh, no, you won't. Our guests might come any minute. No one should see until you make your grand entrance down the stairs. I'll go down and get the drink of water and bring it up here."

On the stairs she met Judith hurrying up to change her dress.

As Barilla's foot touched the hall floor, she heard a knock on the door. Opening it she saw James, Mr. Gordon, and Horace. Immediately behind were the Reverend Blanchard and Pliny.

She stepped back to allow them all entrance, knowing that Pliny would close the door behind him.

In the shuffle of removing overcoats, hats, and mittens, James introduced his father. "Miss Barilla, I'd like to have you meet my father, Andrew Gordon."

She extended her hand. "I am pleased to make your acquaintance."

Abruptly, Horace was beside Andrew, also offering a hand, and said, "It has been a long time, Barilla. I have missed seeing you."

Too stunned to retort and too polite to ignore, she reached hesitantly to touch the proffered hand and immediately withdrew.

Pliny, with natural aplomb, set aside his banjo and moved quickly beside her. He put his arm around her and asked, "How's everything going, my dear?"

She smiled gratefully. "It has been a busy morning, but I believe we are ready." She urged the group to come in and be seated, telling them she needed only to get a drink of water for Else.

In the kitchen she explained to Abigail and William that Else was ready. "Oh my," she added, "Doesn't that turkey smell great."

As she returned through the parlor, the Reverend Blanchard followed her back into the hall.

"How soon before the bride will be coming down the stairs?" he asked.

"About five minutes," she said. "As I remember, you asked me to walk down ahead of her."

He nodded.

As she continued up the stairs, she heard his voice giving orders as to where everyone should stand.

Else drank her water slowly. Barilla noted how pale and disoriented she seemed to be, so she spoke sharply, "Listen here, Else. You are not going to your execution. So let me see a big, happy smile on your face."

Else chuckled, "All right. I'll try."

"You just be thinking of how beautiful you look and how happy you will be making James."

Else sighed, "You are right, dear Barilla, the nearest to the sister I never had."

"Good. Now here we go."

She started slowly, gracefully, down the stairs, one step at a time. In the distance below, Pliny had watched for her. He began to play and sing,

"Many stars at night are peeping

Through the heaven's azure screen"

Barilla flashed him her heartiest smile, as he brought the song to an end,

"Just as many are the moments,

I am dreaming, dear of you"

By that time, Else had reached the hall floor. Tears had formed in her eyes. Tears of joy. She smiled broadly at Pliny.

Gathering her dignity, she advanced to stand at James's left. The smile on her face and the happiness shining in her eyes transcended any beautiful picture Barilla had ever seen. James's expression was also a joy to behold.

Barilla took her place to stand at Else's left. The others, Judith, Mr. Gordon, Pliny, and the Elstons stood behind. Horace was at James's right, so it was conveniently unnecessary for Barilla to see him or be seen by him.

The smell of baked turkey wafted out from the kitchen. Barilla resolved to let nothing mar this happy, festive occasion. She concentrated on the reverend, how tall he was, his face, extraordinarily long because of balding hair, yet the sides of his head, thick with white hair, which blended into an abundant mustache and beard. Evidence that he enjoyed what he was doing came through his light blue eyes. He seemed so delighted to be the agent joining two loving persons in holy matrimony. He finished, saying, "I now pronounce you man and wife. James, you may kiss your bride."

Which James did with the greatest of pleasure.

Immediately, Pliny played and sang in lively rhythm the traditional Scottish tune "Loch Lomond."

Then everyone was kissing and hugging Else, and shaking hands with James. Andrew Gordon stood spellbound, with tears in his eyes, until Pliny finished and had set aside his banjo.

"Young man, that brought memories into the heart of this old man." He grasped one of Pliny's hands in both of his. "I thank ye, most heartily. By yon bonnie banks, eh, that does take me back.

Thank ye, thank ye."

He backed away and turned to kiss his new daughter-in-law, who had broken away from her well-wishers to approach the banjo player.

"Oh, Pliny, what a surprise for me. To hear your clear voice singing one of the melodies of my childhood," she said, as she began to sing, "So viel Stern an Himmel stehen an dem blauen Himmels zelt. I cannot recall all of it in German, but I can clearly see again my father singing that to me at bedtime. Thank you so very much."

Barilla stood behind, observing the two who were expressing their gratitude to Pliny. She felt a glow of pleasure that this man, who gladly shared his beautiful singing voice, was specifically her friend.

"It was so thoughtful of you," she said. "The music, the corsages, and the greenery everywhere."

"My pleasure, Rilla." As he spoke, Judith announced that everyone should be seated for dinner. Thus, Pliny and Barilla were furthest from the group. He took her arm and caused her to halt under mistletoe he had placed there when he and William did the decorating.

"Look above you," He pointed to the green leaves and waxy white berries. "Do you know what that is?"

"No. I don't recall ever seeing any like it before."

"That is mistletoe," Pliny said.

"Oh, isn't that a growth which adheres to oak trees?"

"I suppose so, but do you know the significance of why it is tacked up onto an archway?"

"No," she said, still looking upward.

He swept her into his arms and kissed her lips, not gently, but forcefully, one hand holding her head to press their lips more closely, passionately together. She was vaguely aware of laughing voices from those being seated at the nearby table, but more deeply aware of her own body and what strange reaction caused her arms to encircle Pliny's back, to feel the firm cloth of his frock coat.

When he released her, it took only an instant for her to quietly respond in a reproachful tone, "You should not have done that, in front of all these people."

The expression on his face was not at all apologetic. He pointed to the mistletoe. "That is the reason a man has a perfect right to kiss any lady standing beneath it."

Chagrin came over her, causing a rosy flush to creep into her cheeks. She walked to the table, indicating to Pliny that she would sit at William's right, where William was setting down a large platter of turkey.

"Pliny," she said, "you are to sit here on my right."

By prearrangement, Abigail graced the far end of the table next to the kitchen, with Judith on her right, after both of them had brought in mashed potatoes, boiled onions, gravy, and baked squash. Horace sat at Abigail's left, which placed him on the same side as Barilla. Thus, Else, James, and Andrew Gordon were directly across from Barilla and Pliny.

William picked up a decanter of rosé wine from which he filled the glasses set before him. Barilla and Else, as previously instructed, passed the filled glasses down the line.

Horace, holding his glass, stood up. "It is that time for me to propose a toast to my friend James and his lovely Else. I have known James since we were both attending engineering classes in Cambridge until we both ran out of money So he brought me up to work in Lowell, where I earned enough to return to school. He did not go back. He stayed here, mostly, I think. to court the lovely Else. I observed it was a losing venture, until, to my surprise, she said 'yes' only a few months ago. So, let us all drink to the end of the longest courtship I have ever known."

Horace sat down amid laughter and chiding remarks to an embarrassed Else.

Everyone agreed it had been a great dinner, completed with rum cake and coffee. Barilla and Judith helped William and Abigail clear the table. Then the Reverend Blanchard stood up, thanked his hosts, and announced that he had to leave.

Andrew Gordon turned to his son saying, "It is also the time for me to drive you and the new Mrs. Gordon down to the Merrimack House.

Else repeated the "Mrs. Gordon" in a surprised, but hushed voice.

Barilla realized that those were the first words she had spoken since thanking Pliny for the German music. She seemed so full of herself, so filled with delight, and wonder, and yes, even happiness.

After everyone except Pliny had left, he led Barilla to sit beside him on a parlor settee. The remaining members of the house were in the kitchen.

Barilla looked down to study her hands. Without looking up she said, "You should not have kissed me like that."

"If you expect me to say I'm sorry, I won't." Pliny said.

"What I mean is, that I wanted us to be just friends."

"Barilla, look at me."

She raised her face. Only discomfort showed in her eyes.

At a momentary loss for the right words, Pliny touched a finger to the gold beads. "I never saw you wear jewelry before."

"I bought them for my mother. That is, when I go home to give them to her."

"Just friends, you said. I will always be your friend. Surely you know that."

She nodded.

"Barilla, I don't understand you. You are not timid nor afraid of closeness to men, as I surmise was your relationship to that one," He tilted his head toward where the others and Horace had left, "Just because he gave you naught but a broken heart, you should not believe all men are so callous. If you would allow it, I would give you pearls or rubies, gold or silver, besides my undying devotion. Barilla, what I am trying to say is, I love you."

She cast her eyes downward because her heart had begun to beat wildly.

Pliny reached for her hand to hold it tightly, feeling the rapid beat of her pulse, and spoke gently, "Is it impossible for you to love me in return?"

She raised her eyes to his once more. "Even if I did return your affection, I have to consider my family at home. My sister wrote that they wish me to return to help out."

"Return to Maine! In this weather? That is unreasonable. Barilla, your desire to help is admirable, but don't you have dreams of your own for your future?"

"Oh, I once dreamed of going West. I even began saving money toward leaving in the spring."

Pliny scoffed at what he considered to be a monumental adventure against devastating odds. He added, "It is wise to give that up until the day when there are roads and some forms of civilization." He sensed her discomfort. So, not wishing to disturb her further he stood up abruptly and said, "I'll say good evening now."

She followed him to the coat tree in the hall.

Putting on his overcoat, he reached into its pocket and pulled out a three-inch square box, handed it to her, and said, "Because I won't see you on Christmas day, I bought you a little gift."

In an instant he had donned his hat and mittens, picked up his banjo case, and moved swiftly outside.

Barilla closed the door tightly against the penetratingly cold draft. She felt a rigidity in her arms and legs as though they had turned to stone, which had little to do with the sudden draft of cold air.

Methodically, she moved away from the door, the small box enclosed in her hand. She walked slowly back to sit on the settee in the parlor. She slipped the red ribbon off the box and opened it just as Judith came toward her.

"What have you got there?" Judith asked.

Barilla did not answer as she stared at the contents of the box. It was a beautiful cameo, a lady's ivory-colored profile, enhanced by a small diamond set in a tiny silver necklace upon the lady's bodice, all of this against a caramel-colored background. The whole was entirely encased by filigree silver.

She lifted it out to hold it up by a chain that could be worn about the neck, and handed it to Judith.

"Oh, my goodness." said Judith admiringly. "It's beautiful. Did Pliny give it to you?"

Barilla burst into tears as she nodded, then slumped forward, sobbing bitterly.

"I don't see what there is to cry about. He is a splendid fellow."

"That's just it," Barilla said. "He told me he loved me, and I don't want to, I don't want to love him."

"Well now, you do have quite a dilemma. Frankly speaking, I think you are acting stupidly. Tell me, have you ever known a nicer person than Pliny?"

"No," she stammered weakly.

Judith handed Barilla a handkerchief. Dry your eyes and come to your senses about this."

As Judith spoke, she drew the cameo's chain over Barilla's head, stood back to admire it, and said, "Now, you march out to show it to William and Abigail."

"Oh, no, I couldn't."

"Couldn't! That doesn't sound like the Barilla I have come to know."

In spite of herself, Barilla laughed. She stood up.

"I'll tell you something else," Judith said with deep amusement. "Horace observed Pliny kissing you, just before you both came in to dinner. How I wish you could have seen his face." Then she grabbed Barilla's hand and led her with a definite intensity out into the kitchen.

On Monday morning, Barilla had been at her loom no longer than ten minutes when she felt a tap on her left shoulder. The sound of the voice yelling in her ear could be no other than the overseer, Mr. Lord.

He pointed to Else's loom demanding, "Where's that one?"

She hollered back, "Out until Thursday."

"You take over," were his last words. She knew and he knew that further conversation was futile until at least the noon break. He caught her then at the head of the stairs.

She explained about Else's marriage and that Else had cleared it with the agent, Mr. Avery, that she would not be back until the day after Christmas. Judith waited for her outside. Barilla was not in a good mood as she said, "That bully, Lord, wouldn't even say Else's name when he asked why she didn't come to work."

Judith said nothing. She knew that dealing with an overseer was as useless as pounding her fists against a brick wall.

19

Christmas came on Wednesday. That evening, James and Else came to the Elston's to pick up the rest of Else's belongings. Judith busied herself helping Abigail in the kitchen. James waited in the still-festooned parlor while Barilla went upstairs to help Else pack her trunk.

"So," Barilla asked impatiently, "how is married life?"

"It is fine," she said quietly. "I had been concerned about the union with James. But it was dark and he was so gentle and understanding, I found myself responding to his touch and…" she added in a whisper, "actually enjoying our…union. And I do love him very much."

To this enlightening information, Barilla responded by only saying, "Oh."

She helped Else carry the trunk downstairs. After hugging her and seeing both of them to the door, Barilla said, "I'll see you in the mill tomorrow." When the newlyweds were gone, she felt a strange emptiness, this departing of a true friend.

Later, when Barilla and Judith were in their beds, Judith said, "Else certainly looked happy. She will now have what she wanted, a family of her own."

"She has more than just that," said Barilla. "She loves James and is pleased with what happens between married people."

It was Judith's turn to say, "Oh."

Barilla's thoughts kept her from sleep for a long time, knowing that first of all, on Sunday, she had to thank Pliny for his gift. Any inclination of refusing to accept it would be rude. Her thoughts vacillated to Else's explanation of "union." She thought of the farm animals, of how in every instance, the male seemed to attack the female. Of how, if the males were so forceful and driven to do it, there certainly seemed to be no pleasure for the females. Then again, there was Pliny. He loved her and wanted her and he was hurt, as she well recalled being hurt by Horace last July.

As she dressed for church on Sunday, she knew she must attend the Congregational Church and make some decision with Pliny. However, Pliny was not in church. She looked everywhere for him, even asking James and Else if they had seen him.

Returning to the Elstons, a dejected Barilla walked slowly up the porch steps and into the house. Judith, having gone to Saint Anne's had returned ahead of her. She said nothing as Barilla entered and took off her cape and mittens. Then she said, "You're just in time for dinner, Rilla. Abigail made turkey pie, and it smells delicious."

Not wanting to admit to her feeling of desolation, she answered Judith cheerfully and followed her into the dining room, where Judith hastily set a place for her.

Abigail, with some surprise in her voice, asked, "Where is Pliny? He has spent every Sunday with you since your brother brought him here."

Barilla answered in a calm voice, "Oh, he is too busy helping the Day family move. They all have to be out of the present house by the first of January."

The explanation may have satisfied Abigail, but Judith was not so easily taken in by it.

After supper, Judith asked her to play checkers. She asked no questions, just kept up a cheerful conversation. which she hoped kept Barilla's mind out of the doldrums.

Barilla went through her work at the mill for an entire week, usually being too busy to think.

By Friday, Else, having noticed an unusual seriousness in her friend, asked as they descended the mill stairs, "Are you all right? You seem a bit dispirited."

"I am all right. It's the acrid smell from the oil lamps and the cold." She rubbed her fingers together. "It seems as though my fingers won't even move, then when I must, they do manage to work. I wish there was some fire to heat this damnable place."

"Hah, the only fire you'll get is heated reprimand from mouse-faced Lord."

That brought a smile to Barilla's face. Just then, Judith joined them. The three hastened out to Central Street and parted, Else going to the left, the other two hurrying off to the right.

On Saturday, the fourth of January, Judith asked Barilla to go shopping with her. She needed some warm underwear. "All of mine is too patched up and too thin for warmth."

"All right," Barilla said, "I need some, too."

During the cold, dark evenings, the last bell on Saturdays came at six. Thus, the two girls set off on Central Street toward Merrimack Street. Even in the dim light from the gas lamps, Barilla observed that no light shone from the Day house. Of course not, she thought, they have already moved.

They made their purchases and returned home to a late supper.

As usual of late, Barilla was not herself. To forestall any questions or concerns, she excused herself by informing the others that she was too tired and too chilled for anything but going upstairs to cuddle under several warm quilts.

However, much later, when Judith came up to bed, she found Barilla seated at her trunk, wrapped in quilts, pen in hand, scribbling away diligently by candlelight.

"Writing a letter, or another poem?" Judith asked.

"A poem. It is the only way to release tormenting thoughts."

"I doubt that you are any more tormented than Pliny. If I were you, I would go to him. Go tell *him* your thoughts, not some piece of paper."

"I intend to, tomorrow. That is, if he comes to church."

Judith undressed and climbed into bed.

Barilla reread what she had written.

I could never leave this place and go,
To the land of the far, far west.

I never could forget, oh no,
The one I here love best.
Though time should lend wings to me,
And home to Maine I'd go once more,
Still on my memory you would be,
Engraved fondly forevermore.
Thou, thou rein'st in this bosum,
There, there hast thou thy throne,
Thou dost not know how I love thee.
Yes, ah yes, I am fondly thine own.
My thoughts so tender and true love,
As thou said. thou did'st love me.
As God is my witness from heav'n above
I swear, dear Pliny, I truly love thee.

20

On Sunday morning, Barilla awoke as automatically as if the mill bells had rung. Excitement filled her, at first the thrill of seeing Pliny at church, then the sobering possibility of not. I miss him so much, she thought. I want him. Want to be with him. Want his arms around me. Want him to kiss me. I do love him. Sobs caught in her throat Her lower jaw quivered as she hoped she had not hurt him so much that he chose to avoid her.

She lay still, waiting for the dawn. It gave her time for daydreaming. She saw herself running into his waiting arms. But no, one cannot do that in church. That would have to wait until there was more privacy. Where would that be? Not in a restaurant, surely. Perhaps back here, her temporary home. Oh, would daylight never come.

Distantly, she heard sounds from below. The shaking of grates from the parlor stove. William was up, rustling up the fires.

She arose, wondering why it was still dark. Looking out, she saw only a dull gray sky, which should have shown at least a layer of light beyond the trees.

In the gloom she dressed, putting on the blue dress she had worn for Else's wedding. Then she slipped the cameo's chain over her head and held the cameo fondly in her hand.

Despite the fact that she tried to keep her movements quiet, Judith stirred, yawned, and spoke out sleepily, "Good Lord, what are you doing up so early? Don't you know it is Sunday?"

"Yes, I know, but William is up stoking the fires. If you look out of the window you will see no sunshine. It will probably be a dull, cloudy day." She smiled happily, "But I don't care. In a few hours I will see Pliny again."

She lit a candle, because she knew that descending the stairway without light would be dangerous. She could not allow anything unforeseen ruin her day.

Helping Abigail with the preparation of breakfast, she felt giddy and lightheaded. Because of her resolve, her nerves were no longer as taut as banjo strings.

"You are chipper enough this morning, Barilla," Abigail said. "I'm afraid I don't feel the same. It is so gray outside. I think it will snow, a lot of snow."

To herself, Barilla thought, Who cares? Let it snow.

A sleepy Judith appeared, stifled a yawn, and sat down, then yawned again as Barilla poured coffee. Inhaling the odor of bacon and eggs, she instantly came to life. Between mouthfuls, she said, "Abigail, you are sure one great cook." To Barilla she said, "Miss Smiley-puss, please pass me some toast."

Barilla retorted, "What's the matter with your boardinghouse reach?"

"This is no ordinary boardinghouse. If the mill boardinghouses had an Abigail instead of the Mrs. Merriams, and that last biddy we had before we came here, life would be a lot more pleasant."

Abigail laughed in appreciation, and William looked at his wife with a proud twinkle in his eyes.

The bantering mood sustained them all until it was time to leave for church. William had made sturdy new boots for both girls as Christmas presents, so he admonished them that because of threatening weather, they had better wear them.

Barilla's mother had sent her a knitted wool bonnet with matching mittens, both very near the color of her blue shawl. She felt pretty, she felt alive, and she felt warm.

The girls left together.

"I suppose," said Judith, "you are going to Pliny's church?"

"Of course, and you to Saint Anne's."

"It is best that I go to Saint Anne's. I am surprised you have not been reported as being remiss in your attendance there."

"It was reported to Agent Avery. But I was excused by explaining that I had faithfully attended the Congregational. I even had to get a note from Reverend Blanchard saying so'"

On Merrimack Street, Judith caught sight of a couple of other friends, so before she broke away from Barilla, she whispered, "Best of luck."

Barilla arrived early at her destination to scan the congregation. No Pliny. She stood outside on the steps. Several people passed inside. Soon, James and Else appeared. They greeted Barilla as they entered.

Else turned to ask, "You're not going to stand out here, are you? Come inside with us."

Barilla followed meekly. Seated beside Else, she felt apprehensive. It was time for Reverend Blanchard to appear. Still no Pliny. The service began, Tears threatened, then flowed unrestrained down her cheeks. She used a finger to wipe them away. When that did not suffice, she drew out her handkerchief.

Else noticed, so she reached out her hand in a gesture of comfort. "Rilla," she whispered, "take a deep breath."

Despite being trapped there until the service was over, she became more relaxed, concentrating on exactly what she should do next. In her mind she went over the explanation Pliny had given her about his moving. The only clue, she decided, was to go further out Central Street to where the Days had moved.

As soon as the benediction finished, she arose and moved swiftly down the aisle. A perturbed Else followed as close as she was able because the aisle soon became congested. Outside, gusts of wind swirled violently against their skirts as Else caught up with Barilla. Else grabbed her friend's shoulder. Harshly, she asked, "Don't tell me you and Pliny had a falling out?"

Barilla cast her gaze downward as people, aware of the dark, threatening sky, hastened to walk around them.

"Yes," she answered. "It was my fault. And now I want to go to him so I am in a hurry."

"You can see that there is a storm brewing, so you be careful."

"I will. I am dressed warm. I'll see you tomorrow."

James came up and Else accepted his arm. They hurried away.

Barilla cut across and hastened down Market Street. The snow started before she reached Central, not gentle flakes, but harsh and stinging, like dozens of needles pricking her face Taking long strides, she walked boldly onward, keeping to the right side. After passing the Elston house on the opposite side, she began searching out the street signs that branched off Central. Middlesex, Appleton, Curtis, Union. At each one, her eyes were stung by the pelting onslaught. The rapidly swirling snow began piling up, to drift everywhere. She kept doggedly onward, musing that she must have gone a mile or more. Finally she came to Centre. She crossed Central to a white house. As she carefully climbed the steps, which were indistinct and slippery, she saw the large brass nameplate engraved William L. Day.

She twisted the barred bell on the center of the door, causing it to ring harshly.

Soon, Mr. Day opened the door, trying for the moment to place her. "Oh, Miss Taylor, isn't it? Come in."

Once inside, with the door hastily closed behind, she heard distant laughter of children, and the voice of Mrs. Day asking as she came along the entrance hall, "Who is it, William, out in this weather?"

"I am Barilla Taylor, Ma'am, and I have come to see Pliny."

"You dear girl," said Martha Day, "he is not with us. He now lives with Mister Whittredge."

She turned to Mr. Day and asked, "Where would I find Mister Whittredge's house?"

"It's on Appleton Street," he said.

"I know where that is. I passed it a while back," she said.

"His house is up on the left, the fifth one from the corner. The nameplate is like ours, but engraved Alfred W. Whittredge. But won't you stay long enough to get warmed up? We are about to eat dinner. Will you join us?"

"Thank you, sir. I am too anxious to find Pliny."

She turned and he held the door open for her. Before closing it, he called out, "Be careful on the steps and along the street."

She crossed over again to make her way back to Appleton. She met no one, nor did any carriages pass by. Had she not had a good sense of direction, she would easily have become lost amid the great whiteout. Even the wooden street signs were partially covered with icy snow. Trudging slowly along, in what seemed an eternity, she finally found Appleton.

Groping along uphill, she counted houses. Ah, the fifth. Making slow progress up the steps, she brushed off the brass nameplate enough to discern WHITTREDGE. She saw no bell, so she banged forcefully, repeatedly, on the door.

Finally the door opened about a foot. A whiskered gentleman peered out, "And who be you? A coming out in this storm?"

"I am Barilla Taylor, sir, and I have come to see Pliny Tidd."

"Well, well, now. Do not stand out there." He opened the door to admit her, adding, "You did not pick a good day to come calling."

"I know that, Mr. Whittredge," she said in a rush of words, as she removed her mittens and untied her wet bonnet. "But it is very important to me to see Pliny."

The kindly, whiskered man helped remove her cape and then hung everything on a nearby coat tree.

"My boots are wet, too," she said. "Perhaps I should remove them."

"Oh yes, of course." He indicated a nearby chair for her to sit. She noticed that he spoke in a kindly manner as he added, "I'm afraid nothing can be done about your skirt."

She spent a few moments brushing off the icy patches. Then in her stocking feet, stood tall once more.

Alfred Whittredge, who was not much taller than she, smiled broadly. His twinkling blue eyes showed a deep measure of anxiety.

"Now miss, you just go along through that door." He pointed to an opposite wall. "You will find him in there."

Sing Me a Song

"Yes, sir. I can hear his banjo being played."

The entryway was cold. She opened the door quietly to enter a warm, cozy parlor. Pliny sat in a chair with his back to her. The words he sang, to music completely unfamiliar, caused her to stand quietly and listen.

"Her hair is brown, her eyes are blue.

Her face is fair, her word is true.

The love is deep, from me to her.

No love has she, with me to share."

He stopped to lean towards a table where he wrote something on a paper. Setting the pencil down, he went on plunking out notes, and continued singing,

"They call her Rilla, a pretty name.

Refusing me, has caused much pain."

When he turned again to write on the paper, she circled noise-lessly around to stand a few yards in front of him.

Sensing a presence, he looked up, and his sad eyes flamed with an intensity of disbelief. Awestruck, his jaw dropped.

Barilla knew her cheeks were red from the cold, but they suddenly felt inflamed. Her hands, clasped nervously together, tightened their grip.

Pliny managed to utter, "Barilla!" in a hushed, breathless sound. He quickly set aside his banjo to stand tall. His copper-colored hair was an unmanageable mass of curls. He did not move, merely stared.

"It is really you. Not my imagination?" he said.

"Pliny," she said, placing her thumb and finger up to her quivering chin as words spilled out in a heartwrenching disclosure. "I am sorry I caused you pain. I have also felt pain. The pain of wanting you, wanting your arms around me, wanting you to kiss me the way you did under the mistletoe."

Instantly, he rushed to enfold her in his arms. She lifted her face to his and he kissed her long and ardently. She was aware of the crackling of a fire and of sleet hitting against windows. Then she was too engulfed in emotion to be aware of anything but Pliny's pent up

PLINY TIDD'S SONG FOR BARILLA

WORDS AND MUSIC BY V. C. TAYLOR

Her hair is brown, her eyes are blue, Her face is fair, her word is true. Known as ____ Ril-la; a pret-ty name. To win her heart- that is my aim. The love is deep from me to her. No love with me, has she to share. No o-ther wish, no o-ther gain can re-lieve my heart its ach-ing pain.

hunger and desire, which she felt also penetrating, not only in the arms she held around him, but in her own body.

When he released her lips, he kissed her cheeks, her brow, and hugged her head gently into the curve of his chin and neck.

She managed to whisper, "I do love you, Pliny. It has been awful, my missing you so much."

Thinking rationally, Pliny asked, "My dearest Rilla, how did you find me? In this storm, that is quite remarkable."

"When you were not in church, I recalled your telling me where Mister Day would live."

"Good Lord! Did you go way out there?"

"Yes. I felt that no matter how, I had to find you today."

"You dear, dear girl. I wish I had known."

Now, she, too, began to think more rationally. In a bold, spirited voice, she answered, "You should have come to church."

"I did not feel like churchgoing, knowing you did not return my love."

She pulled her head back to look into his eyes. In both her expression and words, she entreated, "I am ever so sorry. Please, please forgive me."

He kissed her again, a kiss that was shortened by the entrance of Alfred Whittredge.

"Excuse me, Pliny, but since we have long since eaten dinner, Elizabeth and I were wondering if the young lady has had her dinner?"

"Have you?" Pliny said as he drew away from her.

She shook her head and spoke demurely, "No."

"Well, then," said Alfred Whittredge in a fatherly manner, "you just come along and have something to eat."

She followed her host through a dining room darkened by drapes, drawn against the fury of the storm. Pliny followed close behind.

As they entered the kitchen, he clasped her left hand. At the stove, a buxom lady, who wore a lacy, white cap, stirred a pot of gravy. On protruding rods to the right of the stove hung Barilla's cape, bonnet, and mittens. Placed on the floor beneath were her boots.

Alfred introduced Barilla to Elizebeth Mansur. The woman smiled broadly, wiped her hands on her apron, and came forward to shake hands with the newcomer.

"Now, miss, you jes' go back into the dining room and set down. I'll have a plate of victuals ready in an instant." To Pliny, she ordered, "You light candles in there and set some silver for your young lady to eat with."

After following orders, Pliny seated Barilla, then sat down directly opposite, to reach across the table, grasping both her hands.

Alfred Whittredge carried in a bottle of red wine and a tray of four glasses to the table where he set them down and then seated himself beside Barilla.

"A little something by way of celebration." He spoke heartily, addressing Barilla. "Pliny here has been as dull and mad as a wet hen since he moved in here. Now look at him, smiling like a chessy-cat. And it's all your doing, miss."

He proceeded to fill the four glasses with wine, just as Mrs. Mansur placed before Barilla a plate filled with a slab of roast pork, carrots, and mashed potatoes, all covered with steaming, brown gravy. Elizebeth then sat down beside Pliny, directly opposite Mr. Whittredge.

He then passed the filled wine glasses all around and lifted his high.

"To Miss Barilla, who has brought the happy gleam of life back into our Pliny's face."

With some delicacy, Barilla sipped her wine. Although the others were overly jubilated, she felt embarrassed. For the first time since she had left the church, she realized she was indeed hungry. She ate voraciously, now and then glancing up to where Pliny's eyes would catch hers. Seeing in them, and in the warm smile around his lips, such an intensity that, because of the hypnotic attraction, had the others not been there she would have stopped eating to be again enfolded within his embrace. However, she continued eating, occasionally sipping her wine.

Mrs. Mansur, unable to let the subject die down, interjected her own interpretation of lover's quarrels.

"Ah yes," she said in a tone of nostalgia, "Remember, Alfred, when you and I were young, the foolishness of lover's quarrels?"

Alfred nodded. A huge smile of amusement spread across his face. "Oh my, yes. Silly business that. But," he added seriously, "it is something that has to happen so that we appreciate love even more."

A tall clock in the corner struck three. After the third gong, Pliny spoke up. "As soon as you finish your dinner, Rilla, I have to get you back to the Elstons. No doubt they are frantic with worry as to what has happened to you."

She nodded. A guilty feeling washed over her, that of causing Abigail and William to be concerned.

Back in the kitchen, she pulled on her boots. Pliny stooped to tie them up, then helped her don her cape. She thanked Mrs. Mansur profusely for so thoughtfully drying everything.

The young couple proceeded to the door, where Barilla turned to shake Mr. Whittredge's hand, proffering more thanks for the hospitality.

With a protective arm across her shoulder, Pliny guided Barilla against the stormy onslaught as they made their way about a third of a mile back to the Elstons.

Abigail had heard the front door shut, and ran eagerly into the entrance hall.

"Thank God.'" she burst out. "Thank God you are both all right." Suddenly her tone changed to one of reprimand, "What were you thinking of to not come back here before the weather got so bad?"

"That," said Pliny, "is a long story."

Barilla said, "A long story which I will explain some other time. Right now we could both use a cup of hot tea."

Both William and Abigail urged Pliny to spend the night. Because Pliny had told Alfred he might do so, there was no concern there. Abigail brought quilts and a pillow for him to sleep on the parlor floor.

Later that night, in her own bed, Barilla reflected alternately between the day's events to the secure feeling that she and Pliny were united in their love for one another.

She had been intrigued by Mrs. Mansur's open friendliness with Mr. Whittredge. Hadn't Pliny told her that the woman was the cook and housekeeper?

Pliny had laughed when she asked. "Cook and housekeeper, yes. But I have come to understand that one of these days those two, both having lost their mates, will marry each other."

Cuddling into a fetal position, her feet placed cozily against the heated soapstone, she hugged the quilts closely around her, overwhelmingly thrilled with the thought of Pliny sleeping downstairs in the same house as she.

At the sound of the morning bell, she hastened to dress, thinking perchance to see him before going to work. However, while William stoked the parlor stove, he told her that Pliny had already left, He had found it difficult to sleep in a heated room, although the stove had cooled somewhat by morning. The sound of the horse-drawn rollers, packing the snow on the street, had alerted him. He explained that he must hasten homeward in order to clear the steps and path for Mr. Whittredge, then hasten to do the same at their shop.

The mill bells for closing the entrance gates that morning were delayed ten minutes. Yet, because the storm abated during the night, everyone, it seemed, arrived on time.

Barilla did not see Pliny again until the following Sunday when he stopped by to escort her to his church. Thus the pattern became set for the months to come. Even though she was happily in love, nagging guilt about her family's needs plagued her. So when she received her January pay of ten dollars and seventy-three cents, she sent a bank draft of ten dollars home to Maine. She wrote;

Sunday, February 3, 1845

Distant Parents,
It is with pleasure that I seat myself at the Elstons' dinner table to send you my thought along with my pay for January. My health was first-rate until the middle of January when I came down with a cold after being out in a blizzard. It was the sniffily, sore throat, coughing type of cold, which I soon got over, but the cough lingers on. It is worse at night.
We have to report for work, even if we are ill. We dare not complain. The

impure air, polluted by lint from the cotton and smoke from oil lamps, is enough to make even the heartiest of persons choke into coughing spells. And the cold! The only difference between temperatures inside and outside is that inside, there is no wind. There may be some heat from the lamps and the whirring belts and pulleys. Most of us have to manage two looms, and some manage three. So far I have only two and can move around and stamp my feet to gain better circulation.

It would pleasure me a great deal if Mother would knit me a wool undervest to keep my chest and back warm.

We notice an increase of Irish girls taking over some looms. But they mostly work in the carding and spinning rooms. The Irish are treated coldly by many, but I cannot find fault, nor do the overseers, for there has lately been many of our native-born quitting.

I hope that Father is better. Tell Florena that I hope Amos is better, too.

From your absent daughter,

Barilla Adeline Taylor

Pliny often spoke of marriage, but she countered by telling him it would be nicer to wait until spring. However, during February and March Barilla's hacking cough grew worse. Both Judith and Abigail voiced their concern, urging her to see a doctor. At each instance she explained that once spring came, she would be better. An answer to her last letter home came from Florena.

Sunday, March 23, 1845

Absent Sister,

It being the Sabbath, I take time to write you of our doings here. To be truthful, there is not much doing. The snow is nearly up to the eaves of our house. There has not been any thawing of it.

Father is still hobbling about and complaining constantly. Amos is better. He chops wood and carries it in now. He also helps chop wood down home, along with Morval.

We received a letter from Emily telling about her work and how sister Lovesta has adjusted readily. Mother and Father Austin miss them mightily.

We are concerned about your coughing, as are others. Emily received a letter from Judith Fox telling her that you were not well. She told us she was writing to Judith proposing that you come to work in Biddeford, for the work is not so hard there. The hours are the same. Said she would be overjoyed to have you there and certain she can get you a chance. The train stops in Biddeford, so it would not be difficult.

Emily also stated that she felt blessed indeed to have made the acquaintance of a fine Maine gentleman, name of William Morse, who has asked her to marry him. But, of course she has not known him long enough to make a sensible judgment.

Do write to Emily whether or not you calculate to leave Lowell. But as always, you will do as you're a mind to. For now, good evening. Please answer as soon as you get this.

From sister,

Florena Austin

Barilla did not receive the letter until the first Saturday in April. She mused about Florena's comments, not as criticism, but as plain facts of the matter. Of course she would do as she was a mind to. That meant staying in Lowell, near Pliny. She could also excuse Judith's concern. After all, because of their close friendship, she might have done the same under the circumstances.

However, it was now spring. The dirty snow had dissipated in several warm, violent rainstorms during the past week.

Sunday, the sixth of April, dawned clear, with beaming sunshine. Barilla felt better. At least she decided that she felt better.

When Pliny called for her, as she smelled the warm air she greeted him cheerfully, "What a beautiful day."

"It is certainly that, my sweetheart."

She tucked her hand into the crook of his arm. As they walked sedately north on Central, she felt deep pride in his calling her sweetheart. She felt that life was really great.

Horse-drawn carriages and throngs of people, mill girls, families, were all heading for one church or another.

"Church bells," she said, "are more pleasant sounding than mill bells."

Pliny gave her arm a squeeze, then spoke hopefully, "I hope you are in the mood for naming a wedding date."

"Yes," she smiled up at him. "I believe I am. How about June?"

"June?" He grinned widely in surprise.

"Isn't June all right?" she asked.

"Of course, you precious girl. June is fine."

"June twenty-ninth. It is a Sunday, and my birthday. I will be seventeen."

They had reached the steps of the church. Pliny's broad smile of delight was all the assurance she needed.

As April turned to May, Barilla's cough and breathless wheezing became apparent to more than Judith and the Elstons. Pliny was also deeply concerned. One Sunday, the last of May, as they walked hand in hand along the bank of the Merrimack Canal, where the water moved silently along, he stopped to ask, "Have you consulted a doctor about that cough?"

Secretly she hoped he could not feel her trembling, trying desperately not to cough. "No," she said, "because I think I am overcoming it."

"No, you're not," he responded angrily. He turned to face her, "It is getting worse. I want you to see a doctor. How about that Silas Doane? How about right now?"

"Doctors don't want to be bothered on Sundays."

"Because you work twelve-hour days, what other time can they see you?"

She had to admit he had a point. So he took her arm, turned her around, and they walked in silence down Merrimack Street to the doctor's house.

Doctor Silas Doane received the young couple with amiable warmth, being thankful they had not come during his dinner or his afternoon nap. He told Pliny to wait in the parlor, then seated Barilla in a chair, instructing her to unbutton her dress and loosen it off down to her waist.

Overcome with embarrassment, Barilla paled. She had never had a doctor look at her half undressed. Neither had her mother or sister. She knew that for birthing, there had been a midwife. Inwardly, she wished she were not in this ridiculous position.

The doctor thumped her back as he asked questions.

"Yes," she said. "I did have a severe cold in January."

He came around and laid a hand on her chest. "Breathe deep and release your breath quickly, several times."

She obeyed until he said, "That's enough. Tell me, in which mill are you employed?"

"The Hamilton."

"Weave room, I imagine?"

"Yes, why?"

"If this was merely bronchitis it would have cleared up in a few days. But prolonged fits of coughing come because your lungs have filled up with cotton dust. I'll give you some pennyroyal to ease your throat, and some camphor ice to rub on your chest and back."

He asked her name and where she boarded as he leaned over a desk to write out a bill, which he handed to her along with the medications.

"You can pay this when you get your next pay. Now, you may cover up," he said.

He left the room, closing the door behind him. She could barely hear as he asked Pliny about his place of business, and what was his intention toward the young lady. Then in a louder voice there was no mistaking a vehement tirade.

"These young women have no business working here in mills under such unhealthy conditions. They should be home on their family farms. Should be married and having babies. A woman's place is to cook and keep house for her man, and see to his comfort in the marriage bed. That's what those Irish women do. They breed like rabbits every year a baby. The Papist priest sees to that. This country will be overrun with those brats while our Yankee women kill themselves in cotton mills until they are unfit, or dead."

The doctor paused, no doubt to catch his breath. Barilla had not dared to open the door until his voice became more subdued.

The doctor went on to explain, "I'll grant that my views are unpopular with the mill agents and the owners, but I speak the truth."

A chastened Barilla opened the door. Meekly, she moved to stand beside Pliny. She thanked the doctor and they left.

Barilla's thoughts as they walked up Central Street were of the doctor's words. As they crossed the bridge over the Pawtucket Canal, she broke the silence.

"He should not say such awful things about the Irish. Most of them are ignorant of schooling, but they are a kindly people and as good as the rest of us."

"You are right about that, Barilla. We have several working in our shop. Dependable people they are, always singing, seemingly happy despite the fact they live in shacks in the rat-infested acre."

At the Elston house. she asked him to come in because she had something for him.

"This," she said as she handed him a three-by-four-inch case, "is something I had made especially for you."

He unhooked the clasp, and opened the case to study the miniature of Barilla, within a copper-colored frame. A puzzled look came into his eyes. He looked up in amazement, "How is this possible?" he asked.

As he sat on the settee, she stood before him and explained, "One sunny noontime, there was a man who had set up an ordinary wooden box atop three legs. A long line of girls waited their turn to have their likeness made, some of them even missing their dinners. We had been told that there had to be sunshine or the image would not take. You will notice that I could not smile, because I had to hold completely still for six minutes. I was seated in a chair, and had to stare at a short, round piece of pipe in the center of the box. The man then took something out of the back of the box and wrote our names on it. The images were ready for us right after we were paid last evening. I had it done twice, so I could have one for the folks at home."

She had hardly finished talking when she had a fit of coughing. Excusing herself, she said, "Doctor Doane gave me some medicine. I must get a spoon to take some of it." While she was gone, she reflected on the precious one dollar each she had spent on the portraits.

When she returned, Pliny was holding the case against his heart.

"Please sit down here," he said. "I want you to know how much I appreciate this gift. It is a treasure I will always cherish. Thank you very much."

She turned her face closer to kiss him. He held his arm around her shoulder and spoke up seriously, "We have to talk. Your illness is something not to be taken lightly. I think you should stop working in the mill."

She braced herself to answer boldly, "Then how would I earn money? If I don't work Abigail cannot be paid the dollar and a quarter a week for my board."

"I don't want you to work there after we are married."

"Then how will I spend my time'?"

"Alfred Whittredge told me we can live in his house until I find a place of our own. While there, you can help Elizebeth in the kitchen and I am sure you are adept at needlework."

"But for money? I have very little saved up."

"Precious girl, don't you realize that I will be responsible for you?"

"Well," she pondered, "I could ask the agent, Mister Avery, to give me a discharge for the last Saturday in June. That would be the day before our wedding."

"We should talk about the wedding plans."

"Yes, of course. We cannot expect Abigail to do as she did for Else." Barilla thought a moment as how to express a matter so indelicate as Abigail's pregnancy, but found it necessary when Pliny asked, "Why not?"

"Because she has not been feeling well." She continued by whispering in his ear, "There is to be a baby in September."

Pliny squeezed her gently and took her hand in his. Laughing at her as he answered, "You said that as though it was something you should not be discussing with me."

"I have been taught that is something that only women discuss among themselves."

"Or with their husbands," he chided her. "As will I be, once we are married."

She smiled shyly at him as he bent to kiss her with great ardor. Releasing her, he said, "I love you so much."

"I love you, too, Pliny."

Before he left, she asked him about the song he had been singing that stormy January day when she had first declared her love.

"What about it?" he asked.

"You were making it up. May I hear it all sometime?" she asked.

"I will have to think about that," Pliny said, with a mischievous twinkle in his eyes.

At supper that evening, Barilla told William, Abigail, and Judith that she and Pliny planned to be married on her birthday, June twenty-ninth.

"He wants me to stop working in the mill, which I will do that last Saturday. He also told me he would talk to Alfred Whittredge about having the wedding in his house,"

Abigail responded with dismay, "If only I felt better, I would love to have it here. But as you can see, I am already bulging out. It feels like I am growing a watermelon."

They all laughed heartily. Barilla's laughter caused her to choke and cough repeatedly.

When she caught her breath again she took out her medicine and filled a teaspoon. Then she explained about the visit to the doctor.

"It is high time," said Judith, "that you got some cough medicine."

Barilla turned to face Judith, "The doctor also gave me something for you to rub on my back and chest at bedtime."

Barilla did sleep better that night to awaken rested and eager for the day's work. Now, she thought, I will begin to get better.

However, she did not get better. No amount of wishful thinking, or her positive attitude, helped her condition. The aggravation gradually grew worse. It began to sap her strength to the point that she worried about being able to finish working the entire month of June. She grew snappy toward her friends, including Pliny.

One Sunday afternoon, even he lost patience, "Why must you continue working at a job that is destroying your health?"

"I have only a week to go. I can manage that. But I am afraid we will have to postpone our wedding."

He shot her a look of disgust.

"Surely, Pliny," she pleaded with him, "you cannot want me living with you until I get better."

He turned and left her then, not even kissing her or saying goodbye.

She stared at the closed door a few moments before she burst into tears. The agitation brought on more coughing. Because of such prolonged misery, a concerned Abigail hurried out of the kitchen with a spoon and the bottle of pennyroyal. Judith came running down the stairs.

"Come on up to bed," Judith said, "I'll rub your back and chest."

The following morning, Barilla reported to the mill only long enough to explain to Mr. Avery that she was too ill to continue working and asked if she could please have her pay for June.

John Avery stood up. He told her to sit and wait for him as he headed for the door. When he returned, he counted out $9.90, for eighteen days work.

Before he sat down to dismiss her he said, "Mr. Lord said you were a good worker, so we are sorry you must leave. Do return when you feel better."

Pliny left his shop later that afternoon. As he approached the Elston house, he saw Doctor Silas Doane's horse and carriage tied up out in front. He knocked on the door and Abigail admitted him. Her doleful countenance transmitted a deep-felt fear. She explained in a low voice that Barilla had such prolonged bouts of coughing, William had gone for the doctor.

In the parlor behind them, there was no mistaking an angry Silas Doane.

"Back to work. You have to face it, girl. You will never work there again. Your lungs are clogged with lint. There is no cure. I can only advise you as to what will make you more comfortable."

He glanced around to address Abigail. "There are some ways to ease her discomfort. Have her lean over to breathe from a bowl of boiling water, to which you add a small amount of camphor. She should have small, frequent portions of food, rather than big meals, milk, eggnog, baked bean juice, or meat broth with mashed vegetables. And plenty of rest. If in bed, several pillows elevating her head and chest. And, no excitement."

He turned, closed his valise, and strode toward the front door, followed by Abigail.

He stopped to nod to Pliny, "Let me tell you, young man. I do not enjoy seeing such young girls waste away with lung sickness. I have voiced many a complaint against those Boston associates who own these mills, but such a greedy lot they are. Money is their only concern. They do not want to hear about injuries, dyspepsia, fevers, and lungs that have turned brown."

After the doctor had departed, Pliny hastened to Barilla's side. She arose from a chair to wrap her arms around him and snuggle her head against his neck and the side of his face.

"I am so sorry," she sobbed. "Oh, my dearest Pliny, I am so sorry."

"I know, Sweetheart. But you are not to worry. I am here to help Abigail." His gaze caught the eyes of a concerned Abigail to relay his assurance.

He then directed Barilla to sit at the dining table, while he followed Abigail into the kitchen. As they waited for water to boil he laid out a plan saying, "My employers have set hours of seven to five, with time off at noon for dinner. I will come in the mornings then at noon, and after five, to help out."

"Thank you, Pliny. I am sure Judith will help at night."

He brought the bowl of pungent camphor fumes to the table and set it before Barilla. He said, "Apparently you did not work today."

"No. I have stopped for all time. I went only to get my final pay." She pulled gold and silver coins from her pocket and laid them on the table. "I had to pay the doctor three dollars. All that's left is six dollars and ninety cents. I do have some money in the Railroad Bank."

He placed a hand on her shoulder, "Now you stop talking and breathe in that stuff."

Thus a pattern for her care was set, at least for the next few weeks.

Many visitors came when they could, Else and James, Climena Bradbury, Louisa, Malvina, Audrey, and Minerva. Even Jamie came a couple of times after school.

On her first day of idleness, Barilla had written a letter to the family back home.

22

June 24, 1845

Beloved Parents,

It pains me to tell you that my health is not good. I can no longer work in the mill. The sickness is in my lungs. I am obliged to rest, to do nothing strenuous, and depend on medicaments to ease my coughing. Abigail and William are such first rate folks, they see to my daily needs. Judith is a great help in our bedroom at night.

There is an attentive and helpful gentleman, a friend of brother Byron's who stops by each day bringing me comfort with his music. It is indeed a great satisfaction that I am surrounded by generous and loving people. Surely my cup runneth over.

I hope Father's leg is better. Did you have help with the spring planting? Kiss the little boys, Bub and Gene, for me. I send bear hugs to the other four. Please write and tell Florena to write.

From your loving daughter,
Barilla Adeline Taylor

Eventually a letter came from home.

Sunday, July 13, 1845

Dear Daughter,

I now sit down to answer your letter. Your father is still unwell. He can bear little weight on his bad leg. Con came home to see to the planting. Amos comes down when he can. Of course the boys, Morval, Stephen, Melchoir. and Jack have all worked like full grown men.

We are indeed sorrowful that you have such a misfortune. If you'd a stayed to home like we wanted you to, you would not now be in such a state. You must make a plaster of mustard, flour, and water to rub on your chest. You remember I always gave you children a cough syrup of honey and vinegar. These things help more than any medicine a doctor can give you.

The lilies you planted have grown most up to the eaves of the house. They are budded, ready to bloom.

From your affectionate mother,
Melinda

On July 23, Pliny told Barilla that Alfred Whittredge and Elizebeth Mansur were to be married the following day.

"They will be away for a few days. However, they both send you their greetings and prayers for your recovery. Alfred showed me a reclining chair he had made for his daughter Nancy. She had consumption and had found the chair helpful with her breathing. I can use a cart from the shop, and with William's help, we shall bring it here for you."

On Sunday, the two men brought the heavy chair into the parlor, so rearranged that it fit nicely where Barilla could also look out the window. Taking her hand as though conducting a princess to a throne, Pliny helped her into the bulky recliner.

He bowed low, sweeping his hand in a wide gesture, "Your every wish is my command, fair lady."

"My dear Pliny, you do spoil me."

"My pleasure. Now, what is your wish?"

"To hear you sing me the song you were making notes about that stormy day in January."

Pliny dutifully picked up his banjo, which he had left there since Barilla had needed his daily help.

Abigail, Judith, and William moved discreetly aside to listen from the dining room. Pliny sat down, advising Barilla to look out the window as he sang.

"Her hair is brown, her eyes are blue.

Her face is fair, her word is true.
Known as Rilla; a pretty name,
To win her heart, is my aim.
The love is deep from me to her.
No love with me, has she to share.
No other wish, no other gain,
Can relieve my heart its aching pain."

He rested the banjo in his lap and cast his eyes downward, the tick of the clock the only sound until Barilla turned her head. Tear-filled eyes looked in his direction. She spoke in a soft tone.

"Thank you, Pliny. I understand more clearly now the error of my ways, the ways of foolish stubbornness I held onto until I missed you so terribly."

She smiled then, to say less seriously, "Thank you for the song. Now you will have to rewrite it."

He looked up, studying her intently, then smiled. "Of course. I rather like the tune. I'll work on revising the words."

He laid aside the banjo and came to lean over her. When their lips met, she felt waves of delight engulfing her weakened body, feeling overjoyed with the wonder, the magic, the happiness, this man had brought her.

Abigail announced that supper was ready. She handed Pliny a cup of pea soup for Barilla, which she was able to handle herself, and she urged Pliny to join the others at the table. Because the Whittredges were away, Abigail had insisted Pliny have his meals with them.

Supper finished, Pliny returned to find Barilla asleep, the cup and spoon placed neatly on the table beside her. He told Abigail it was best to leave her that way. He would come back in time for breakfast.

At bedtime, Barilla stirred and opened her eyes to see Judith watching over her. Judith reached out to touch Barilla's arm, as she spoke softly, "You look so peaceful and comfortable. Would you like to have me bring down a nightgown and a pillow so you can spend the night here?"

Barilla nodded sleepily. She had not coughed at all since being seated in the chair.

Judith, concerned that Barilla should not be left alone downstairs, asked if the mattress from her own single bed could be brought down so that she could sleep near the sick girl. This was accomplished, yet after a couple of weeks, the strain took its toll on Judith, who after working a twelve-hour day, began to get weary and droop.

Barilla had weakened to the point that she was no longer changed to a daily dress. Nightgowns were both her day and night apparel.

It had become the norm for Judith to nap after supper until the Elstons would retire. Pliny was always there to read to Barilla or to entertain her with music.

Then it happened one night the first week of August that Abigail could not waken the soundly sleeping Judith. She spoke to William, asking what should be done. William came down the stairs and explained the dilemma to Pliny.

"If you have no objections," said Pliny, "I will stay and sleep on the pallet."

"By Jove, that is an excellent idea. Sure you don't mind?"

"Not at all," said Pliny.

Secretly, he was delighted. Because he always wore work clothes, he removed only his shoes. With just the light from an oil lamp in the dining room, he lay down to sleep. The constant wheezing from the sleeping Barilla did not disturb his sleep.

A sudden choking sound alerted him as at the same time, Barilla spoke out, "Judith, could you please get me the hot water and camphor?"

Instinctively, Pliny darted for the kitchen. The striking clock resounded twelve times. He returned in a short time, carrying a steaming bowl, to hold her face above it.

"Where is Judith?" she managed to ask, between the deep breaths she took.

"Upstairs, my dear. She needs unbroken sleep."

"So do you."

He answered her as though it was some sort of joke. "She works twelve hours a day. I work only nine. Besides, she loves you like a sister, but I love you as a man." He added in a somber tone, "a man who loves you dearly, and prays constantly for your recovery."

She lifted her head. With her hand she indicated that he should remove the bowl. Reclining once more in the chair, she looked at him seriously.

"Would you please apply some of the mustard plaster on my chest?" she asked.

"Of course," he answered without thinking.

She unbuttoned the nightgown. Using both hands, she pulled the material aside almost to her waist.

Pliny picked up the container of mustard mixture. In the subdued light, he proceeded to spread the material on her chest. Inadvertently, his right hand slipped across her breast. His fingers paused to lightly press a nipple between his thumb and forefinger. He did not withdraw, nor did she protest.

The sensations so awed them both that their eyes clung in the sudden knowledge of desire. They looked fiercely into each other's eyes as though seeing there the very souls of one another.

With reluctance, he withdrew his hand and cast his eyes downward.

Mesmerized, Barilla still stared at his face, then buttoned up her gown. "Pliny," she whispered, "your touch caused a strange sensation throughout my body."

"I know, Sweetheart. It was the same for me."

"What does it mean? That is, if I were not ill, and we were already married, and you continued doing that, what would happen next?"

Being as naive as she, he could only answer, "I'm not sure, my dear. Your being so ill prevents us from finding out. Now, if you are comfortable, please go back to sleep."

He laid down again on the pallet beside her chair. Sleep evaded him for a long time, while he conjured up various visions of how a man and woman consummated their urgency. After the clock struck three times, he slept. His dreams gave him no answers, only more frustration.

At Barilla's request Pliny had obtained a power of attorney for her to sign, allowing him to withdraw her money from her bank. At eight percent interest, her balance amounted to forty-five dollars.

This enabled her to pay the necessary five dollars a month to Abigail for board, and three dollars for the weekly visits of Doctor Doane. She wanted Pliny to manage it for as long as necessary.

She knew she would never regain her health. She came to realize, as she drifted in and out of consciousness from the tincture of opium the doctor gave her, that she would not live much longer. There were things she must write before death took its final grip on her weakened heart. Judith brought her pen, ink, and paper, which lay on the table beside her. During periods of rational thinking, she placed the paper on her writing board and wrote. All her thoughts were of Pliny.

Do forget me. Why should sorrow,
O'er that brow a shadow fling?
Go onward. Forget me, and each morrow,
Brightly smile and sweetly sing.
Smile though I cannot be near thee.
Smile though I no longer see thee.
May thy soul with pleasure shine.
Lasting as the last gleam of mine.

She turned it face down on the table and rested. She closed her eyes and drifted into sleep. When she awoke, she reached for another sheet of paper and began to write.

When I am gone, sing me a song.
Shed not a tear o'er this friend's early bier.
Smile when the slow tolling bell you may hear.
When I am gone, I am gone.
Sing me a song as you stand by my grave.
Grieve not, sorrow not, beloved, be brave.

Come at the close of a bright summer day.
Come when the sun sheds its last ling'ring ray.
Or come when the leaves have all blown away.
Be not sad that I could not stay.
When I am gone, just sing me a song.

On Saturday morning the ninth of August, Pliny told her he would have a surprise for her at the end of the day. Even in her wildest imagination, she could not conjure up what the surprise would be.

At suppertime, Judith gave her clear beef broth. Of late, liquids had become her only source of nourishment.

It was after eight o'clock that evening when, in the dusk outside the window, she saw Pliny and another man approaching the house.

Together, they soon entered and came into the parlor.

"Byron!" she whispered in unbelievable wonder. She reached out her hand to him as tears welled up in her eyes.

Byron knelt beside her chair, laid his arm gently across to her shoulder, and kissed her cheek. Pliny stood on the opposite side.

Overcome with emotion, she tried to suppress the coughing that engulfed her. Pliny sprang to action to hold her upright until the coughing ran its course. He then gave her a spoonful of what her mother had recommended as cough medicine.

Relaxed again, she laid back once more and smiled at her brother to ask, "How did you get here?"

"By boat down the Penobscot, then by sea into Boston Harbor. From there I came up on the train."

"But why? How did you know I was ill?"

"Pliny wrote me a letter."

Even though the sight of her pitiable condition tore him apart, he began telling her about work being slack in the woods in August. He went on to say, "I have a good carpenter helping, so our house building is in good hands."

Her eyes had closed. The rhythm of his voice had lulled her to sleep. The wheezing sounds, which Pliny had become accustomed to, shocked Byron. He said, "She is so pale, so blue-colored."

Pliny nodded. As he explained the sleeping arrangement, he also told Byron he would take him up to the Whittredge house where he could sleep in his bed there, because he spent every night on the pallet beside Barilla's recliner. He turned away to pick up his banjo.

"At Christmastime I wrote a song for Barilla at a time I feared she did not care for me. Recently, I had to change some of the words." He motioned Byron to follow into the dining room where he sat down and began to play and sing.

Her hair is brown. Her eyes are blue.
Her face is fair. Her word is true.
They call her Rilla, a pretty name.
Refusing me, caused me much pain.
Naught on earth, I wish to gain.
I'd give my life to spare her pain.
Why, oh why is life such strife?
Oh dear God! Please spare her life.

Thereafter, Byron took over the daytime vigil. One day Barilla asked him to promise her something.

"Of course, dear sister. What is it?"

"Those two poems on my table underneath the cameo. Fold each one up the size of an envelope. Keep them until I die. Then give them to Pliny. I want Father to have my Bible, also all of my belongings sent home."

In the days to come, Barilla's strength ebbed. No longer able to feed herself, her caretakers had to force her to sip liquids.

In the still-dark of early morning on August twenty-second, with great effort, she reached out, speaking to Pliny, "My love…so good to me…must say good-bye."

He knelt by her chair, leaned over to lay his head lightly against her breast, one hand gripped tightly to one of hers. Her free hand came up to thread her fingers into his curly red hair.

"Sorry," she whispered, "So sorry…to leave…my true love."

The wheezing stopped and so did her heart.

William, Abigail, and Judith came down in the morning to find

Pliny bent over Barilla's silent form, shaking with uncontrollable sobs. Simultaneously, Byron arrived.

Pliny turned to William. "Will you tell him his sister has...died."

Thus it came about that Byron and William made arrangements. Barilla's casket was moved onto the funeral director's hearse. William sat beside the director. The Reverend Blanchard's carriage came to transport Pliny and Byron to the burial site.

Judith had gone to work as usual, where she told Jamie of Barilla's demise. Just as the cortege started up, the boy came racing up Central Street.

Pliny stepped down to encase the sobbing boy in an enveloping embrace. He lifted the sobbing boy into the carriage, placing him between himself and Byron.

At the cemetery, Pliny tried to sing a hymn, but found he could not. He thought of the poem she had written, "Sing me a song," and knew he could not possibly sing while there was such a quivering in his jaw. As the small group stood in a semicircle around the Reverend, Jamie looked up at Pliny and said, "I loved her best of all the people in the whole world."

Pliny laid his hand on the boy's shoulder and said, "So did I, Jamie. So did I."

23

Letter from Joseph Convers Taylor (Con) to Byron in Lowell.

Roxbury, Maine August 25, 1845

Distant Brother Byron,
I now seat myself to write a few lines. We are well, except Father. His leg is so lame he cannot walk without a cane. We received your letter on Sunday, August 24th. We was glad to hear that Barilla was alive, though afraid the next news may be her death news. We all hope she will get well and come home. Father says that if there is not enough money to pay her bills, that you must try to pay them.
Joseph C. Taylor

(This letter probably did not arrive in Lowell until September, long after Byron had returned to Bangor, Maine.)

Born to Abigail S. (Kimball) and William Elston:
September 11, 1845	Barilla Adeline Elston
September 22, 1847	Ruth Adelaide Elston
March 18, 1849	Josiah Amos Elston

Pliny wrote to Barilla's parents:

Lowell March 5, 1846

Mr. Taylor,
Excuse the liberty I have taken to address one to whom I am in a measure, a stranger. Although not personally aquainted with you, I trust my

name will pardon my writing. I would ask to learn anything of my friend Byron. I have no tidings of him since he wrote me in September that he had arrived back in Bangor.

I have had Barilla moved to the park-like cemetery about two miles out on the Lawrence Road. That was done on the 14th of November. Also a stone put up. It is a good straight stone four and a half feet high. It is engraved with the following inscription-

BARILLA A.
Daughter of Stephen B. and Melinda Taylor
Died Aug. 22, 1845 age 17 yrs.
Is there a thought, sad sorrow healing.
Which can a while your grief suspend
Yes! There is a sweet, a holy feeling.
'Tis the remembrance of a friend
Of Roxbury, Maine

The total cost for putting up the stone and the engraving is $12.75 of which I paid $2.75 which will leave a cost to you of $10.00 The moving and excavation cost was entirely my own.

We have quite a body of snow now, but in respect it has been a light winter.

If you should write me, please write in care of Day, Converse and Whittredge, 137 Central Street.

Please accept my best wishes for good health. Also my respects to Mrs. Taylor. Barilla was truly a fine young lady.

Yours Truly,
Pliny Tidd

(There was no mention of where her body had first been interred. Possibly at the old Lowell Cemetery, on the corner of School and Branch Streets.)

Afterward

In 1980 I was able to locate the gravestone in the Lowell Cemetery on Lawrence Street. After photographing the stone, which is now flat on the ground, my husband, Ruel, and I made a rubbing of it. While we worked at it, I thought of the treasure which would have been lost had all that pertained to Barilla been carelessly destroyed. For there we were, a hundred and thirty-five years after this brave girl's untimely death, filled with the feeling of having known her, my husband's great-aunt.

Ruel asked me what song I would sing as was her request in her final poem. The oldest song that came to mind was "Aura Lea."

"When the Blackbird in the Spring, On the willow tree

Sat and rock'd I heard him sing, Singing Aura Lea.

Aura Lea. Aura Lea, Maid of golden hair;

Sunshine came along with thee, And swallows in the air."

Ruel was suddenly moved to say, "Wouldn't it be fascinating if she could somehow communicate with us?"

"Oh, but she has," I stated with definitive assurance. "She has most certainly communicated."

About the Characters

Emily Austin married William Morse (one son)

George Dana Austin married Mary Bradbury (no children)

Jamie Quinn: An imaginary character; an example of Irish waifs in that period.

James Gordon: An imaginary character.

Else White, Judith Fox and Horace Gailey actually lived. I have been unable to find out what happened to them.

Pliny Tidd presented my greatest mystery. Besides the letter to Barilla's parents, March 1846, I found record of him in Lowell directories as a resident in 1844 and 1845. Extensive research in Massachusetts Archives and the Family History Library in Salt Lake City was futile. A search of records in the Woburn, Massachusetts Cemetery turned up at least 60 persons named Tidd buried there. No Pliny Tidd!

My romantic inclination leads me to believe that, nursing a broken heart, he either went West, or possibly to Alaska or Australia.

The Taylor family record is an open book.

Stephen Burleigh Taylor b. 1797 d. 1879.

His wife, Melinda (Hinkson) b. 1802 d. 1887.

Their children:

1. Florena b. 1823 d. 1905 married Amos Austin (six children). In 1858 they went to Petaluma, California. I am in touch with descendants in Atlanta, Georgia.

2. Byron Chesley b. 1524 d. 1854 m. Charlotte Gregory (two children). He is buried in Levant, Maine.

3. Joseph Convers b. 1826 d. 1866 (Con) unmarried. He was a circus clown and musical entertainer. Played a 5-string banjo.

4. Barilla Adeline b. June 29. 1828 d. Aug 22, 1845.

5. Morvalden A. b. 1830 d. 1925 m. Sarah (Barnard) (three children). They settled in towns near Minneapolis, Minnesota. I am in touch with descendants in Atherton, California.

6. Oliva Maria b. 1832 d. 1837.

7. Stephen Marvin b. 1834 d. 1920 m. Elizebeth (Maly) (two children). Went to Minnesota. Met her there.

8. Melchoir E. b. 1836 d. 1913 m. Philena (Dean) (one child). Only one to remain on the farm. "Home Place" house is gone.

9. Orellana F. (Jack) b. 183b d. 1920 m. Fanny (Small) (one child). They lived for a while in Levant, then moved to Norway, Maine.

10. Renaldo Eugene (Gene) b. 1840 d. 1917 m. Mary (Hodgen) (four children). R.E. only one to serve in the Civil War. Company H. Maine Regt. Later went to California, buried in Gridley.

11. Philand Delano (Bub, P.D.) b. 1843 d. 1919 m. Addie (Thompson) (four children). Lived across the road (Rt. 17) from the "Home Place" on property deeded him by Melchoir. One of their children was Ruel E. Taylor Sr. Thus the connection down through the present generations.

12. Araminta Adelia b. 1846 d 1889 Born six months after Barilla's death. m. first, Joseph Gleason, second, David Lebroke (one child). Buried in North Waterford, Maine.

Among Barilla's possessions, besides her letters and poetry, was one photo of her, a Bible, inscribed with her name, gold beads, and a cameo. The cameo had both a chain and a pin clasp to be worn as a brooch. That and the gold beads were sometimes worn by my mother-in-law, Nellie (Mrs. Ruel E. Taylor Sr.).

At present, besides the writings, I have the original photo, the Bible and the cameo. Nellie gave the gold beads to her daughter, Christie in New Jersey, from whose house they were stolen. (Undoubtedly worth far more than the seven dollars Barilla paid for them in 1844.)